A Day in the Life of
A Camden City Drug Dealer

Mike Smooth

PROLOGUE

Camden, New Jersey is but ten square miles and divided into four common parts: North, South, East, and Central Camden; yet, it has practically been the "wet dream" of national news reporters for consistently being ranked as one of the most dangerous cities in the nation. Even now, in 1995, which was a few years after the fall of the infamous Sons of Malcolm X, Camden was still a focal point of the media's obsession with poverty stricken cities. It's true enough that violent crimes happen to people in my city on a regular basis, but it's almost impossible for me to fathom that a small city like Camden could achieve such a fearsome reputation.

It is mostly when I'm getting high, times like now, that I take a moment or two to sit and contemplate how such a thing could happen - I mean, we have New York and other North Jersey cities to the north of us, Philadelphia to the west of us, and both Baltimore and Washington D.C. to the south of us; yet, despite these large and more infamous cities that surround my beloved Camden on all sides, this particular section of New Jersey somehow manages to stand apart from them all.

It was a most intriguing concept for me to ponder. Metaphorically speaking, I guess a swimming pool full of piranha is a bit more fatal than an ocean filled with sharks; and with nearly every street of this city being infested with some sort of criminal activity, I doubt that I could have made a more accurate comparison.

Within these four sections of Camden, scores of different "sets" (slang term for designated drug territories) subsist, all of them co-existing amongst one another with an ever-fragile understanding of each other's independence.

Such wasn't exactly the case for my neighborhood.

Parkside, which is a neighborhood located on one of the outer edges of the Central section of Camden, borders with the more southern segment of the city. The section of Parkside in which I lived, via Haddon Avenue, is the southernmost section of Parkside and was actually right on the borderline between South and Central Camden. With Wildwood Avenue, Parkside's most central street, being a good quarter mile away from our neighborhood, there was always a sense of disenchantment between our section of Parkside and theirs. The distance between us wasn't great, but it was vast enough for the two of us not to feel so closely related. The time had eventually come when my neighborhood had decided to defect from Parkside by claiming its own independence; and the first thing hustlers in our section of Parkside had to decide upon would be a new name.

Just as Wildwood Avenue was roughly a quarter mile away from our neighborhood, South Eighth Street, a central street in a neighboring set on the downtown side of Camden, was roughly a quarter mile away from us in the opposite direction. With our neighborhood being stark in the middle of both Downtown and Parkside, it seemed more than suitable for our local hustlers to rename this area "Mid Town."

The southern section of Camden is perhaps the largest section of the city, which means that South Camden consists of a great deal more sets than any other part of Camden. Downtown, which is what we call the greater portion of South Camden, begins at South Ninth Street and intersects with Pine Street as it extends all the way down to the Delaware River. Literally, Downtown was huge and its sets uniquely designed. Eighth Street, Sixth Street, and the rest of the streets numbered all the way down to Second Street, were long roads that ran parallel with one another, all the while stretching from one side of Camden to the other. In turn, scores of smaller streets intersected with these large roads, consequently, giving birth to an incalculable number of street corners where hustlers drew the lines of their respected territories.

Nearly all of these Downtown sets were interdependent, meaning that while despite them all drawing separate identities, they still recognized their relation to one another with regards to them being a part of Downtown, which as previously stated, is one of the bigger and more respected sections of South Camden. Their past and present reputation in this city's underworld definitely preceded them.

South Eighth Street was one of the Downtown streets closest to Mid Town; moreover, it was home to a multitude of sets, all of them based on the smaller streets which ran adjacent to South Eighth Street itself. Stragglers from these sets, along with others from the South Sixth Street sets as well, made it every bit as much of their business to make us prove our right to be a legitimate 'hood as Parkside did.

It was a test that, no matter how strong the effort, we somehow always failed to surpass; needless to say, it only made us seem weaker in the eyes of both our rivals. These defeats made for bitter pills that all the hustlers in our neighborhood had no choice but to swallow; and these particular issues help combine with other ingredients to help perpetuate a beef between us and a prominent hustler from a Downtown set on Fourth and Chestnut Street who went by the name of Jay-Dollar.

It began when India, a twenty-something year old single mother from the East Camden section of the city, had moved into our neighborhood on Haddon Avenue. She was a tall, brown-skinned female with long legs and a pretty face that went all too well with an amply shaped figure. Above all was the fact that India's reputation of promiscuity did indeed precede her; there were a few hustlers from outside of my 'hood that could personally vouch for her sexual prowess, and the look about India's eyes verified as much. Such gossip and curiosity about the "new chick on the block" was more than enough to entice nearly every thug in our area, myself included.

Putting a halt to all of our advances, however, was India's off-again on-again lover, Jay-Dollar. He was a relatively tall, brown-skinned "pretty-boy" who was always dressed in the latest, most expensive clothing; his flashy wardrobe and flamboyant swagger made him easy to recognize as a visitor among us. And rest assured, everyone was surely keeping an eye on him.

Unlike most outsiders who'd move into our neighborhood, Jay-Dollar didn't simply limit his activity to just coming and going in and out of India's house. He'd spend a lot of time hanging out on her porch step with some of his cronies, one of them in particular being a friend of his whom we all came to know as "Little Stu."

Little Stu was one of Jay-Dollar's closest cohorts and well-known for carrying out a variety of Jay-Dollar's errands, all of them ranging from simple drug runs to the sometimes violent enforcement of street policies. He was a short and barrel-chested hustler from the downtown section of Camden whose reputation was built more so on his association with others rather than his own personal doings. The faint-of-heart may be easily fooled by Little Stu's rough-and-tumble demeanor, but to those like myself, who had already been battle-tested, Little Stu was nothing more than a larger-than-life bluff artist; and his presence, along with Jay Dollar's, was more than an aggravating sight to witness.

Needless to say, we were all quick to notice the great deal of traffic flowing to and from India's home, all of them being friends and associates of Jay-Dollar. A sea of unfamiliar faces was popping up to converse with Jay-Dollar, nearly all of them trading hard stares with me and my gang of thugs as they talked. Furthermore, Jay-Dollar would also spend a lot of time on his stoop with Little Stu, the two of them seeming as if to be keeping a watchful eye on just how great a "flow" (a flow being the amount of income a set generates) we had. It was only a matter of time before rumors of Jay-Dollar plotting to dip his hand into our drug trade had begun to surface, and we, already struck with an inferiority complex when facing conflict with a set from Downtown, were beginning to feel overly defensive.

Jay-Dollar's set on Fourth and Chestnut Street was far on the other side of Downtown Camden and had absolutely nothing to do with our contention with the sets on Eighth and Sixth Street; still, our cynicism had already been aroused. A heavy sense of hostility was in the air between us and them, and Jay-Dollar knew it. Jay-Dollar not only knew it, but didn't seem the least bit concerned about it, and it was this blatant expression of arrogance that moved to enflame us even more. It would only be a matter of time before the tension between us escalates into violence, and thanks to Donnie, one of the younger and more volatile thugs in my neighborhood, the stage had already been set for a most violent presentation.

Donald Biggs, more commonly known to us as Donnie P, was practically born and raised in our neighborhood; he was the only child of a heroin-addicted mother and a father who, while in between stints in prison, was heavily addicted to base cocaine. Needless to say, it was only a matter of time before Donnie found himself hanging out in the streets at an early age, and he had done so with a vengeance.

Barely eighteen years old, Donnie had already made quite a name for himself as a bona fide tough guy. He was quick-tempered, overly aggressive and more than capable of backing up his tough talk. Never having the patience for drug dealing, Donnie dealt mostly in armed robberies and only moonlighted with the drug racket in between money schemes. Soon, his reputation had grown beyond the boundaries of our meager 'hood, and for better or worse, all, of us appreciated his presence in our part of town.

I emerged onto Haddon Avenue just in time to witness Donnie, while amongst a crew of younger hustlers, send Little Stu to the concrete by way of a strong right hook.

From a short distance away, I could see the quickness and full extension of Donnie's punch. It was a blow that forced Little Stu's head to jerk hard up into the air and then lead his body into a complete three hundred sixty degree spin before plummeting hard down to the pavement.

I walked swiftly up the street, my pace quickening with each time I saw Donnie smash the heel of his Timberland boot hard against what I figured to be Little Stu's unconscious body. The one or two onlookers I saw watching from their porch tops had now swelled to crowds; Donnie's entourage, now excited by their leader's abrupt show of force, proceeded to follow suit by kicking and stomping Little Stu as well. Seeing far beyond the excitement of what was now going on, my brain had immediately began making a complete analysis of what was sure to happen after this melee finished playing itself out.

The fuck! I said to myself while hastening my way towards the scuffle. *This is some bullshit, man! This is some fuckin' bullshit! This shit ain't good for the set at all.*

I had long ago made my mark in this neighborhood by way of fist fighting, and I was no stranger to gunfire; therefore, my worry about the extent of Jay-Dollar's reaction to all of this had nothing to do with my worries about what I knew was sure to follow. My concern, more importantly, was that of a financial one.

Fighting and carrying on in the streets will only bring the police into our neighborhood, and the presence of the police will undoubtedly bring any and all criminal activity to a halt. With a pause from drug dealing comes a pause from me making any money in the streets, and I definitely couldn't afford to take a break from making money at this present time.

"Aye, yo!" I said while fighting to end their vicious assault. "Chill the fuck out, yo! Y'all niggas gotta chill the fuck out before the mafuckin' cops come!"

I was now in the midst of the melee, grabbing some members of the mob by their shoulders and pushing them aside.

"Word up, yo!" I hollered out to seemingly no one but myself. "Ya'll niggas gots to chill the fuck out an' get the fuck out of here before the cops come! Y'all making the set hot as hell wit' this bullshit!"

Donnie was the only one of the pack who hadn't adhered to my advice.

There were countless times when everyone in my 'hood, myself included, had very much admired Donnie's fierce-of-heartedness. To be honest, we constantly found ourselves relying upon it to help put our foot down against rival neighborhoods. At other times, like now for example, he was again proving himself to be more of a liability than an asset. Knowing how savage Donnie can be while immersed in the heat of conflict, I took great care in trying to quell his wrath; still, it would be no easy task.

"Hey, yo!" I remarked softly but firmly while grabbing a handful of his army coat. "That's enough, yo . . . the nigga's done, yo . . . for real . . . it's over with."

"Da fuck is you doin', nigga?!?" Donnie snapped while snatching his coat from out of my grasp. He then took a step in my direction, bringing all of his anger and emotion directly in front of my face.

"Go 'head with that bitch shit, Don Juan ," he huffed. "Aint nobody tryin' to hear that bullshit you talkin' right now, yo . . . word is bond."

The distance between us was so close that our noses nearly touched. I could smell the alcohol on Donnie had been drinking as he fought to catch his breath while staring me directly in the eyes.

"You see me puttin' in work over here, nigga! The fuck is you doin' comin' around here all on some scared shit, yo?!"

To the average eye, one would think Donnie and I were about to square off and begin slugging it out, but no such thing was going to happen. He was the temperamental little brother, and I was the smarter, more sensible big brother. It was a role that I often enjoyed playing with Donnie, but now was not the time.

"Man, listen," I said with a mixture of both impatience and exasperation. "You all out in the open wit' this nigga on the ground all bloody an' shit. Look at the heat you about to bring around this mafucka. We gots to get the fuck out of here, yo . . . an' I mean NOW."

Through our brief exchange of words, Donnie had found a moment to calm down, and with that came a moment of rational thinking. He was beginning to take my argument into consideration, and just like that, in a mere matter of seconds, he conceded.

"True, true, true," Donnie agreed while taking a few steps backward. His complexion had returned from red back to high yellow. "I'm a get the fuck out of here, yo. I'll holla at you later."

And just like that, Donnie was on his way across the street towards a burgundy late-model Jeep Cherokee that he had rented from a drug addict for just a few bags of base. Before turning and starting back towards the corner, I took a look down at the bloody mess that Donnie had so casually left behind. Little Stu was still unconscious. His face, which was horribly swelled and bloodied-up, appeared a gruesome mess as his broken body lay twisted on the sidewalk.

My moment of sympathy for what had just now happened to Little Stu was short lived; the ear-piercing sound of shattered glass had come from out of nowhere, catching me completely by surprise and scaring the hell out of me.

"What the fuck?!" I said out loud while cringing from a repeat of what I had just heard a few seconds ago.

I looked over to find Keifey, a fellow hustler who was a year or two younger than Donnie, but every bit as prone to violence, standing near the street with a handful of stones. He narrowed his eyes while flashing a most devious smile that was every bit as black as the complexion of his skin; then, he took aim and pitched another. I turned and watched as a window on the second floor of Jay-Dollar and India's house shattered, its shards falling down onto the porch roof and smashing into even smaller pieces.

"Yeah, nigga!" said Keifey, seeming as if to relish in my dread and dismay of what he was now doing. "Fuck that nigga, yo. This Mid Town, bitch! Fuck Jay-Dollar!"

There was no need for me to try preventing Keifey from wrecking India's home any further. The damage had already been done: Jay-Dollar's right-hand man has been beaten to a bloody pulp, and the house in which he and his girlfriend lived had now been seriously vandalized.

Donnie, through his rash and utterly impulsive behavior, had undoubtedly used his "tough guy" rhetoric to enflame the more hot-blooded hustlers and administer a call for war that Jay-Dollar would absolutely have no other choice but to answer. My concern was not so much as to whether or not Jay-Dollar would answer the call, but when, and most importantly . . . HOW?

How hard will this nigga retaliate? I wondered to myself hustling around the corner and towards my own car. *How hard will this nigga retaliate and what exactly will his inevitable act of revenge cost my neighborhood?*

Little did I know that I would receive the answers to all of these questions much sooner than I'd care to imagine.

8:00 a.m.

After another failed attempt to remain asleep, I now lay half-awake in bed lazily entangled in my bed linen. While still fighting to enjoy what little rest there was for me to have, I stayed put in my bed, struggling to rejuvenate some of the energy I had lost from another long night of weed and alcohol abuse. It was the feel of Lakeisha's body being absent from mine, however, that had fully brought me to consciousness. For the Camden City School system, it was still Christmas break; therefore, I groggily figured that she may have already awakened and was off tending to our four children. I forced myself upwards and onto the edge of the mattress, and then, while holding my head in the palms of my hands, began piecing together last night's most recent events.

It was another neighborhood get-together, this time involving some of the key characters in my 'hood. B.J., Keifey, Irvin, Puerto Rican Mannie, Justice, Peace-Peace and I had all agreed to meet up to discuss and determine what course of action to take against Jay-Dollar, the culprit who had riddled our neighborhood with bullets just a few days earlier.

Donnie, the individual most responsible for provoking this war, didn't bother showing up. What's done is done, and as far as he was concerned, there was nothing more to discuss other than when we planned to do the shooting and who was coming with us. The issue amongst other hustlers, much to the contrary of Donnie's point of view, was not about what should be done, however, but more so rather when and how.

It was a discussion that will undoubtedly show the true colors of everyone who claimed to be a part of our set; and it was by way of these conversations that everyone's degree of courage, determination and intelligence will be measured. Some hustlers will argue for us take our time and exercise extreme caution before retaliating, while others will argue for a quick, more hasty response. While those directly involved with the politics of our neighborhood sat and argued about this, that and the other, it was the mental, physical and financial state of Mid-Town that was suffering most.

I was once told that, in ancient times, Chinese generals would celebrate and party with those whom they distrusted most, for a festive occasion allows one to drop their guard, and intoxication encourages them to express their truest feelings. Watching as everyone argued their points of view while heavily under the influence of drugs and alcohol, I couldn't have understood this ancient Chinese strategy any clearer.

Jay-Dollar's act of revenge was a most disparaging attack which not only left one of our local residents wounded and many more intimidated, but it had practically decimated our ability to generate an income as well. An increase of undercover officers, routine police raids and the regular sight of both marked and unmarked patrol cars gave the law an intense feel of omnipotence in our 'hood. As a result, both drug dealers and drug addicts alike were reluctant to be seen on Haddon Avenue, which was much to the satisfaction of our tax-paying neighbors who, until their property had recently been torn to pieces by gunfire, had begrudgingly tolerated our criminal activity.

Keifey and Irvin were brothers whose resemblances are so similar that one could easily mistake them for twins rather than simply being a year apart. They were both black-skinned with short wiry builds, their eyes large and mouths wide and toothy. If not for Keifey's wild, braided hair, which contrasted sharply with Irvin's clean cut and wavy hairstyle, it would be near impossible to tell the two apart on face value. Keifey was the oldest, but, surprisingly enough, it was the younger brother who proved to be the more level-headed of the two.

Malik Anderson, more commonly known by us as either "Leak" or "Leaky-Leak" was the youngest in attendance. At barely eighteen years of age, he had the size and girth of a grown man; sadly enough though, he had the temperance of a young adolescent school boy. Lacking any credible street ambition, Leaky-Leak was a low-level jack of all trades with regards to hustling; in fact, he was more a car-thief than anything, and even that was more so for joyriding than anything else.

Rashon and I were the same age, yet he's had an earlier start in the street life than me. His older brother, Ismael, was one of the older kids from our neighborhood who had helped play a pivotal role in our 'hood's early struggle for independence. That was a few years ago, and Ismael had joined the Navy since then, subsequently settling down somewhere in South Carolina. Rashon remained in the 'hood with the rest of us, living off of what his brother had done in the past more so than what he was currently doing in the present, which was basically the same as me: living the street life, pushing one package after the next.

B.J. was undoubtedly the eldest of all those in attendance. He was the same age as those who had fought for Mid Town's right to be recognized as an independent 'hood in the years before our reign. We all knew that B.J.'s role throughout those trying years were minimal, but nevertheless, we acknowledged him being there; which subsequently allowed B.J. to enjoy a small measure of respect from those like myself who had come up in the streets after their struggle.

On face value, one would never guess Mannie to be Hispanic. He was a chubby kid in his early twenties with coal-black skin, a large fleshy nose, full lips and thick wool-like hair which was always kept in an array of braids.

Being the darkest of his family, Mannie was ostracized by his siblings and most of his classmates, but he found himself welcome amongst the blacks, who were more than impressed with his "bilingualism." He was jokingly dubbed "Puerto Rican Mannie" as a novel reminder that he was more than just an ordinary black kid, but a Puerto Rican black kid; it was an inside joke that was shared and understood only by those within our more intimate circle.

Puerto Rican Mannie was a "people person" in every sense of the word and got along with addicts to the point where they'd buy from him regardless of the size or quality of his product. This, along, with Mannie being vigilant about selling every last bag, could have easily lent to him becoming an above-average dealer, but his faint-heartedness and incompetence during times of crisis made him unsuitable for anything greater than being a simple worker.

Our partnership consisted of me buying the product, packaging the product, and then passing it off to Mannie for him to sell. It was also my job to iron out the eventual squabbles that would often occur between Mannie and other dealers in the midst of them fighting amongst each other for sales. In return for my employment, which some argued to be nothing but more than "protection," he diligently sold whatever amount I gave him and would often finish off my own personal stashes free of charge. Despite the cynicism and criticism of fellow drug dealers, our partnership, to both Mannie and I, was a beautiful thing.

Peace-Peace was a year or so younger than B.J. but older than the rest of us. He was a local thug with a reputation for violence before landing his self a stint in prison where he returned more than five years later as a Five Percenter. He had also acquired more than twenty-five pounds of bulk, which gave his physical frame a rather hulking appearance. On the left side of his face was a thick, almost grotesque scar that stretched vertically from the top of his brow to the corner of his mouth. This scar also snaked down over a gray and white marble where his left eye used to be, which only added to his gruesome exterior. In short, Peace-Peace was horrible to look at. He was never much for words, and his quiet, foreboding demeanor only helped lend to a most dubious air of intimidation.

Justice was the only one of us whom wasn't born and raised in Mid Town. He was a Five Percenter whom was originally from New York and had met Peace-Peace while incarcerated. He had moved into our neighborhood upon his release and has been living amongst us ever since. Despite the years he had spent living in Mid Town, still, no one fully trusted Justice. He was aloof and impartial to neighborhood politics, only choosing to fraternize with a select few in the 'hood; and this few just so happened to be me, Donnie and Peace-Peace once he had been paroled.

The congregation was held at Rashon's one bedroom apartment in East Camden. His stereo system was at full tilt; the killer sounds of the Infamous Mobb Deep filled every room in the apartment. Still, it wasn't enough to overpower the sounds of the music booming from the apartment beneath us. We were all gathered inside the kitchen area, some of us around the table, some either sitting in a dining room chair or standing. The fog of nicotine and marijuana smoke filled the room as everyone argued their opinions.

Keifey reflected the sentiment of Donnie and the younger, more hot-blooded hustlers in our neighborhood by advocating the need to strike hard and strike fast, as always, proving himself to be arrogant, stubborn and dangerously foolish. Murder or attempted murder is a crime that calls not only for courage, as Irvin had pointed out, but extensive planning and precise execution was even more important; the slightest mistake could, and undoubtedly would, land an individual in prison for the rest of his or her natural life.

Irvin, by nature, was a soft-spoken, non-confrontational person. His laid-back and easy style of conversation could easily give one the misconception of him being afraid of his much more aggressive and animated older brother. As sensible as Irvin may have sounded, his argument was easily overwhelmed and overshadowed by Irvin's more colorful personality.

I wasn't the least bit surprised to find Mannie intimidated by the very thought of him being involved in a particular situation that lent to the possibility of him landing in prison. His subtle agreement on Irvin's behalf was silenced not only by Keifey pointing out various examples of Mannie's cowardice, but also by challenging Mannie's right to be a part of our neighborhood. Irvin had even gone so far as to threaten Mannie with physical harm right there on the spot if he were to say another word. Much to no one's surprise, it was more than enough to keep Mannie quiet.

For all of B.J.'s self-proclamation as an "O.G." and a true veteran of Mid Town's original struggle for independence, he was extremely reticent throughout the entire argument. Keifey's hard line demeanor and enflaming demands for everyone to show courage in the face of death forced B.J. to accept the reality of him being nothing more than a family man who was merely fantasizing about what he once strived to be as a youth. Instead of his usual boasting, bragging or bluffing, B.J. settled for the job of refereeing the argument between Keifey and Irvin when things became too heated. In all reality, it was all he could do without being called on his own cowardly ways.

Knowing that Mid Town would forever be paralyzed with deciding a course of action, Peace-Peace, Justice and I had already made secret plans to deal with the hustler from Fourth and Chestnut Street on our own. The three of us only showed our faces that night for cosmetic purposes.

Always a person to define himself more by actions rather than words, Peace-Peace could only stand but so much and left almost immediately. Justice excused himself less than an hour later. I, on the other hand, chose to stay and indulge in my ability to read everyone's personality as they increased the amounts of intoxicants being consumed.

Needless to say, the night was long, and I enjoyed the sight of all these clashing personalities, all of them running high on emotion and intoxicants. Boy, was it something to see.

*   *   *

The sight of my cell phone missing from its place on the nightstand had instantly snatched me away from some of last night's more dramatic events. Moreover, I noticed that my pager wasn't in the same position I had left it. Someone had tampered with my belongings while I was asleep, and it wasn't hard for me to figure out who the culprit was.

While reaching for and lighting a cigarette, I vaguely recalled shutting off my cell phone after I had ignored both her pages and calls for the thousandth time. She had chosen to pick a fight during my attendance at Mid Town's neighborhood meeting. Although we had both agreed that my cell phone was strictly for business; yet, it was the heat of battle that caused us both to ignore this cardinal rule. Consequently, Lakeisha was left without a means to get in touch with me which undoubtedly helped fuel the flames of her anger

Not answering the phone whenever Lakeisha calls will undoubtedly jump-start her sense of jealously, and the fact that I had turned it off in the midst of an argument will have definitely set her emotions into overdrive. Knowing how Lakeisha's mind works, she will absolutely suspect that I had been spending the night in the arms of another woman. The fact that she had taken my cell phone and pager was proof enough of the thoughts running through her mind. It was a wonder that we weren't having it out already, let alone last night upon my return home. There would definitely be a reckoning before I left the house this morning.

The thought of facing Lakeisha in all her rage and jealously so early in the morning was more than enough for me to desire another cigarette, yet I thought better of it and began to start my day. After checking both my pant pockets to find all one thousand eight hundred and eighty-five dollars of yesterday's earnings present and accounted for, I clicked on the stereo by its remote control and then slipped out of my boxer shorts and wrapped a towel around my bare waist.

Before heading to the shower, I stopped short at the mirror to half-admire my physique while pondering the irony of how much I resembled my father who had now been deceased for more than a decade and how Tommy, my only other sibling who has been dead for about two years now, had resembled my mother. It seemed a cruel joke for the only two survivors of a small family to resemble their dead relatives instead of one another. I continued staring at the reflection of my dark yellow-skinned complexion which complimented my short, athletic build and almost hairless facial features. I was a clear-cut likeness of my father, and the thought of it was enough to make me smile.

While making my way to the bathroom, I stopped to peek inside of Serenity's bedroom where she was sitting upright on her bed, watching her two younger brothers battle against one another on their video game system. Serenity was nine years old, Marco was eight, and Milton, whom we all nicknamed "Milky," was six. I found it amazing how, despite them all having different fathers, each one of them resembled their mother to the point where they were almost identical. They all shared Lakeisha's rich, chocolate-brown complexion, her slanted eyes, her small button nose, and most of all, they had inherited Lakeisha's full, jet-black Indian-like hair.

Although Dijuan Jr., mine and Lakeisha's two-year old son, looked exactly like me when I was his age, I still harbored the fear of him growing up and taking more of Lakeisha's genes than mine. My brother died without having any children, and with little Dijuan Jr. being my family's only grandchild, he unknowingly bore the burden of preserving the Ingles' family traits.

With the exception of the son that both of us shared, none of Lakeisha's children know who their fathers are, and although knowing I wasn't responsible for their physical birth, her children were all acutely aware of me being responsible for providing the necessities of life; therefore, they acknowledged me as their dad and adhered to my wishes without much grief.

"Hey, daddy," said Serenity while staring in my direction.

"Hey, baby," I replied while scanning the bedroom. "Where's Juannie?"

"He's still sleepin'," Milky answered, not bothering to turn his eyes away from the television screen. He was far too involved with the video game to turn around and acknowledge me for the time being.

"You gonna buy our sneakers today?" Serenity asked.

"It depends on how good y'all are," I answered while silently cursing myself for forgetting my week-old promise to buy them all new sneakers. "It depends on how all of y'all act and if y'all listen to your momma. Do what y'all are supposed to do and don't give her no grief, and I got y'all covered."

"Gettin' our sneaks ain't gonna take away from our Christmas stuff, is it?" Marco asked while pausing the video game to look into my eyes as if to search for any signs of untruth. He was incredibly shrewd for an eight-year-old boy and never ceased to amaze me with his pragmatic approach to even the simplest things.

"I got you, Marco," I said with a slight smile. "Just be easy."

I left all three of the children to their early morning activities and headed to Marco and Milky's bedroom where Dijuan Jr. was sprawled out on his stomach, still deep in slumber. Watching his tiny body constrict and expand while sleeping always filled me with a sentiment that I find hard to explain. The thought of being responsible for bringing such a fragile and precious form of life into this world gave way to feelings and emotions that I still have yet to understand. I wondered how any man, or woman for that matter, could abandon and leave such an innocent creation on its own to fend for itself. I'd rob, steal, cheat and even murder to support my child.

Come to think about it, I was practically doing most of these deeds now.

I smiled while continuing on my way to the bathroom, and once there, I stripped free of my towel, placed it on the towel rack, and then started the shower before stepping into the tub. While standing beneath the hot streams of shower water now beating against my naked body, I could feel a keen sense of rejuvenation surging about my being.

With a clear mind and a renewed sense of spirit, I began assembling a mental list of things that needed to be done today while at the same time arranging a schedule in which to get it all completed. As always, I started with a tally of what I had amassed so far, and then assessed the progress I've made from the last "flip" (a flip being the act of selling the entire amount of product previously purchased and preparing to purchase more with its proceeds).

Seven hundred to eight hundred and fifty dollars was the average price for an ounce of base, which would first be bought, sliced apart, cut into small pieces, and then packaged and sold according to its size. "Nickels" and "dimes" were trademark sizes for the average drug set. "Dubs" were for the more well-established and booming drug areas, while "fifty-cent pieces" are usually reserved for special clientele.

In my case, fifty-cent pieces were exclusively for customers whom I dealt with through my pager. These customers were usually law-abiding citizens with jobs and careers who feared the risk of being caught up with the riff-raff and hassle of neighborhood predators, robbers, con artists, and police alike. This special clientele consisted of some of our city's teachers, municipal workers and civil servants, all of them entirely grateful for my fast and fair door-to-door service.

A drug dealer's profit is made only after he has met the cost of buying the product; whatever is left after that is then considered to be his gain. The bigger he makes his bags, the smaller his profit; the smaller he makes his bags, the bigger his profit. Both methods have their advantages and disadvantages, which ultimately determines the personality of the neighborhood.

For example, the advantage of those who make their bags bigger may appear more attractive to the addicts and sell a bit faster, but the profit is guaranteed to be few a hundred dollars less, and in this line of work, every dollar counts. A smaller income demands one to spend his money wisely, which means indulging in too much of anything before meeting his quota is a cardinal sin.

Everything in life costs money, and dealers who choose to make their bags bigger must be careful to keep these things in mind when spending on miscellaneous items. Aside from the basic needs of food, clothing and shelter, guns (which are arguably the most necessary ingredient of street life) costs serious money - not to mention the need to save money and make one's self able to buy a bigger package. After all, the bigger the package, the bigger the flip; the bigger the flip, the bigger the profit, and profit is what it is all about.

Dealers who make their bags small in order to inflate their profit usually find success through clientele and customer service. With patience, a good quality of product and a steady flow of customers, this particular dealer will normally have a chance of turning a decent profit; however, the average addict is always out to get the most for his or her money and will usually gravitate towards the bigger and more attractive bags of the "quick-flipper." At times, he'll even run the risk of being "beat" (slang term for being conned) and experiment with an unfamiliar face, all for the sake of a potentially bigger bag. Thus, the dealer who chooses to stretch his product is usually stuck with his merchandise a bit longer.

His greatest advantage though, is that the "long-term flipper" will usually have product left over while those involved in the quick-flip will have eventually sold out, leaving the addict with no choice but to buy from the dealer with the smaller bags. However, the time in which he has spent waiting for this moment will usually have taken its toll; in other words, the need to meet certain financial obligations will most likely have taken away from the hefty difference of what he expects to make and what he actually brings in.

Due to a most generous drug connection, I was buying four and a half ounces of base at six hundred and fifty dollars an ounce, which currently costs me twenty-six hundred dollars a flip. On the strength of my patronage, the half-ounce was free of charge. It was a dirt-cheap bargain that allowed me to bag up large nickel bags of base while at the same time, turn a generous profit.

Although I'd normally package close to sixty-five hundred dollars' worth of base, I'd owe twenty-six hundred dollars of it to the next purchase, leaving me with a gain of roughly four thousand dollars from each flip. In order to establish some type of financial stability while satisfying my own obligations, I created and implemented a system that would enable me to successfully meet my responsibilities and, at the same time, ensure a bit of security for me and mines.

"Droughts" (periods of time when drug suppliers are unable to distribute product to drug dealers that sell hand-to-hand) are one of the most detrimental setbacks to those like myself whom are involved with the quick-flip; therefore, I made it my business to repurchase product as soon as possible, whether materializing my profit or not. Saving money was an option to be considered only after the amount of base I had stashed away matched the amount of base I was currently buying. For me, having product will always outweigh the need to have money.

It was a slow, grinding process that demanded every fiber of sacrifice and discipline, yet after six months of adhering to such a strict means of budgeting my earnings, I had at last begun to achieve a solid sense of financial stability without arousing the attention of fellow dealers, who in all reality, are nothing more than fierce and sometimes dangerous competition. From personal experience, I've come to learn that a great deal of robberies, murders, and incarcerations are caused by the closest of friends, those who can't help but to harbor envy of the other's benefits from using proper judgment. With that particular lesson, I was quick to learn that secrecy was every bit a tool for survival as it was for success, and deception was most definitely a means of exercising its power.

I never once boasted about the cash I made or bothered to flash the profits I earned from hustling, nor did I ever speak braggingly of my success. More importantly, I made sure to keep any information of how much "weight" (the term used for any amount of drugs greater than an ounce) I bought, or whom I bought it from, a complete and total mystery. Even now, my dress code was less than flamboyant, and I kept no more than a few hundred dollars in my pocket at a time. While everyone guessed that I may be scoring one or two "onions" (slang term for ounces) per flip, contrarily, I was moving close to four and half ounces through Puerto Rican Mannie and doing quite well.

After my purchase of more than six thousand dollars' worth of product, I would cut and package it into six individual "G-packs" (a G-pack being one thousand dollars' worth of packaged narcotics) and then hand them to Mannie once at a time, receiving seven hundred dollars in return for each package. Our relationship enabled him to earn three hundred dollars for each G-pack he sold while the average worker earned only two hundred. The slightly higher pay was an induced incentive for him to appreciate my generosity and work even harder to keep things in their proper order.

Mannie's hustler ambitions were pretty much the same as Donnie's, to make a name for his self, but lacking Donnie's courage, Mannie wouldn't dare overstep his boundaries nor place himself in a situation where his toughness would be tested. By no means did he want to fight with anyone for a sale. With that being said, Mannie had no choice but to rely on his people persons' skills; still in all, it more so a blessing to both me and him instead of being a curse.

Mannie was attuned to the concept of money being the "end all - be all" for those living the street life, and with a comprehension of that idea, Mannie lost little time with finding out what works well for him when dealing with the competition of other hustlers. He not only understood the difference between his pay and others', but he also understood the danger of flaunting it as well. In short, he religiously followed my instructions to stay clear of the limelight.

As of today, I have managed to accumulate eight thousand, seven hundred and sixty dollars, not including the money I needed to re-up, and three ounces of base, which lay tightly sealed in clear plastic wrapping. Unlike most dealers who would either rush off to buy a bigger package or indulge in a bit of shopping, I saw my modest savings as a near infallible means of protecting myself against the many unseen impediments that forever lurked about in the lifestyle we lived.

If, by chance, I were to ever get "cased" (slang term for being incarcerated), I'd possess the means to bail out of jail, hire a respectable lawyer and have a substantial amount of product stashed away in order to sell and get back on my feet; as soon as the opportunity for bail presents itself, I'll be back on the streets and in the mix of things almost as if nothing had ever happened.

Due to the imposing presence of an ever-vigilant drug task force, it wouldn't have been such a bad idea for me to relax from the streets for a while, but the pressure I felt to make ends meet only strengthened my urge to challenge the wits of Camden City's Police Department. Dealers and addicts alike may fear harassment from local authorities, but addicts will be addicts, and their need to buy and abuse drugs was every bit as great as my need to profit from them.

My attention was now diverted towards Lakeisha, who had violently, and without warning, snatched back the shower curtain. The rage about her eyes was projecting a most murderous glare.

"Yeah, motherfucker!" she spat, mistaking my fear of the knife she was holding for surprise to see her holding my cell phone in the other hand. "What the fuck was you so busy doin' last night that you had to turn off your phone? "

A sigh of exasperation had escaped my lips. I was all too familiar with Lakeisha's possessive and sometimes explosive ways; therefore, I knew that it was best for me remain quiet while she was in the midst of having one of her fits. Lakeisha was a fervent woman, impassioned and energetic and never hesitant when expressing how she felt. Although she and I have never physically fought one another, there were several incidents when I thought such an altercation would occur, and this instant seemed like such a time.

"Let me get out the shower first," I said while shutting off the water. "We can talk while I'm getting dressed."

Lakeisha's facial expression was now a mixture of both humor and disgust.

"Talk?" she mocked. "Are you fuckin' serious, Dijuan?! Talk? There aint nothin' for us to talk about! You're gonna tell me where the fuck you were at last night, and you're gonna tell me what the fuck you were doin' . . . and you're gonna tell me now, yo!"

I stepped out of the tub and reached for my bath towel, stealthily watching Lakeisha through the corner of my eye as I began drying myself off. Now semi-dressed and with my soaking wet feet planted firmly on the bathroom rug, I felt a bit more secure and able to challenge the momentum of our conversation.

"Things was gettin' hot and heavy at Rashon's crib, last night," I heard myself half-lie. "Niggas was fightin' and the whole shit, and through it all, I was tryin' to re-up, so I ain't really have time to keep goin' back an' forth wit' you over some shit that's not even worth us fighitn' over. There . . . you fuckin' happy?"

I could slowly feel my anger began to kindle while explaining myself. The two of us both knew that our dialogue was about to take a turn for the worst; however, like Lakeisha, this is something that I knew and understood, but, still, I couldn't help but to go on.

"You know how I am when it comes to you askin' questions about me hustlin' an' shit, so stop tryin' to make somethin' out of nothin', yo. This is the shit that got us fighin' wit' each other last night, and it ain't even worth it, Keisha, so please . . . just cut it the fuck out, yo . . . please."

Lakeisha didn't reply but instead, remained quiet. I could tell that she was only searching for a way to continue venting her suspicions.

"Oh, so that's how you think you're gonna do me when you don't feel like talkin'?" she asked with sharp, distrustful eyes. "You mean to tell me that you gon' use them niggas out there on the streets as an excuse not to straighten out your problems at home?!?So you're tellin' me that them niggas out there are more important than your fuckin' family, Dijuan?"

Lakeisha knew full well that I placed her and our family above anyone else; everything I did in the streets, including all the risks and consequences that were involved, were all for the sake of us having a better life. She didn't have to break a single sweat nor spend one green dollar to feed, clothe, or shelter anyone under our roof. These were all responsibilities that I assumed, and I hadn't let her down once. The fact that Lakeisha would continue on with such a blatant untruth as a means to argue, to me, was disrespectful, and I had little patience for it.

"What?!?" I asked angrily, this time, matching her evil gaze with one of my own.

Lakeisha had just now lost her footing in the argument, and the two of us both knew it. A slight trace of defeat was now beginning to surface through the rage once storming about her eyes; yet, Lakeisha and I have been together long enough for me to know that she would not concede without a fight, despite it being all in vain.

The momentum had shifted, and I had now transformed my defensive position into one of offense in a swift matter of minutes.

"Dijuan, why you . . ."

"Come on, man," I interrupted while brushing my teeth. "It's early as hell, and you're on some fuckin' bullshit. Da fuck are you bitchin' about, Keisha?"

I spat a huge mixture of toothpaste and saliva into the bathroom sink and then rinsed my mouth clean before continuing on. "It's too fuckin' early for this bullshit, Keisha, I'm tellin' you."

With that, I pushed past her and started towards the bedroom where Lakeisha had suddenly began to follow behind me, not bothering to say a word. She remained silent while taking a seat near the edge of the bed, watching as I applied lotion to my body before slipping on a pair of boxer shorts and then a pair of black denim jeans.

"I know you're out there trickin' (slang term for being adulterous), Dijuan," she mumbled gloomily. "I do everything I can to make you happy, Dijuan. All I want is for us to be a family, but you actin' like you don't even give a fuck, and that's fucked up, Dijuan. I swear to God, Dijuan . . . that's fucked up, yo... you ain't right."

Lakeisha was harping on the same argument from last night, and today, I had even less patience. We both knew there was absolutely no truth to the point she was determined to argue. I was trying my best to ignore her and remain silent, but we both know that such a method never works. Lakeisha is the type of person to always test my will, and me being silent was more or less a form of giving up, and giving up ground in any way, shape, fashion or form will only invite her to try and force me to compromise somewhere else. We've been down this road one too many times already, and I knew far better than to give in.

I had already moved to discard our previous spat and was now fighting to sort out my obligations for the day. The possibility of getting cased by the police was at an all-time high, yet the children's need for new sneakers and nice Christmas gifts wouldn't allow me to rest; not to mention the bills, a two hundred and twenty-seven dollar phone bill and a three hundred and seventy-five dollar electric bill to be exact.

All of these things, including the thoughts on my plans to retaliate against Jay-Dollar later on tonight, were working my nerves at a most terrific pace. Everything, including my very own life, was a stake. Lakeisha's so-called doubts about my commitment to our family's well-being seemed terribly insignificant, and she was aggravating my nerves more and more with each passing moment. She nearly jumped out of her skin when I, without warning, turned around and lunged in her direction.

"Man, gimme this fuckin' phone!" I raged while snatching it from out of her grasp. "I go through too much shit for you and the mafuckas that live here to be goin' through some bullshit about some fuckin' phone, some fuckin' phone call, or anything else you fuckin' bitchin' about! I run the streets all fuckin' day and do what I gotta do to make ends meet around this mafucka! How're you gon' come at me bitchin' on some little kid shit shit when I'm out here riskin' my life and my freedom for us? Man, get the fuck out of here wit' that shit, nigga! I don't want to hear that bullshit!"

I raged on for the next five or so minutes, allowing myself to be lost in all of the frustration I was now venting on Lakeisha. It was only when recognizing the undeniable look of defeat in her eyes that I took notice of just how verbally abusive I was being. Lakeisha remained quiet while sitting on the bed with her arms crossed and looking off into another direction, seeming as if to hide the humiliation of her being berated and reprimanded like a child. She was nervously biting away at her bottom lip, which was a tell-tale sign of her struggling not to reply with some sort of snappy comeback. Her feisty spirit had been temporarily defeated, which made my own victory bittersweet.

In fact, it was more bitter than sweet.

I loved Lakeisha with all of my heart, and I hated to see her unhappy, especially when knowing that I am the reason for her sadness. Stricken with guilt, I turned away from the sight of her being in such dismay and continued to get dressed for the day. I slipped a white tee shirt over my tank top before putting on my favorite sweatshirt and then carried my Timberland boots with me as I walked over and sat on the edge of the bed opposite to Lakeisha. By now, she was stretched out along the edge of the mattress with her back towards me, facing the wall.

This was the "break-up to make-up" segment of our argument, in which passionate love is to be made after some of our most heated quarrels. I knew what she wanted, but the course of today's events demanded my immediate attention. Once checking the clock, I felt even more inclined to set things into motion; therefore, I started towards the closet to retrieve both my pistol and my army coat.

I pulled my Glock-nine millimeter handgun, along with its cartridge, from off the top shelf of the closet and inspected its bullets before loading and tucking it into the waistband of my jeans. I then snatched my army coat from off its hanger, all the while staring at Lakeisha, whose body was silently screaming out for my attention. I was dressed, armed and ready for the day, but the thought of leaving her alone in such gloom felt totally wrong; no, it felt totally unacceptable.

Despite the super-macho image that I had been so successful with promoting amongst my peers, I was really soft and tender at heart, especially for the woman I love; therefore, I had no problem with giving in to the emotions I try so hard to conceal from the elements I co-exist with out in the streets. I withdrew my pistol and placed it in on the dresser before sliding onto the bed beside Lakeisha, easing the crook of my arm beneath and around her neck to fully caress her.

"This fightin' shit is corny as well," I said softly while kissing along the nape of Lakeisha's neck. "Let's make up and be friends."

"Don't be tryin' to downgrade my status, nigga," she replied sharply. "I'm your mafuckin' wife; fuck that 'let's be friends' shit."

The feel of Lakeisha arching her buttocks hard against my crotch had aroused me just enough to momentarily forsake the entire world for an instance to be with her. Everything between us seemed to be in perfect peace, and in that very moment, all the pain, all the anger and any hard feelings that had once existed were now totally erased. I sensed her need to be cherished and appreciated, to be reminded that I cared for her; and in turn, she sensed my need to fulfill them.

"Stop playin' tough, nigga," I growled with her earlobe pinched sharply between my teeth. "Now, turn around and kiss a mafucka."

She twisted herself on top of me, and I, always the one to be in control, rolled with her momentum and flipped myself on top of her.

"I'm gonna go lock the bedroom door," I said after kissing Lakeisha on the lips.

"Go lock it then, punk," she replied while kissing me back.

I matched the loving look in her eyes with a playful sneer of my own while rising up to go and lock the bedroom door. In a mere matter of seconds, I was at the foot of the bed, beginning to undress. Lakeisha watched with hungry eyes as I wasted very little time with stripping down to my boxer shorts, which did little to conceal my now stiffened erection. Before making my way to the bed, I took a moment to grab the remote control for our stereo system and switch to a more romantic radio station. Jodeci's "Forever My Lady" was playing, and it couldn't have been better timing.

At twenty-nine years of age, Lakeisha was still a ravishing beauty. Despite a slight droop of her breasts and the few stretch marks she kept hidden by not taking off her tee shirt, Lakeisha didn't possess the body of a woman who had borne four children. Her limbs were sinewy and well-defined; her stomach was flat, her buttocks, round and firm. Her thick, jet-black hair was long and styled in a ponytail, accenting the sharp, slanted look about her eyes which were now peering out from beneath a smooth set of eyebrows.

Lakeisha's face was aglow, and as her pink, fleshy lips parted into a broad white-toothed smile, I fell in love with her all over again.

"Stop playin' an' take your shirt off," I said while sliding back onto the bed beside her. "You act like I ain't never seen you naked before."

"You're the man of the house, right?" Lakeisha teased. "Won't you come over here and take it off me your mafuckin' self."

I smiled to myself while easing on top of her, and then, with every ounce of love I felt beating from within my heart, I kissed her ever so gently on the lips. The seductive gaze we held after our kiss, along with the flutter of Lakeisha's eyes as I worked my way inside of her was the purest definition of lovemaking that I had ever partaken in thus far; and the soft gasp that escaped Lakeisha's lips as we began to enjoy one another only urged me to further thank God for another chance to experience the pleasure of pleasing her.

9:30 a.m.

Like South Camden, East Camden is very much a huge section of the city; it, too, consisted of countless streets that, in turn, gave birth to scores of neighborhood drug sets within its interior. Twenty-Fifth Street is one of many East Camden neighborhoods that, throughout the course of time, had made quite a name for itself in the city's criminal underworld.

I lived three doors down from the corner of Twenty-Fifth and High Street, which just so happens to be the southernmost end and heart of what was more popularly known as "Two-Five" or "Two-Fifth Street." It is, without a doubt, a high crime area where drug activity is a twenty-four hour a day business and where the cliché, "being at the wrong place at the wrong time," is an absolute reality.

Thugs hung out and conducted their illegal activities in broad daylight, unfettered by the ever-lurking presence of the police. With the evening came a personification of Twenty-Fifth Street's criminal culture. Everything considered to be the exact opposite of what's good and righteous seemed at its full glory of being during the day, but even more so during the evening hours. Cars frequented the area with rap music booming loudly from their speakers at all times of the night; drug dealers, addicts and local hoodlums, alike flourished in whatever manner of business they were involved in. It all seemed like an on-going 'hood movie that never ended.

While lying in bed, Lakeisha and I could overhear a great deal of what was going on outside of our home. We were left with no choice but to listen in on their conversations, their laughter, their arguments and every now and then, even their plans for war. The sound of police cars racing about with their sirens aloud was a routine occurrence. The ear-piercing reports of gunfire were sometimes heard, but far from surprising.

Needless to say, Lakeisha absolutely detested this neighborhood and made it her business to tell me so on a regular basis. She complained bitterly about the neighborhood ruckus being too close to our home and she even went on to vent about the criminal activity that was going on next door to our house. She griped about the wandering eyes of drug dealers and feared for the safety of her children . . . OUR children . . . as she would so fervently state.

I, too, did not like where we lived, but not so much because of the abundance of criminal activity. Camden's criminal element is prevalent just about anywhere in the city; it's just an unfortunate reality. My concerns were more so about us being outsiders in the eyes of one of the more violent-prone neighborhoods in Camden rather than the random criminal activity that existed around us. In short, my concerns were Lakeisha's fears multiplied to the highest power; and had she'd seen things though my eyes, her stress level would be in heart attack range every day of the week.

As long as we lived in neighborhoods we aren't native to, Lakeisha and I will always be considered outsiders, and in any inner-city neighborhood, outsiders were always prone to the hostility of local riff-raff. Appearing a bit too lavish gave way to the chance of us arousing the attention of those whom are always hungry to make a few extra dollars, no matter what the method. Armed robberies, home invasions, extortion, and even kidnappings are crude but common methods of taxing those particular residents who weren't homegrown. On the other hand, projecting a peaceful, neighborly image could easily be mistaken for weakness and would only entice the same shady individuals whom we try so hard not to bump heads with. In short, life in a foreign neighborhood is perilous. No matter where Lakeisha and I moved in the city of Camden, we were sure to encounter the same scenario.

I disliked living in this neighborhood every bit as much as Lakeisha, but I didn't think the time was right for us to just up and move. Even drug addicts celebrated Christmas, which meant that a portion of what they'd usually spend will go to family members. Business will be slower this time of year, and with my own neighborhood being a place of interest for the police, it was definitely a strain for me to acquire what little profit there was to be made.

It was during these times when Mannie's services, along with my pager clientele, proved invaluable; still, it was just barely enough to keep me financially afloat. Aside from this month's rent and utilities that had yet to be paid, my family was no doubt expecting a good Christmas. And that didn't include my week-old promise to buy the kids' new sneakers.

Letting my purchase of their sneakers be considered as Christmas gifts may undoubtedly be a more economical solution, but to the children, it would not only be unfair, it will be totally disappointing as well. I loved being their "daddy," and the thought of straining such an impression because of my own shortcomings was unbearable.

*   *   *

It was a sunny, but extremely frigid morning; yet it did nothing to slow down the everyday business of Twenty-Fifth and High Street. From where I was standing on the porch, I could see local hustlers clustered together on nearby street corners, all of them bundled up as best they could against the weather. The black, navy-blue and brown colors of their ran-down wardrobes only reflected the drab atmosphere of this East Camden neighborhood; these were the local hand-to-hand to drug dealers still fighting tooth-and-nail to meet a quota. Such was the same for every neighborhood in Camden, Mid Town included. I was instantly struck with an urgency to get into the streets of my own 'hood.

I stood at the top of the porch steps as a clear-cut example of color-coordination; my black denim jeans, black knitted cap, and black army jacket, which remained open to expose a thirty-inch gold and diamond-encrusted necklace, served to accent my oak-brown Timberland boots and matching sweatshirt. My wardrobe may not have been expensive or brand new, but the manner in which I put it all together gave me the look of being an official hustler. The pistol I kept tucked in the waist band of my jeans, along with the large wad of cash in my pants pocket, however, verified as much.

All feelings of love and intimacy that I had so freely shared with Lakeisha and our children were now left behind the doors of my home. A family man had no place in this fierce, competitive, and often deadly world of drug dealing. No longer Dijuan Ingles Sr., a man who deeply loves his woman and his children, I departed home as "Don Juan," a drug dealer from Mid Town that will do whatever he has to do in order to get paid.

*   *   *

At least once every month, Archie, my drug connection, will disappear for two or three days. I assumed that it was probably during this time that he was making his move to "re-up" (term used for renewing one's supply of product). It was now "day-two" of his hiatus, and I was beginning to grow a bit antsy. With the exception of the two G-packs I had given to Mannie, my flip was nearly finished; all that remained of this current flip was five hundred and forty dollars' worth of base which I was quite sure would be sold sometime by the end of the day. The thought of running out of product and waiting at least another day or so to re-up wasn't good. Sitting still wasn't one of my favorite things to do; I feared idle time as if it were the devil itself.

While driving down Federal Street towards Mid Town, I was still debating whether to wait around for Archie or bag up some of the base that I already had stashed away for a rainy day. Dipping into the base I already had saved away would take away from my "rainy day fund," and by discipline, I would be inclined to put back into that stash before seeing any profit. Needless to say, it was a setback that I really didn't care to experience at this present time.

After a sharp turn off the Federal Street Bridge and onto a highway ramp, I was now cruising past the Campbell Soup Administration building and only a few minutes away from my neighborhood. My struggle to decide whether or not to wait for Archie was growing more intense by the second.

My neighborhood was terribly "hot" (slang term for being under pressure from police surveillance), which greatly increased my chances of being arrested. The money to be made during these trying times will most likely fail to match the expense of getting knocked, but the livelihood of my family depended upon how much money I brought home every night. I couldn't afford to be afraid of the police right now. While turning onto a cobblestone back road which lie adjacent to my end of Haddon Avenue, I decided to "bag up" (package drugs) one of the three ounces I had saved and stashed away. There was absolutely no way I could go a day without making money; I was determined to keep my hustle going whether I saw Archie or not.

I recognized Mannie standing at the corner of Haddon Avenue and Pine Street. His trademark goose-down jacket and paisley-print skullcap was unmistakable. Mannie is, and always has been, a more nocturnal type of individual. Although much preferring the peace of the midnight shift, Mannie would occasionally flirt with the morning hours if he only had a little bit left. Seeing him out and about at this particular time of the morning was a clear indication of him either being finished or a few "bundles" (a bundle being one hundred dollars' worth of packaged product) away from being finished. I smiled while blowing my horn to get his attention while pulling over by the curb.

"What's up, my nigga?" Mannie asked while entering my car through the passenger side door; I almost shivered from the pre-winter chill that he had brought along with him.

Mannie's face was tight from the sharp December winds, and the dull glaze I saw from within his reddened eyes told of a long night of smoking and drinking.

"Ain't shit," I replied while pulling off and crossing Haddon Avenue towards Mt. Ephraim Avenue. "I was hopin' you'd tell me."

"You know what it is, big homie," he replied with a tired, but triumphant smile. He then handed me a huge roll of dollar bills. "That's fourteen hundred."

Careful not to be spotted by nosy neighbors and our ever competitive "co-hustlers," I turned the corner and pulled over onto Mt. Ephraim Avenue, just in front of Division Street.

"You finished?"

"Nah," Mannie replied. "I still got a couple bundles left."

My pager began to sound off as I finished stuffing the cash Mannie had just now given me down into my pants pocket. The screen read 7465-400, which was a cryptic code from Mr. Benson for a delivery of four hundred dollars' worth of base.

"I need a ride, dawg," Mannie said while relighting his blunt.

"Where?" I asked while silently cursing Mannie for his inconvenience.

"Out East," he replied.

"Out East?" I retorted while declining to indulge in the weed Mannie was trying to offer me. I was now visibly perturbed. "I just came from out East."

"Come on, man," he pleaded from behind a cloud of marijuana smoke. "I'm tryin' to get on Rand Street. That's right over the bridge."

"Rand Street?" I questioned while pulling out and starting back onto Mt. Ephraim Avenue. "Who you fuckin' wit' out there?"

"This bitch named Randi."

"Randi?" I inquired. "I know you ain't talkin' about the chick that got a baby by that dude, Bamboo."

Again, Mannie flashed a most victorious smile.

"Hell yeah, nigga," he answered triumphantly. "She's the truth. Why, what's up? You hit that?"

I've known Randi Thompson since my days in junior high school, before she moved from Parkside to East Camden. With a cute face and well-developed body, Randi was the apple of every young boy's eye; consequently, she was one of the more popular kids in school. But like many popular school kids, times change and fortune had eventually turned against her. Randi wound up dropping out of school while in the tenth grade and went on to mother five children by five different deadbeat dads, one of them being Bamboo, a local tough guy whom had recently been released from prison.

"Nah," I replied. "She ain't really my type."

"Sheeeit," Mannie declared. "She's everybody's type, nigga! She's a mafuckin' freak!"

"You better watch out for her baby-dad, yo," I warned. "You know he just came home an' shit."

"Who? Bamboo?" Mannie sneered. "Man, he don't give a fuck about that bitch. And even if he did . . . man, fuck that nigga. He's a snitch anyway."

Once again, Mannie had proven to me why he'd never be anything more than a bottom notch on the criminal food chain. A great deal of his decision making was poor and based more on his lack of discipline.

"Right there," Mannie said while pointing at a shabby row home. "That's her crib, right there."

"I'll holla at you later," I said to Mannie while shaking his hand. "You be safe out here, nigga . . . and I hope you're 'strappin' up' (using condoms for safe sex) wit' this chick, too, yo."

Mannie only smiled.

"Peace my nigga. Get at me when you get straight."

I lit myself a cigarette and watched as Mannie strode up the walkway towards Randi's house, half-expecting him to bump into Bamboo who may very well be on his way out. With Randi being known for her porn-style sexual prowess, and Bamboo being famous for his "act now-think later" state of mind, I definitely saw trouble in Mannie's future.

While pulling off and starting up Rand Street, I retrieved my cell phone and dialed Mr. Benson's phone number.

"Hey, Mr. B."

"Is this my buddy?" he affectionately joked.

"The one and only," I replied. "What can I do for you?"

"You didn't get right back at me, so I figured you were unavailable."

"Nah, Mr. B," I replied, hoping that he hadn't already made a move to buy from someone else. "I was caught in the middle of some bullshit, but everything's straight now. You still need me to bring you somethin' back from the store?"

"Of course," he answered.

"Alright, cool," I replied smoothly. "Gimme like ten to fifteen minutes."

There was now a brief pause between Mr. Benson and my dialogue. The hesitation on his behalf was based more so on his eagerness to get high. He'd been waiting long enough for my services and didn't want to wait another ten to fifteen more minutes. Mr. B.'s impatience would inevitability lead him to go elsewhere if I couldn't persuade him to sit tight and wait patiently for me.

"You know how I do, Mr. B.," I remarked with a hidden sense of desperation. "It'll definitely be worth the wait. I got you covered, my man. Trust me. Hold still for a minute and you'll be happy that I came through for you."

"All right, bud," said Mr. Benson while sounding a bit dejected. "Make 'em healthy."

"No problem," I replied while feeling a slight touch of relief. I really couldn't afford to lose a sale for four hundred dollars' worth of base; and knowing that I had won him over had instantly helped smooth out my trepidation. "I'll see you in a few."

The two of us had both hung up the phone, and in a matter of minutes, I was back on Haddon Avenue heading southbound toward my neighborhood. Despite being pressed for time, I decided not to turn down Spruce Street and instead continued down Haddon Avenue for a quick look at what may be going on around the way.

Both Rashon and C-Gutter were local thugs who had little to no ambition in the business of drug dealing. C-Gutter was more or less one of the stragglers in our 'hood; for the most part, he didn't do much more than hang out and get high, at times, selling a bundle or two for Rashon whenever Rashon was able to employ him . The two of them were standing on the porch of an abandoned home, sharing a blunt as I neared the corners of Haddon Avenue and Pine Street. They greeted me with upraised fists when recognizing my Honda station wagon as I cruised through. I honked my horn in acknowledgment of their welcome before continuing on making a left onto Pine Street and then another left onto Mt. Ephraim Avenue before parking my car near the alley which serves as a shortcut from Division Street to Spruce Street.

MidTown may have a been a small, almost minute neighborhood, but its complex network of alleys, which coincided with an array of streets, made our 'hood a tiny labyrinth that provided us with numerous escape routes from impending drug sweeps, which we all called "raids." It was by way one of these routes that I would travel and make my way to see one of the oldest and closest friends I have.

10:00 a.m.

I've known Tamara McGee, more commonly known to everyone in the 'hood as "Tammy," since I was a child. She and her older brother, Marquis, lived across the street from my family with their aunt, Ms. Beatrice, who also just happened to be best friends with my mother. Ms. Beatrice and my mother had been close to one another since grade school, which iswhat ultimately begat the fusion of our two families. She and my mother were like sisters, my older brother and Tamara's older brother considered themselves brothers, and I was left alone with nothing but a tremendous crush on Tammy, who was nearly five years my senior.

What both families had in common, besides poverty, was a heartbreaking string of tragedies; and with each calamity came a closer binding of all our individual lives to one another. Ms. Beatrice was diagnosed with terminal cancer less than a year after my father's untimely death, and my brother was killed years later during the same botched robbery that landed Marquis in prison with a life sentence. Ms. Beatrice died not too long afterward, leaving Tamara alone with an empty home and dozens of unpaid bills; and such was the same for my mother.

With sharp, beautiful features, a well-toned physique, and a passionate, almost domineering personality,

Tamara was undoubtedly the most attractive woman in our neighborhood; however, she was extremely reclusive and practically remained hidden from nearly everyone and anything involving the 'hood. Her life consisted of working at night and spending her days alone and absorbed in what appeared to me as a dark, brooding world of melancholy. All attempts to bring her out of this state were met with an open barrage of attitude and hostility, and that was definitely too much for the average person to bear. In other words, it was best for most people to simply leave her alone.

Luckily, Tamara had known me since childhood and considered my mother and me to be the only family she has left, and this allowed me to enjoy certain privileges that were vital to my livelihood as an effective hustler. Despite Tamara's adamant protests, I paid her quarterly house taxes and half the utilities; in return, she'd given me an extra set of keys to her house and a key to one of her spare bedrooms as well. Tamara's home was the perfect place of sanctity. She was such a privy and unpleasant individual, that no one would ever imagine, let alone prove, that I was using the house in which she lived as a stash house.

With both Mr. Benson and Archie weighing heavily on my mind, I couldn't wait to get inside of Tamara's house. After returning back to the 'hood and parking my car near the corners of Division Street and Mt. Ephraim Avenue, I walked swiftly through the maze of alleys and side streets to reach her home. I was moving speedily but stealthily, almost as if someone were following me. The rush to go and handle my business was reduced to a slow, casual stroll as I entered through the back door to find Tamara standing at the kitchen stove, dressed in her pajamas.

As always, her beauty was radiant. The swell of Tamara's breasts were pressed ever so teasingly against the fabric of an over-sized sweatshirt, and her shorts revealed a strong and well-defined set of legs, both of them being thoroughly lotioned and emphasizing a smooth, honey-brown complexion. Blonde and light-brown strands of hair fell from beneath a handkerchief which was tied and knotted on the front of her head.

I was but nine years old when Tamara had slapped me senseless for attempting to grope her, and despite that happening more than a decade ago, I'd instantly relive the humiliation of that event whenever she so happened to look into my eyes and almost discover that I was ogling her.

"What's up, Dijuan?" she asked while whipping a batch of eggs around in a large, black frying pan.

"I gotta beep somebody from your phone real quick," I replied while heading towards the cordless phone lying atop the kitchen table. I then grabbed a beer from inside of the refrigerator while at the same time dialing Archie's pager number. Despite me not looking in Tamara's direction, I could all but feel the heat of her eyes staring me down.

"Don't you have a phone upstairs?" she asked smartly.

"Yeah," I replied while opening the beer bottle. "But it couldn't wait . . . I had to beep dude now. I put in my upstairs number, so don't trip. I ain't gon' have nobody callin' here for you an' shit."

Tamara flashed a smirk while turning her gaze back to the eggs she'd been preparing.

"You hungry?" she asked. "I put cheese in 'em."

"Yeah," I answered while on my way out of the kitchen. "I'll be back down in a minute."

My only form of paradise was straight up the stairs and to the rear of the house, protected from the outside world by a bolt lock and key that I, and I alone, possessed. Just to be safe, I made sure to keep a spare key hidden in a place in the house that only I knew of. With a swift turn of the key, I was soon about to enter. An involuntary sigh of relief had escaped my lips while making my way inside. I couldn't help but to absolutely adore the sense of comfort I enjoyed when being here.

The first sight upon entering inside my bedroom is a queen-sized bedroom set, two end tables, and a bureau which were all coated in black lacquer. The wall to the right side of my bedroom played host to a string of posters which I aptly dubbed my "Wall of Fame." There were posters of Bruce Lee, Tupac Shakur, Malcolm X, and an enlarged photograph of my father and older brother which was encased in a bronze picture frame with "**R.I.P. MY NIGGAS: SEE YOU WHEN I GET THERE**" engraved at the bottom.

My mother would have gone ballistic if she had seen such an inscription. As a black woman who had grown up during the civil rights era, she absolutely abhorred our use of the word "nigga." With her, there was no rationalizing the difference between a "nigger" and a "nigga," and to be honest, I couldn't really justify it either. I understood the history of Black people in America, and therefore, I tried as best I could to guard myself against indulging in the use of it. Sometimes, however, the word would occasionally slip from off my tongue, and I would silently burn with shame for doing so.

Despite her petite size and pious appearance, Mrs. Lorraine Martha Ingles was the exact oppositeof what she may appear to be on face value. My mother is, and always has been fiercely aggressive and extremely opinionated, wasting little time with expressing how she felt. More so than not, my mother would demonstrate her will in a cold, almost tyrannical fashion. There was no arguing with her, let alone winning. Mrs. Ingles' word is, and always will be, final and absolute.

My mother was very much aware of the illegal activities I was involved with in the streets, and she had given me more than an earful of reproach for engaging in such "niggard-ness" and "stupidity." Now, years later, her ear-scorching reprimands came only when she was in the mood to do so; this undoubtedly gave whatever time we'd spend together an edge of awkwardness and uncertainty. Mrs. Ingles was definitely a dangerous and arbitrary person to converse with, very much like Tamara, and it is probably why the two of them got along so well with one another.

Once inside the bedroom and after locking the door behind me, I emptied the contents of my coat pockets onto the bed and then placed my beer and pistol on top of the dresser where a half bottle of Scotch had been sitting since early yesterday afternoon. I reopened the bottle and swallowed a good portion of liquor and then followed the taste of it with a healthy guzzle of beer while fumbling around the top drawer of my bureau for whatever was left of my flip.

Ever the cautious type, all eight thousand-seven hundred and sixty dollars of my savings was locked in a fire-resistant deposit box, which was safely hidden away in Tamara's basement. The spare key to my deposit box was placed on the very same ring that held the spare key to my bedroom.

I had just finished counting up all the money from my last flip when the phone rang; its caller I.D. read "NUMBER RESTRICTED," which meant that it was Archie.

Had he still been on hiatus, Archie would have never answered my page. Words couldn't explain how relieved I was to learn that I wouldn't be forced to tap into my stash of base. I took another swallow of liquor and then answered the phone.

"Yo."

"D-Block, what's good?"

"You tell me," I replied, answering to the codename he'd given me. "I'm tryin' to handle my handle an' shit. What's good wit' you?"

"Same ol' shit?" he asked.

Same ol' shit," I replied.

"I'll meet you out P.S.M., at papi's house. Gimme an hour."

"True."

"Peace."

"Peace."

And just like that, in a mere matter of seconds, I had placed an order for four and half ounces of base; the agreement had been made for us to meet at a Dominican grocery store in Parkside within an hour to make the purchase.

With my order for four and half ounces now arranged, delivering Mr. Benson's four bundles of base was my next order of business. Given a little more than sixty minutes of allotted free time, I then made the decision to get a haircut after seeing Mr. Benson. I separated his portion of base from the total amount I had left and placed it into its own plastic bag, finished the rest of my beer, and then took another swallow of liquor before lighting a cigarette. The alcohol was now finding its way throughout my body, and with the smooth, resonant state of mind it bought, came the understanding that my day had now officially began.

While tucking the pistol back on my hipand sliding back into my army coat, I simultaneously began to conduct an assessment of my earnings from this past flip. Paying Mannie for selling two G-packs, along with the minor expense of day-to-day living, amounted up to a seven hundred dollar expenditure. That, along with the twenty-six hundred dollars it costs me to re-up, combined for an outlay of thirty-three hundred dollars. After subtracting all of this from the sixty-four hundred dollars' worth of base that I had "bagged up," I'd be left with a profit of thirty-one hundred dollars, which didn't include the money needed for this month's rent and utilities, and that will be another thousand dollars. On top of it all, I still hadn't bought the children's sneakers and Christmas gifts.

With it all being said and done, I'd be stashing away a little more than a thousand dollars, which was hardly worth the stress of running these streets. But then again, I was one step closer to having ten thousand dollars stashed away, which would undoubtedly place me in a rather advantageous position. I would soon be able to entertain the thought of doubling my purchase of base with the comfort of knowing that everything else was safe and secure. I took one more swig of liquor, finished my cigarette and then gathered my drugs and money before locking the door behind me and starting my way down the stairs.

Tamara was curled up in a corner of the sofa, reading a book when I made my way down the stairway. She was peering at the pages in her book through a pair of black-framed reading glasses.

"You got some weed?" she asked, not bothering to look up from whatever was capturing her attention.

"Nah," I replied while heading towards the kitchen. "I'm sayin' though, where's my eggs? I know you ain't play me out an' shit."

I looked back to find Tamara staring at me with a show of agitation.

"It's in the kitchen, mafucka," she snapped. "And stop tryin' to play me on some 'housewife shit, too, nigga. You shoulda made sure your baby-mom fed yo ass this morning' if you was that damned hungry."

Totally amused with Tamara's customary sarcasm, I only smiled while starting back towards the kitchen.

"Rasheed called," Tamara said as I began helping myself to the sandwich she had already prepared for me.

While holding the egg and cheese sandwich firmly in my hands, I froze dead in my tracks. All plans for the day had suddenly gone on pause. I immediately turned and began making my way back to the living room.

"When?" I asked, still holding the sandwich firmly in my grasp.

"You'd better not drop none of that shit on my carpet, nigga. I'll tell you that much."

It was now my turn to express a look of agitation.

"Stop playin', man," I replied dryly. "When did he call?"

Tamara's facial expression went smooth, her eyes hardening by the second, and at that very instant, I was face to face with my mother.

"First of all," she said coolly, but forcefully. "Do I look a fuckin' man to you? No! So don't fuckin' address me as one."

Being all-too familiar with Tamara's "hissy-fits," I decided to concentrate more so on the delicious taste of the egg and cheese sandwich instead of her anger and irritation. In between bites, I thought of Rasheed Daniels, Mid Town's neighborhood legend, who had managed to capture Tamara's heart before landing a thirty-year prison sentence for two counts of burglary and two counts of aggravated assault.

It was the harshest prison sentence that I, or anyone else for that matter, had ever heard of. The judge declared that it was the nature of his crime, along with Rasheed's blatant disrespect for the courtroom that had inclined him to impose such a punishment. It was said that Rasheed had constantly laughed at some of the witnesses' testimony, cursed them, and at one time, even spat on the floor throughout the course of the trial.

I was but a child when Rasheed was loose on the streets and for the most part, I had only heard of him by word of mouth. From the lips of old timers and those a few years older than myself, Sheed was a monster, a highly intelligent, no-nonsense type of criminal whom was often betrayed by his own seething temper. Everyone, including my older brother, idolized him.

It wasn't hard for me to imagine how both Rasheed and Tamara wound up moonlighting with one another; after all, he was Mid Town's "Thug of all Thugs," and she was the most beautiful and sought after female in the 'hood. What I couldn't understand though was how Rasheed had managed to acquire such an incredible grip on Tamara's mind and body, so much so, that she was serving Rasheed's thirty-year sentence right along with him. Instead of enjoying what life has to offer her as a young and incredibly attractive woman, Tamara, instead, chose to live a life similar to that of a convict.

With my egg and cheese sandwich now thoroughly devoured, I tuned back into the "here and now," where Tamara was still fussing and telling me off. The vibrating sensation of the pager against my waist was a reminder of my need to satisfy Mr. Benson's appetite to get high. Listening to Tamara's attitude was all too reminiscent of this morning's episode with Lakeisha, and I, like my earlier spat with Lakeisha, was now beginning to grow impatient.

"Listen," I interrupted rather gruffly. "I got somethin' to do. We'll have to talk about all this other shit later, all right? You want me to bring you some weed back, or what?"

Tamara's face drew tight and then relaxed, all within an instant.

"Fuck it then," she said while returning all her attention back to the book she'd been reading. "I'm good."

The atmosphere between us had grown ice-cold, leaving the last two words of Tamara's reply hanging in the air like a dark cloud of bad news. She was now in her *Fuck me? No, FUCK YOU!* state of mind, and there wasn't a single thing I'd be able to do to remedy how she felt.

I was more than tempted to try and reconcile, but I didn't have the time. For the second time today, I was setting my sentiments to the side, all for the sake of doing what I had to do out in the streets. And just like that, I brushed off any sense of regret I may have felt for dismissing Tamara's feelings.

"I'll see you when I get back, Tammy."

Tamara didn't bother to respond, and instead, continued reading as if I hadn't said a thing. Without bothering to utter another word, I turned and started towards the back door.

10:15 a.m.

Eighty-five dollars is the going rate for a bundle being sold on the streets, which means that those who'd purchase one hundred dollars' worth of base all at once will receive a fifteen dollar discount. Dealers whom were merely selling product for someone else usually couldn't afford to make such a bargain and would usually sell their bundles for ninety dollars instead of eighty-five. With the intense pressure brought on by the police, and the Christmas season taking away from our business revenue, deals for a bundle were practically nonexistent. Only a few hustlers, one of them being myself, could afford to do so, and that was just barely.

In order to outdo my competition, I sold my bundles for eighty dollars instead of eighty-five. This was another reason why I appreciated my pager clientele so much, for none of them knew or even cared to know about the "bundle deals." After much suffrage from the slew of bad experiences by way of these customers having to rely on shifty drug runners, they were all too happy to finally be in touch with the actual drug dealer himself; it was too much of blessing for them to have a direct line with the source for them to complain about paying full price for their product.

Just as I had figured, Mr. Benson was more than satisfied with my delivery. In fact, he was overjoyed. I made sure that all four bundles he had requested were as healthy as they could be, and he was more than thankful for my services. Mr. Benson was one of my more subtle customers who paid the full price for my product, and he was all too easy to accommodate, which was very much unlike the next customer whom I was now on my way to see.

Scrappy Shine was an addict who lived in a run-down row-home on the eight hundred block of Cherry Street, which lies between both Eighth and Ninth Streets in the Downtown section of Camden, right beside Mid Town. By Scrappy Shine's own admission, he was a one-time cocaine dealer who, like so many others during the early eighties, had fallen victim to the crack epidemic. His once eminent function as a stand-up hustler and ladies' man was now reduced to nothing more than a measly addict, respected by a new generation of dealers only for his expertise in transforming powder cocaine into base.

With powder cocaine, a decent portion of baking soda (preferably one-third the amount of powder cocaine)and near-boiling water, converting powder cocaine into base cocaine is a relatively simple task. All one needs to do is stir the two ingredients together in boiling water until they are both merged into one jelly-like substance, to which it is then removed and placed onto a plate so that it may harden from its exposure to air. The greatest attribute of a "chef" (the title given to one who converts powder cocaine into base) is not so much as being able to formulate cooked-up cocaine, but more so his ability to "stretch" (add extra grams to the product while converting it into rock) the product as much as possible without ruining its quality.

When stretching cocaine, an increase of baking soda is needed to thicken the substance and add weight to the product, but it will undoubtedly neutralize the potency of the narcotic; therefore, an extra ingredient is needed to boost its strength. There are a wide variety of elements one could use for this procedure, yet only a true chef knows which item to use for the best results. Stretching the cocaine is a delicate and complicated procedure that could very easily prove disastrous for an amateur chef. This was a concern more so for those who sold weight to the dealers rather than hand-to-hand hustlers like me who sold directly to the addicts.

With the ability to transform twenty-eight grams of powder cocaine into at least thirty-five grams of good quality base, Scrappy Shine proved himself to be a premier chef, yet his dubious disposition, along with the filthy environment in which he lived, made it near impossible for me to endure his company. It was a big enough struggle for me not to vomit while doing business with him, let alone sit beside him for hours on end as he cooked up and dried my product.

After parking in front of Scrappy Shine's shabby abode, I removed the Glock nine-millimeter from the side of my waist, removed its safety, and then placed it in the front pocket of my army coat before exiting the car; making sure my weapon was easy to get to was a key element of survival in these parts.

Scrappy Shine's home was a weigh station for a multitude of criminal activities. Drug addicts, prostitutes, drug dealers, and all other types of characters were prone to dwell within his house, and there was absolutely no telling who or what type of situation may materialize while inside. Once, while making a late night delivery, I was unarmed when bumping into a clique of rival enemies who were at his home for a reason unbeknownst to me. Despite there not being any type of conflict, still, the entire situation was extremely too close for my own comfort. The fact of the matter remained that I was beyond the borders of my neighborhood, unarmed and outnumbered; it would be a mistake that I was sure not to let make a second time.

The door was answered on the first knock by Blue Bird, a nondescript drug addict who often served as a courier between drug dealers and big spending addicts. He was a short, muddy-skinned man with raggedy braided hair, large bulging eyes, and a thick, uncombed beard.

"What's happenin', cap'n?" he asked with a dull, yellow-toothed smile. "Shit, it's colder than a son of a bitch out there. Come on in, so I can shut this door."

Within seconds of entering inside, my nostrils were instantly arrested by a wretched stench so strong that it seemed to be an entity of its own. It was a putrid combination of cigarette and base smoke, mixed with the repugnant coupling of body odors which were left by an incalculable amount of people who had traveled to and from this residence. I followed closely behind Blue Bird, all the while guarding the breaths I took for fear of ingesting the filth I felt sinking into my skin and clothing.

"Come on in, you jive mafucka, you!" said Scrappy Shine in response to my knock at his bedroom door. "It's about god-damned time!"

The obscene stench that I had endured while on my way through his home seemed to be condensed and concentrated into this one tiny room. The floor was littered with dirty clothes, food wrappings and a host of other things one would easily classify as garbage. Soiled sheets instead of curtains were nailed to the wooden frames of the windows which helped cast a dim light on Scrappy Shine, who was seated on the edge of his sheet-less bed, busying himself by cleaning a makeshift crack pipe. A skeletal female figure lay on the bed opposite to

Scrappy, the constant flittering of her eyes from me to Scrappy signifying her eagerness to get high.

"Damn, nigga," he said while concentrating on the task at hand. "It's bad enough that you ain't even got the whole two bundles, but you take forever to get here."

The source of Scrappy Shine's dissatisfaction was more so because of me only having one hundred and forty of the two hundred dollars' worth of base he wanted. My timing, however, wasn't an issue; in fact, I was a few minutes earlier than what I had originally promised. I despised being in the midst of such filth and was getting even more irritated by Scrappy Shine's senseless complaints, which were only holding me here longer than I desired.

"Listen, man," I bluffed, making sure to express my irritation. "I just turned down a bundle sale on my way over here. If you don't want this shit, let me know so I can hurry up and catch the mafucka, know what I'm sayin'? So, what's up, yo? You want this shit or what?"

I had the best product on this side of town, and both of us knew it. Of course, he wanted it; every base smoker in this area wanted it.

Scrappy Shine stopped what he was doing to turn his gaze in my direction, the keen sense of focus in his eyes sharply contrasting the ineffectual condition of his body. A dingy, over-sized tank top hung loosely over his withered and shrunken body, exposing a rather sickly physique. His skin was horribly blemished and clung tightly to a fragile and brittle bone structure. He was completely emaciated.

Scrappy took a moment to scratch through his gray, uncombed afro. One side of his overgrown mustache curled upward, giving the slight indication of him smiling.

"Here you go, young blood, said Scrappy while rising up to his feet. "Ain't no need for you to get all testy wit' a brotha."

He reached deep into the pocket of his sweatpants and extracted a raggedy roll of crinkled dollar bills. I, in turn, exchanged my plastic bag filled with his one hundred and forty dollars' worth of base for the collection of soiled bills he was now holding.

Careful not to leave without making sure all one hundred and forty dollars of Scrappy Shine's money was there and accounted for, I proceeded to count out the money he had just now given me while he, in turn, dumped the contents of the plastic bag onto the mattress and began counting each individual bag of base. The two of us finished our count at the same time, which was very much to my relief. In less than ten seconds flat, I was down the stairs and out the door of Scrappy Shine's pigsty of an establishment.

Despite my never wanting to support any illicit business of a rival neighborhood, I stopped at a local drug area Downtown and purchased three dime bags of weed. My usual place of patronage was clear across town, yet I didn't quite have the time to travel. I now had less than an hour before meeting with Archie, which meant that my plan to get a haircut must be enacted with haste.

With Tamara's attitude weighing somewhat heavily on my mind, I hoped that she would accept one of these bags of weed as a peace offering. Just as she sees me as her younger brother, I, in turn, see her as my older sister. Being in Tamara's presence always made me feel like a kid again, and as a kid, I desperately didn't want my big sister to be mad with me, especially over something so trivial.

10:45 a.m.

With some of the city's most talented barbers at the helm, Universal Cuts was one of the most premier barbershops in all of Camden. Despite the going rate for a haircut being somewhere between fifteen and twenty dollars, once could easily jump ahead of the line for a few extra bucks. In the heat of customers bidding to be next in line, I've witnessed one hustler pay as much as ninety dollars for a simple shape up. It was an act that, at times, could easily stir up hard feelings for everyone that had been waiting ever so patiently for their turn to be seated in the barber's chair.

As popular as Universal Cuts was, I wasn't the least bit surprised to enter inside the barbershop and find it completely filled; however, it was every bit of a shock for me to recognize two of my rivals now sitting amongst the crowd.

Richie-Rich, who is originally from Sixth and Mt. Vernon Street, was a relative of Little Stu. With his square, meaty face and fleshy, box-shaped nose, anyone could easily see their family resemblance.

Casper was a well-known drug dealer from Fourth and Chestnut Street and also a close associate of Jay-Dollar. He was a black-skinned man who, despite his hardened and haggard appearance, was only in his early twenties. Long, ratty dreadlocks fell from beneath a black skullcap, which was pulled down just above his brow. A hard set of eyes seemed to beam out from beneath his wool hat and broadcast an open willingness to subject me to bodily harm.

Despite Casper's threatening and seemingly menacing disposition, he is, in fact, a stone-cold coward. I've witnessed firsthand how he had buckled under the pressure put on by younger hustlers whom I knew personally; in the streets, Casper was a joke.

Richie-Rich, on the other hand, was a completely different story. Not only is he overly known to be quick-tempered and terribly fierce at heart, Richie-Rich was also an adamant troublemaker with street-fighting skills praised by nearly all that know him. There was absolutely no doubt the damage we had done to Casper's cousin was now weighing heavily on both of their mines as the three of us all exchanged glances, and it only intensified my feeling of uncertainty even more.

The atmosphere between us was electric.

I masked my nervousness with an outward air of nonchalance while forcing myself to return their glares as I walked past them and towards Burgers, a tall dark-skinned man, who was currently at work on a customer's hairline.

"Don Juan, what up?" he asked, not bothering to break away from concentrating on his masterpiece.

"How many you got in front of me?" I asked.

Burgers took a brief second to scan the row of waiting patrons before promptly returning his attention back to the customer in his chair.

"Four," he replied.

"Who's payin' top dollar?" I inquired.

"Nobody," he answered.

"I got twenty-five for a shape-up."

"I got a twenty-five banger," Burgers immediately announced while brushing the loose hair from off his customer's neck and face. "What's up?"

A few of the waiting customers began to shift uncomfortably in their seats. Richie-Rich and Casper's faces went rigid, their eyes reflecting an overwhelming urge to do me physical harm. The weight of the pistol now tucked on my hip seemed to increase with each second I stood still in front of the unhappy crowd.

"Thirty," said Richie-Rich while staring me directly in the eyes.

"Okay," Burgers remarked, this time with a mixture of both greed and sport for the bidding event. "We got thirty, Don Juan. Do I hear thirty five?"

"Forty," I declared.

"Forty dollars," Burgers broadcasted out loud, this time with a slight touch of excitement.

Richie-Rich sat back against the cushion of his chair, trying hard not to express how angry he truly was. And then, with a simple wave of his hand, he had withdrawn from the contest. There was slight feel of disappointment from the spectators. From Casper and Richie-Rich, however, there was nothing but vehemence. As hard as Richie-Rich may have tried to seem unfazed by his defeat, there was no concealing the rage now storming about in eyes.

I closed my own eyes as Burgers slung the cape around my neck and reopened them to find Richie-Rich rising from out of his seat while staring intently in my direction. My first thought was that he was setting out to try and attack me, but instead, he told Casper that he'd be back while making his way out the door.

Richie-Rich returned no more than ten minutes later with three of his fellow cronies. Two of the three henchmen were relatively unknown to me, but the third individual was dreadfully familiar.

Standing well over six feet tall with strong shoulders and muscular arms, not only did Lazy Eye possess the build of a professional boxer, but he was unofficially considered to be one as well. He was terribly ill-tempered, violent-prone, and dangerously unpredictable. With a devastating punch that had scored countless knockouts in his day, Lazy Eye's name rang bells from nearly every street in Camden to every prison in the state of New Jersey. In a tense atmosphere such as this, he was definitely bad news.

My heartbeat increased tenfold as they filed into the barbershop, all the while glaring at me with what seemed to be an intense passion to pounce upon me as I sat coolly in the barber's chair. I forced myself to lock stares with them a bit longer than I wanted to before cutting my gaze away, trying as much as I possibly could to appear nonchalant and unfettered by their presence.

The waiting customers whom were already seated beside Casper instinctively made room for Richie-Rich and his entourage. From experience, I've come to learn that Downtown's battle tactics were to simply overwhelm their enemies by either outnumbering or out-gunning them; location was rarely an issue. For all I know, I can be ambushed while sitting in the chair or while on my out the door. To see them multiply in such a short period of time indicated peril, and the look of anticipation on Richie-Rich's face warranted extreme concern; Lazy Eye's presence, however, was more so a declaration of war which could very well materialize at any given moment.

He sat edgily with his hands clasped, his elbows resting on his knees and with a slight lean forward as if prepared to lunge forward and attack me at any given second. In an effort to be heard over the loud buzzing of Burgers' clippers, my voice boomed much louder than I cared for; consequently, each and every word I had spoken was heard clearly by those seated before me, including my enemies.

"Burgers, don't turn my back to these niggas, yo . . . mafuckas might try an' roll me an' shit . . .you know what I'm sayin'?"

Patrons now began to stir uncomfortably at the sound of my proclamation. Casper, on the other hand, smiled. Richie-Rich and his two unknown cronies, however, remained stone-faced. Lazy Eye simply clicked his tongue, his eyes never leaving mine. I was peaking with anxiety, and they seemed to know it. They seemed to know it, and they seemed to feed from it.

Embarrassed by my own feelings of unease being made public, I immediately decided to make them pay a most grievous penalty if they so happened to rise up against me. I stretched my fingers out towards the butt of my gun, which was still tucked on my hip and in the waistband of my jeans, and then slowly caressed its handle with my fingertips. Careful to not only keep from disturbing my barber's work, but also for the sake of remaining as inconspicuous as possible, I very slowly and deftly eased the weapon from off of my hip and was now holding the Glock-nine millimeter ever so slightly against my thigh. As a hustler's rule of thumb, I always kept a single round loaded in the firing chamber of my pistol, and with a smooth and careful flick of my thumb, the safety pin was off. I was now prepared for whatever may transpire.

God knows that I didn't want to shoot anyone in such a closed-in and crowded area. The barbershop was filled with people, which means a dozen potential witnesses and quite possibly a few innocent bystanders-turned-victims were sure to materialize if something were to go wrong. I wasn't a professional gunman and was quite sure that at least none of my enemies were neither, which meant things had the potential to get quite messy; when weapons are used in a closed area full of people, stray bullets normally give way to dreaded situations.

Now, with both my eyes and my pistol locked onto Lazy Eye and his crew, I was beginning to ponder the consequences of what may soon come about.

Was my pride and the reputation of my neighborhood worth me taking the risk of losing my life or becoming a man wanted for murder?

A verse from one of Tupac's rap songs had begun to play over and over inside of my head, not so much as to encourage me, but to remind me of what this was all about.

I'd rather die like a man, than live like a coward; there's a ghetto up in heaven, and it's ours . . . Black Power!

I loved Mid Town with all of my heart. It was the source of all of my childhood memories and of a happiness that had replaced the longing for a father I had never gotten the chance to know. It also helped quell the sorrow and mourning for a brother I'd never see nor speak to again; moreover, the 'hood accepted me. It accepted my pain and all of my shortcomings; and the very thought of anyone disrespecting or scoffing at the place that had done so much good for my peace of mind was infuriating, the sight of them, maddening.

Like so many others from my neighborhood, I harbored a deep and passionate hatred for those who'd sneer at our fortitude and challenge our ability to defend its honor. But unlike many of my weak-hearted compatriots, not only was I ready to uphold the reputation of my 'hood, I was more than willing to do so - and I was definitely able. Again, I began to weigh the pros and cons of my situation; and while staring into the faces of my enemies, I came to the ultimate conclusion.

Yes, I said out loud in my head. *Yes, I'll do whatever I have to do to make these niggas respect my 'hood. And yes, I'll make them pay the ultimate price for underestimating me just because my 'hood is nowhere near the size of theirs.*

While blinking away any thoughts of reluctance, I decided to shoot Lazy Eye first if they decided to move against me. He was their leader and their strength; therefore, he would bear the brunt of my counterattack. I'll shoot him dead, and then I'll gun down the others before fleeing to Tamara's house as fast as I could in order to retrieve my entire savings and give it all to Lakeisha for the keepsake of a family I'd be leaving behind. There wouldn't be any prison time for me. I'd rather die in a hail of gunfire before spending the rest of my life barred from the people and things that I hold so dear to me. Fuck that.

A thin film of sweat had now begun to form between my finger and the gun trigger. Whether as a satisfied customer or a soon-to-be fugitive of the law, I was determined to walk out of this barbershop untouched. With my finger still on the trigger, I slipped the gun back into the waistband of my jeans just as Burgers snatched the cape from around my neck. I rose to my feet with my eyes trained on all of my rivals, never bothering to look away as I peeled off two twenty dollar bills and hand them over to the barber.

With my head up and with my chest out, I made my way out of the barber shop, and it was only then that I was finally able to exhale a sigh of relief. Never before had I experienced a situation so intense, yet it would be nothing compared to what was set to take place later on tonight. I checked my wristwatch to find that I was five minutes late for my rendezvous with Archie, but the fact that he had yet to page me was an indication of him not being there either.

Satisfied that, despite the fact of so much happening in such little time, I was still on schedule to meet with my connect. I smiled to myself while lighting a cigarette.

It ain't even twelve o'clock yet, and shit's fuckin' hectic as hell, I thought quietly to myself while heading towards the car. *This fuckin' life is crazy as hell, man . . . it's fuckin' crazy as hell.*

11:15 a.m.

As a child growing up in the eighties, black-owned grocery stores, clothing stores and other businesses were a common sight in the inner-city. In those days, nearly every resident living in their respective neighborhoods were well-acquainted with one another, so much so, that children could go to the store with nothing more than a handwritten note from their parents and return with a bag full of groceries.

It was a golden era of my childhood; it was a time when everyone knew each other, and children feared discipline from their neighbors every bit as much as they did from their parents. In hindsight, I could sadly admit that it was a time that now existed only in the back of my mind. Times have changed, and the once familiar faces of local shop owners were now replaced with a different culture and a radically diverse style of people.

The Hispanic community seemed to explode from out of nowhere and swiftly monopolize the grocery store market, while at the same time, affirming their presence in the ghetto. Store names like "Roses'," "Ernie's," and "Silver Gallon" were now changed to names that the average English-speaking citizen would find difficult to pronounce. The kind and familiar personalities of Ms. Rose or Mr. and Mrs. Johnson were gone and now replaced by sharp, business-minded Latinos who had clearly taken the term "ghetto-entrepreneurship" to an entirely different level.

Homemade cheeseburgers (which were no more than generic beef patties topped with a slice of cheese), single pieces of chicken, pork chops, and hot pockets were all sold for a dollar each. They sold T-shirts, socks, hats, bootleg movies, c.d.'s, and even sneakers for reasonable prices. Some store owners even pawned and sold jewelry.

Puerto Ricans and Dominicans had managed to transform what it meant to run a place of business in the ghetto, and they were all-too effective at doing so. In a swift matter of years, nearly every corner store in the city of Camden went from Black-owned to Latino-owned.

Some of these store owners spoke good English while others could barely pronounce a single sentence, yet they all possessed good fashion sense and donned what seemed like a ton of the most expensive jewelry. Most importantly, they tolerated the presence of criminal activity that existed in their neighborhoods, which was something that store owners of the past would never have done. Drugs were allowed to be sold directly in front of their establishment and at times, inside the store as well. To be honest, some store owners were drug runners themselves; in fact, I know a few of them personally.

With these new-style corner store owners turning a blind eye to such prevalent criminal activity, their business establishments soon became a valuable part of a drug dealers' local territory, and these same drug dealers were now quick to defend them against the threat of outsiders who may attempt something along the lines of robbery.   After all, what self-respecting drug dealer would allow a foreigner to rob any place of business where they hustled and lend to the possibility of them being placed under intense scrutiny by the police? Retaliation for making a hustler's neighborhood "hot" was practically a guarantee, and it proved to be quite an effective deterrent for those who preferred to make their money the "ski mask way."

*   *   *

Regardless of whatever section of the city we'd agree to meet, Archie and my ritual of doing business always remained the same. I'd enter inside the corner store and greet the cashier with my usual "what's up, Primo?" before purchasing a one liter bottle of orange soda and having it placed inside of a brown paper bag, to which I'd then slip the twenty-six hundred dollars inside it while making my way to the rear of the store. Archie was already there, totally engrossed in a game of Ms. Pac Man as I approached. While making my way towards the back of the store, I began thinking back to when I had first met Archie.

I was moonlighting with a girl named Sheryl Braxton a little while back, and Sheryl just so happened to be the mother of Archie's two children. I could see quite clearly that Archie was bothered by the sight of me lounging inside Sheryl's home, but the energy of him being a coward far outweighed his jealousy. Whether it was when he occasionally showed up at Sheryl's house unannounced or when he and I would randomly cross paths with one another in the city, the most Archie would ever bother to do was stare at me from the corner of his eye while pretending to look the other way.

Tired of Archie's nonsense, I pulled my car over and approached him one day as he stood on the corner of Eighth Street and Carl Miller Boulevard talking to a group of hustlers. He was completely shocked, and it showed all over his face as I approached him. Archie's apparent surprise had immediately transformed into grave concern when I asked to speak with him in private. I inwardly laughed at Archie's struggle not to appear so blatantly afraid; he was a far cry from the rough-and-tumble, no-nonsense gangster that Sheryl was so deathly in fear of.

"What's good, my nigga?" he asked while fighting not to seem overly afraid while standing in front of me. I, in turn, was struggling not to laugh out loud in Archie's face and take advantage of just how much of a coward he really was.

Despite how deep Sheryl's feelings may have gone for me, I already had a woman at home, and more importantly, Sheryl already knows this. My approaching Archie had nothing to do with whatever business they may be having with one another when I wasn't around, nor was it some foolish attempt to prove how tough I was. My approaching Archie was more so out of concern about him having the urge to make some type of trouble with me because of my dealings with his children's mother. After meeting him face to face, however, I was quite sure that he wouldn't be a problem; and now, it seemed as if my more immediate concern was for me to not appear as if I was looking for any trouble with him instead.

Even though Archie was a bona fide coward, he is, in all reality, a hustler whom was higher up on the criminal food chain than I. Despite him being indeed faint-of-heart, Archie was still very much established in the streets; and, if pressed to do so, I was quite sure that he could send a few troublemakers my way. Although I had absolutely no fear of confrontation, I was all too interested in making money to be out in the streets trying to prove just how tough a guy I really am for the sake of a female whom I cared little to nothing at all about.

"Ain't nothin' serious," I remarked rather smoothly. "I just wanted to holla at you about Sheryl an' shit."

Archie's face went tight. His top lip twitched a bit, and from behind the tint of his designer sunglasses, I could tell that he had instantly become fearful. I moved quickly to ease his nerves.

"I'm sayin'," I began swiftly and smoothly. "I just wanna know if you feel some type of way about me fuckin' wit' your baby-mom an' shit. If y'all on some 'break-up to make-up' shit, I can respect that and be on my way, you dig what I'm sayin'? Cause it ain't that serious. I ain't tryin' to be all in the middle of whatever y'all got goin' on an' what not."

Within a mere matter of seconds, Archie had grown cool and nonchalant; his instant change of demeanor was evidence of him being overly relieved that I hadn't approached him on a more hostile note.

"Nah, it's all good, my man," Archie lied. "Go 'head an' do you."

"All right," I replied not quite liking how Archie had so quickly slipped into his hot shot persona. "I just had to come at you some real man-to-man type shit, you know what I'm sayin'? I ain't tryin' to make somethin' out of nothin' over no female an' shit."

Archie, now in full recovery of his internal panic, merely pursed his lips.

"Nah, my nigga," he said while extending his hand towards mine. "Go 'head an' do your thing, homeboy. I ain't worried about her."

The two of us shook hands and then parted ways, and I began making my way back to the car in a rather agitated mood. The thought of appeasing Archie's false sense of being someone worthy of my respect had most definitely irked my nerves.

Being steadfast against my anger, however, had paid off in a big way. Archie had approached me a few days later with a most generous price on the weight he was selling. The rest, as they say, is history; and subsequently, we've been doing business with each other ever since. Needless to say, Sheryl and I had soon began losing interest in one another and had eventually agreed to go about our own separate ways, but it made no difference to me. For a drug dealer, money takes precedence over ANY romantic endeavor, and I couldn't have found a greater trade-off for Archie's woman than Archie's product.

All thoughts of the past had dissipated to the back of my mind as I drew nearer to Archie. Like myself, he'd often adopt the inclination to dress opposite of the success he enjoyed from drug dealing, but his rag-tag and shabby choice of wardrobe was a bit too over the top. In short, Archie looked a royal mess.

The leather on Archie's Timberland boots were scarred, dirty, and worn down to the point where the sides of his footwear sagged droopingly against the soles of his boots. His blue denim jeans were too short and too slim; the lack of looseness in his pants accented the lankiness of his tall, wiry frame in a most ridiculous fashion. The saggy, almost deflated Nautica goose-down jacket he wore was a little too over the top and helped Archie appear far more poverty-stricken than a drug addict. He looked like a complete bum.

On the floor beside his worn and weathered work boots was a brown paper bag which contained a one liter bottle of orange soda with four and a half ounces of base inside of it. Our routine exchange was soon to be underway in a swift matter of seconds.

"You're late," he muttered with his attention fixed firmly on the game he was still playing. "You gotta stay on point, yo . . . you comin' here all late is bad for business, you know what I'm sayin'?"

Although I was but a few minutes late, it was indeed the first time that I had been so. In fact, there were a few instances when Archie, himself, had been late. I was far from being in the mood to be lectured, especially from someone preaching from such a hypocritical standpoint. More importantly, I absolutely can't stand for someone to talk to me without bothering to look me in the face while doing so; I take such behavior as condescending and terribly disrespectful.

My nerves had instantly given off the sensation of them being plucked, and I now found myself struggling to remain cool. The episode with Lazy Eye and his crew at the barbershop had left me feeling a bit hot and bothered, and I was still very much on edge.

Archie's criticism of my being late was threatening to unravel what little wits I had already fought so hard to keep. It was solely for the sake of business that I hadn't drawn my pistol to rob him right here on the spot. The very thought of him shaking in his boots at the sight of me brandishing my pistol gave way to a sense of giddiness that I could really do without at the present time.

"What's good?" I asked, figuring it best to ignore Archie's comment and press on with the issue of buying the base so I could hurry up and be on my way.

"Everything," he replied while frowning as Ms. Pac Man fell victim to a group of enemy ghosts.

Like a scene from an espionage movie, the exchange was swift and inconspicuous. I knelt down and switched his bag with mine while pretending to fiddle with my boot lace. I then rose to my feet with a package that outwardly looked like the one I had just purchased at the counter, but with different contents.

Seeing the most incriminating evidence now in my possession instead of his own brought great relief to Archie's conscience, and it showed all over his face. I was instantly reminded of how spineless a person he was when I had first met him. How a person as cowardly and as soft-hearted as Archie could score such a high position on the criminal food chain was beyond me.

The idea of him cooperating with the authorities to avoid jail time was difficult for me to accept, yet overwhelmingly easy to imagine. Threatened with the concept of Archie sooner or later setting me up to be arrested, I made the decision to start shopping around for a new supplier. That, however, would happen only after I'd increased my purchase from four and half ounces to nine.

Nine ounces of base was an abundant amount of weight to be bought, and I couldn't just buy that amount from anyone; countless people have been robbed, scammed, and even killed for much less than that. Doubling my purchase would allow me a generous amount of time to shop around and select Archie's replacement. With that in mind, I promptly made known my plans to increase the quantity of base for the next purchase.

"Yo," I began. "Next time you holla at lil' Joe, tell that nigga to double up next time I see him."

"True indeed," Archie replied while dropping another quarter into the video game slot, again, his attention not once veering in my direction.

And with that, our need to meet and converse with one another had come to an abrupt end. Having made my purchase and putting in for the next order, there was nothing else left for me to say. Without bothering to speak another word, I turned and started out of the store.

12:45 p.m.

Bagging up sizeable amounts of base cocaine can sometimes be one of the less favorable tasks of a drug dealer; it is a duty that requires extreme patience and the utmost forbearance. Large quantities of base are usually sold from drug suppliers to hand-to-hand drug dealers such as myself in the form of large, solid chunks. Once purchased, these chunks are then chipped, preferably with a single-edged razor, into smaller pieces whose size is normally dictated by the personality of the neighborhood in which it was to be sold. In short, bagging up base is a process which demands astute attentiveness, and for one stuck with the unfortunate duty of bagging up four and a half ounces of rock cocaine, it can prove to be a grueling activity.

While most dealers may prefer a dinner plate to chop their base upon, I favored a mirror, a large sixteen by sixteen-inch mirror to be exact; its reflective surface enabled me to distinguish and gather every last crumb. Everyone who chops and bags rock cocaine has their own particular method. Mine was systematic and functioned more like an assembly line. After the base is cut and chopped into "nickel-sized" rocks, they are then arranged into rows of twenty, to which they are then prepared to be packaged.

Empties aren't just needed for packaging the product; they also play an essential role in a dealer's need to distinguish his self from the competition as well. Although one street corner can be inhabited by a multitude of drug dealers, all of them may not be selling the same quality of product; consequently, one must find a way to separate himself from the opposition. Satisfied customers will return in search of the dealer from whom they previously bought their product, and if that dealer happened to be absent, they'd buy from anyone selling the same color bags with hopes of getting the same quality of base they'd bought earlier.

With the chunks of base now cut into small nickel-sized rocks and divided into long lines of twenty, the strenuous task of "bagging up" was only halfway to completion. There was still the job of packaging and sealing the bags that remained, not to mention the need to clean up afterwards. A simple twist of my thumb and index finger would open the bag, to which I would then scoop the rock inside, fold the top of the bag down to where the rock rests, press its crease against a hot iron, and then quickly but gently press my fingertips against the heated fold of the bag in order to seal it closed.

Once packaged and sealed, the bag would then be tossed to the side, and the process will achingly repeat itself until the one bag soon became a pile of twenty, and the one heap of twenty bags multiplied into dozens of piles, each pile containing twenty bags apiece. The end result of my labor will be a legion of nickel bags, all of them packaged, sealed, organized into one bundle per pile, and then awaiting a scrupulous recount.

*   *   *

It had taken me nearly an hour to bag up the four and a half ounces of base I had just recently bought from Archie. The tightening of my back, the stiffening of my arms and the dull, cramping of my fingers were all telltale signs of how painstaking the task of bagging up base cocaine really is. Despite my overbearing sense of fatigue, the sight of seven thousand, one hundred and sixty-five dollars' worth of base packaged in fresh, chunky nickel bags was indeed a sight to behold. Archie had obviously given me more than four and a half ounces, and that was one of the many reasons why I had always remained on the up-and-up with him. My decision to nullify our acquaintance was now striking me with a feeling of melancholy, so in an effort to maintain my good spirits, I dwelled more so on my gain of today rather than my impending loss in the very near future.

At this present time, I stood to reap a profit of nearly forty-six hundred of the seventy-one hundred dollars of base that I had just now packaged; it is the most I had ever bagged up from four and half ounces. Each plastic sandwich bag was filled with five hundred dollars' worth of base; two of these "five hundred packs" will be placed in a slightly larger plastic bag, making it an official "G-pack."

With my entire package of base now cut and packaged, I took two G-packs and placed them on top of the dresser where I was now standing and then took another healthy swig of Scotch. Along with the two G-packs on the top of the bureau was a sandwich bag containing four hundred dollars' worth of product; another member of my pager clientele had called in for an order just as I had finished recounting my profit.

Soon, I'd have four hundred more dollars to go along with my eleven hundred dollars for Christmas shopping. Eager to get things underway, I wiped the mirror clean, scraped off any excess plastic which may have melted onto the iron's surface while sealing the bags, and then placed everything back into their hidden areas before dialing Mannie's cell phone number.

"Who?" asked Mannie in what seemed to me as a standard version of "Who is it?" for every Latino I had ever met.

"It's me, Don Juan," I replied while taking another sip of liquor. "Where're you at?"

"On Haddon," he answered. "Why, what's up?"

I smiled at Mannie's answer.

When it came down to business, he seemed to always be at the right place at the right time.

"I'm about to shoot through an' hit you off," I said smoothly.

I could feel his urge to hustle come into play almost immediately; the receiving end of my cell phone was now surging with energy. He, too, was just as anxious to get things going.

"That's what's up," he replied. "It's tryin' to flow a lil' somethin' out here, too. On top of that, I'll be the only nigga out here wit' coke, too, so shit should be lovely."

Mannie's response of being the only person on the block with coke struck me as odd and for some reason, a bit unsettling. I didn't like the idea of Mannie being the only person on the avenue with product and making money in front of a gang of hungry, cash-strapped hustlers.

"Who's out there?" I asked.

"Everybody," he replied.

"Everybody?" I asked, not really caring for Mannie's vague way of answering my question. "What do you mean, everybody? Everybody like who?"

"Well, not everybody," he snickered. "But damn near everybody: B.J., Donnie, Meka, Keifey, Irv, Lil' Pete . . ."

"Lil' Pete?" I interrupted. "He just got shot like a week ago!"

"Yeah," Mannie concurred. "That nigga's on crutches an' everything. Mafuckas be tryin' to tell him to take his lil' ass home, but you know how he is, man. . . . nigga loves the 'hood like a mafucka."

Lil' Pete was barely fifteen years old and the only local resident that had taken a bullet in the midst of Fourth and Chestnut's retaliation against our neighborhood. Shooting someone, being shot by someone or, just coming home from incarceration is like returning home from Vietnam or something; it's a tremendous badge of honor. For Lil' Pete, a kid who had no family, the love and attention he had received for catching a bullet was undoubtedly intoxicating.

After all of the love and attention he had received, it definitely wouldn't be hard for Lil' Pete to fall in love with the streets, and that's what worried me most about him. The streets are finicky, and if he wasn't careful, the same 'hood that Lil' Pete loved so dearly could, and would, bring his life to a tragic end.

"All right then," I said, ready to bring our conversation to an end. "I'll be there in like ten or fifteen minutes."

"All right then, peace," Mannie replied. "Hey, yo!"

Mannie's sudden interjection had immediately snatched my attention, preventing my thumb from pressing the end button on my cordless phone.

"What's up?" I asked, now starting to feel an oncoming sense of aggravation. This conversation was now beginning to go on a bit longer than I desired and was now threatening to impede me from conducting business. I had four hundred dollars waiting to be made.

"M's home," Mannie said.

"M?" I remarked smartly. "Who the fuck is M?"

"M, nigga!" Mannie said as if he had the nerve to be losing his patience with me. "You know whom I'm talkin' about. M-16, nigga . . . you, know . . . Moses."

"What Moses?" I asked. "You mean Moses from around the way?"

"Yeah, but he don't go by that name no more," Mannie answered, this time with a stark trace of humor in his voice. "He callin' his self Musa an' shit."

"Musa?" I asked, not meaning to speak that particular question out loud.

"Yeah," Mannie replied. "That nigga done came home on some fake, jail-house Muslim shit."

"Yo," I replied dryly. "Moses was Muslim before he got locked up. In fact, I think his whole family is Muslim an' shit."

"Yeah, but it's different this time," Mannie countered. "Everything that comes out that nigga's mouth is 'Al-

Hamdu-Allah' an' 'Allah-u-Akbar'. This nigga even rockin' one of those big-ass terrorist beards an' shit!"

Mannie chuckled as he continued to make fun of Moses. I, on the other hand, frowned at his sarcastic jab at the Muslims' religious and traditional cultures. Still and all, I had far more important things to do than lecture Mannie about the need to respect other people's customs and beliefs.

"That's it?" I asked.

"Yeah," Mannie confirmed. "That's it."

"Peace, then," I said."

"All right, yo," he said. "Peace, my nigga."

The taste of alcohol had now begun to settle in my mouth and immediately began provoking my urge to smoke; yet, with the residue of cooked-up cocaine still on my fingertips, I figured it a bad idea to light myself a cigarette. While heading towards the bathroom, my thoughts traveled back in time to when I had first met Lakeisha.

She was akin to one of B.J.'s many mistresses and often accompanied the two of them whenever they rendezvoused on Haddon Avenue. Donnie was the first to approach Lakeisha, but he was young, lacking both tact and composure. "Aye, baby girl! You gon' let a nigga get at you, or what?"is usually not the best way to make a good impression on a woman. I, skillfully and with a bit more class, made my approach a short while later, and the two of us hit it off immediately.

It didn't take long for me to learn of Lakeisha having three children by three different men, but by then, it really didn't matter. Warnings and words of caution against me dealing with her had come from both friends and "old heads" alike. Even my mother, who had long ago made known her disapproval of my decision making, expressed her condemnation of what she called "foolish" and a "jack-assed" decision.

Everyone except Tamara remained fixed on forcing me to "smarten up." Instead, she simply declared that I was hung up on some "sucker-for-love" type of shit, but it was okay. From her perspective, I was just young and experimenting with a fast ass girl, and that it was only natural for a "whore" like me to lay down with a chick who she so aptly defined as "raunchy" and "smutty." Tamara had said that she only hoped that I'd be smart enough to wear a condom in the midst of it all.

Everyone's pleas for me not to get so seriously involved with Lakeisha had fallen upon deaf ears. She was the classic older woman – attractive, witty, and above all, sexually obliging. In short, there was nothing anyone could do or say that would deter me from satisfying my appetite for her. At seventeen years of age, I was soon head-over-heels in love with a female who was not only a "baby-mom" to three different men, but she was also eight years older than me as well.

It was the talk of the neighborhood, and my relationship with Lakeisha was treated more so like a scandal than anything else. It was news that had traveled everywhere except behind the walls of Northern State Prison, where Moses, her one-time pen pal and aspiring soul mate, was sitting behind bars wondering what on earth had happened to his and her correspondence.

Moses was a few years older than me and credited for being one of the original hustlers from my neighborhood, yet whatever he had going on with Lakeisha prior to me dealing with her hadn't been made known to me until she and I had become an item. Had I known of their involvement prior to our relationship, I would have broken ties with her immediately.

With the exception of money, nothing brings more complications to male friendships than when the two both share a common interest in the same woman. How Lakeisha, or B.J. for that matter, could neglect to fill me in on such a potentially explosive issue would fuel arguments between the three of us for months to come. I faulted B.J. more than Lakeisha for this lack of information simply because of him knowing firsthand how explosive these "love-triangles" can be. I reasoned that it was somehow on the strength of his own benefit that he had neglected to fill me in on Lakeisha and Moses' dealings with one another.

My contention with Moses, unlike B.J.'s more complex and conniving ways, was a bit easier for me to understand.

In hindsight, I think it was more so the sentiment of Moses having a bruised ego by way of him losing his "woman" to a "young boy" from around the way that had motivated him to confront me with such aggression. Needless to say, a heated encounter came about, and in a mere matter of minutes, the conversation between the two of us had quickly become a hair away from turning violent. Had it not been for Irvin and Keifey, Moses and I surely would have come to blows, and in the 'hood, fighting over a woman is something that is very much frowned upon and deemed "un-macho."

For Moses to act in such a hostile fashion over something so trivial as a "piece of pussy" made him look very, very bad in the eyes of our peers. The two brothers scolded him harshly, and as a result of their unforgiving rebukes, Moses had opted to hold his feelings in check and pretend to make amends with me. Despite the atonement we had made, it still wasn't hard for me to see that he had taken my unintentional transgression a little too close to heart.

Moses never had any tangible luck with hustling on the streets, and to no one's surprise, he soon wound up going back to prison. And now, three years later, he was back in the 'hood.

While scrubbing my hands in the bathroom sink, I wondered if Moses still harbored any sense of ill-will towards me. Time stands still only for those whom are incarcerated, and while inside the confines prison housing, some inmate can spend their prison sentence dwelling on one thing or the other. Moses could very well have been one of those people.

For me, however, things had definitely moved on. Not only was Lakeisha now the mother of my child, we were also living together as a family. I am much older than when I had first gotten into it with Moses, and above all, I am definitely less tolerant of his or anyone else's attempt to prove their manhood at my expense. In short, Moses will pay a most costly price if he were to attempt any foolishness.

A lit cigarette dangled loosely from my lips as I re-entered the bedroom and began preparing to make my exit. I slipped back into my army coat and stuffed a G-pack into each one of my front pockets. I then took a moment to exhale a stream of smoke before tucking the Glock-nine back against my hip in the waistband of my jeans. O.J.'s four bundles of base were tossed into a plastic sandwich bag and then stuffed into my jeans pocket. The eleven hundred dollars in cash was folded and placed in the other. With everything accounted for, I clicked off the stereo system, locked the door behind me and then began making my way down the stairs.

Tamara was in the kitchen, presumably doing dishes, when I reached the bottom step. She peeped from out the doorway as I started towards the front door.

"Where're you goin'?" she asked.

"I got a couple runs to make," I answered, half-hoping that she wouldn't seek to be in the way of me handling my business. "Why, what's up?"

"I need you to come back in like a half hour."

I inwardly sighed at her request.

"No can do, big sis," I replied earnestly. "Can't promise that I'll be back in a half . . .I got a whole lot of shit to do, Tammy, for real."

"You gots to come back," she pressed. "It's a surprise yo, for real. You won't be disappointed. Just come back around at like one-thirty . . . please."

There was absolutely no way for me to get out of granting Tamara's request, and we both knew it. She was politely refusing to take "no" for an answer.

"All right, then," I replied while hiding my exasperation. "I'll see you in like a half hour."

With nothing else to say, Tamara returned to whatever she was doing in the kitchen. I, on the other hand, turned and started out the front door to get my day underway.

1:00 p.m.

Words can't describe the feeling a hustler experiences when hitting the block with a fresh package of product; the closest I can get to explaining such a sentiment would be something like the rush of a professional athlete when receiving an adrenaline shot before going back into the game. I exited out of the alley from Spruce Street onto Division Street and began making my way up towards Haddon Avenue, my blood surging with the excitement of opportunity.

Just as Mannie had told me a little while earlier, nearly everyone in the neighborhood was out and about today. I could see them more and more clearly as I approached the corner of Division Street and Haddon Avenue. All of them, except for a few, were occupying the front porch of a neighborhood drug addict's home. Lil' Pete was sitting on the step with his wounded leg fully extended, his crutches standing erect alongside the porch.   As always, though, it was Donnie who had taken center stage.

Sitting atop the hood of his newly-acquired luxury car, Donnie was the picture-perfect image of a young inner-city hustler. He sat coolly on hood of his jet-black Acura Legend as if he was shooting a rap video. The tints of his car windows were as dark as the color of his car, the chrome of its sparkling twenty-two inch rims glistening every bit as brightly as the jewelry on his neck, wrists and fingers.

Spotting me as I neared the corner, he raised both his arms in acknowledgment. Donnie's gold watch and bracelets drooped down his wrists and into the sleeves of his coat as his arms remained high in the air.

"Don Juan!" he exclaimed loudly. "What's good, my nigga!?!"

Everyone on the porch fell in suit with Donnie's greeting.

I was quite sure that the unfamiliar ladies I saw standing on the porch with the rest of my cohorts were friends of B.J.; he was incredibly notorious for using our terse inner-city environment as a backdrop to impress women from out-of-town.

The females' current interest in me was undoubtedly aroused by the reception I had been given from everyone on the porch; I could feel their stares of appraisal as I made my way across the street towards them. That, along with the warmth of everyone else's welcomes, boosted my feeling of importance a hundred times over. It gave an extra pep to the swagger in my step.

Despite the warmth of everyone's greetings, I remained conscious of the perils of me being in a well-known drug area with both a gun and an already-packaged amount of product on my person. The bullet-riddled skeletons of a few abandoned cars and the bullet-scarred walls of the houses in our neighborhood reminded me that almost anything could happen at any given time. The feel of the gun on my hip and the packages of base bulging against my pockets were beginning to make me feel a bit too antsy. I had to get rid of this gun and all of these drugs, and I had to do it quickly.

But first, I had to greet and personally accept Donnie's welcome. Donnie was undoubtedly the wildest out of the bunch, and moreover, he loved me to death. As pressed as I may have been to relieve myself of this incriminating evidence, I was more so inclined to take a brief moment to indulge in an exchange of love between him and myself.

"What's up, yo?" he asked out loud against the music pounding from the speakers of his expensive car stereo system. Everyone on the porch was bobbing their heads to the music; also, I could spot a few of the neighborhood hustlers on the porch, free-style rapping to the rhythm.

While holding the blunt in one hand, Donnie extended the other.

"Ain't nothin'," I replied while clasping his one free hand and simultaneously hugging him with my other arm. "What's good wit' you?"

"Ain't shit," he said rather casually. "Just chillin' an' shit. You know how I do mines, my nigga."

It took only a matter of seconds for me to scan the crowd and find Mannie absent from the scene. I accepted the blunt from Donnie while turning my attention not only towards the cars traveling up and down Haddon Avenue, but towards the many vehicles parked here and off into the distant as well. The fear of being caught with an overwhelming degree of illegal merchandise was weighing more and more on my conscience with each second I stood on the street smoking with Donnie.

From where I was standing, I could hear Keifey rapping to the beat booming out of Donnie's car stereo system. Lil' Pete was bobbing his head and smoking a blunt of his own as Keifey lyrically spun his tale of gun slinging and drug dealing. It sounded all so good. His skills of rhyming on time with the scheme of the instrumental's base line were impeccable; he undoubtedly deserved a record deal. I looked up and acknowledged Keifey with a smile when hearing him mention my name in his rhyme.

Satisfied that I had fulfilled Donnie's need to be recognized, I figured it was now best for me to get things going. I took one more toke of the blunt before passing it back to him.

"Where's Puerto Rican Mannie?" I asked.

Just as Donnie moved to answer, I spied Mannie exiting the corner store from up the street. He, in turn, spotted me as well and threw up both his hands in acknowledgment. I left from in front of Donnie, but stopped short to acknowledge Lil' Pete for a quick second before meeting up with Mannie.

He smiled while accepting my handshake, the hardness in his eyes starkly betraying the youthfulness of his young, hairless face.

"What's good, lil' homie?" I asked. "The fuck is you doin' out here on crutches an' shit?"

Both me and Lil' Pete already knew the answer to that question. With an absentee father and a heroin-addicted mother for parents, there was absolutely no love waiting for the poor teen at home. Behind the closed doors of the run-down rowhome at 907 Haddon Avenue where he lived, there were no household values being taught and instilled, no everyday elements of life that middle and upper class families took for granite. The basic essentials of life like electricity and running water, let alone food, were scarce to come by where Lil' Pete laid his head. No one could blame him for not wanting to be there, not even me.

Mid Town was Lil' Pete's home, and those like myself who hustled on these streets were his only siblings. Win, lose, or draw, Lil' Pete's fate would be tied in with the streets; and to be perfectly honest, I couldn't imagine him reaching the age of twenty-one without further incident. It was a harsh and tough reality for a great deal of us to accept, but nevertheless, life can only be what it is.

Lil' Pete's smile only broadened when hearing my question, this time, his facial expression being tough and matching the hardness of his eyes.

"Damn, yo," he remarked sourly. "Everybody actin' like I ain't supposed to be out here an' shit. I only got hit in the mafuckin' leg an' shit. What the fuck, yo? Niggas actin' like I took fifty rounds in the chest or some shit. The fuck is up with that?"

Admiring Lil' Pete's fortitude while at the same time worrying about his future, I flashed a closed mouth smile.

"Be right back," I said while turning around to meet Mannie.

"Gimme a cigarette, yo" said Lil' Pete.

I pulled out my box of Newports and extracted a single cigarette from its pack and handed it to him; then I began making my way towards Mannie. I met him two houses down from where everyone else was congregating, neither one of us bothering to say a word to each other. I turned and started up the steps of an abandoned home; Mannie dutifully followed behind me as I went inside. Every outlet, save for the door, was boarded. Light crept inside from in between the cracks and crannies of the wood-covered windows, giving a damp illumination of the trash that lay scattered about the place; the darkness of graffiti writing was barely seen upon all the walls.

This was mine and Mannie's stash spot.

Once inside, he and I got straight down to business. I immediately retrieved the two G-packs from inside my jeans pockets and handed them over to Mannie.

"Here," I said in a rushed tone. "One is yours and the other one's mines. Make sure you put mine in a safe place an' shit. I'll come back for it in a couple hours."

Mannie accepted the packs. As he turned to find a safe place for both of our packages, I pulled the pistol from off my hip. I used the end of my sweatshirt to wipe it free of any fingerprints before giving it to him.

"Here, yo" I said while handing him the firearm by way of my sweatshirt. "It's off safety, and it already got one in the head. Keep an eye on my shit, yo, for real. Don't let nothin' happen to it."

Mannie had hastily stashed the product and then accepted the semi-automatic handgun with a look of complete confidence. "Man, why you act like we just started doin' this shit, yo? Ain't nothin' gon' happen to ya shit, nigga . . . don't even start tryin' to trip."

The stale odor of urine and trash had quickly grown too much for me to bear; my impatience with Mannie's overdose of self-confidence was beginning to work my nerves as well. Just as I was about to chastise him for talking too much, he disappeared into the darkness of the house, only to return a few seconds later.

Again, he was smiling.

"Okay, my nigga," Mannie announced. "Let's get the fuck out of here."

Deciding against my urge to scold Mannie for speaking so freely and foolishly, I instead, fished myself another cigarette from its box while making my way out the door. Mannie started down the steps while I opted to hop one banister after the next until arriving onto the porch where everyone still remained huddled amongst one another, continuing on with their drinking, smoking and grooving to the beats bumping from out of Donnie's system. Again, everyone greeted me warmly; this time, it was with hugs, handshakes, and pounds from those whom I knew.

From the corner of my eye, I could spy Mannie crossing the street and disappearing down Division Street. Satisfied to know that he was well on his way to make money for the both of us, I felt a bit more comfortable with taking a few moments to indulge in whatever good time everyone on the porch was now having.

Standing well over six feet tall and weighing more than two hundred plus pounds, B.J. held the physical stature of a professional football player; with his towering height, booming voice and award-winning acting skills, he could easily fool those whom didn't know him to be a hardcore street hustler. Consequently, like now for instance, he was able to keep a flock of females outside of a home where he lived with a fiancée and two children.

Despite the controversy that had taken place between me, Lakeisha and Moses being more than three years ago, I still couldn't help but to somewhat dislike B.J. for the part he played in the entire scenario. That particular situation had revealed to me just how tight he and I really were, which proved to be a gross overestimation on my behalf; it was a harsh lesson about life that couldn't help but to wound me every time I saw him.

"Don Juan!" said B.J. out loud, playing off to the girls like he and I were the best of buddies. "What's goin' on wit' you, my dude? What's the motherfuckin' word, yo?"

"Ain't nothin'," I said smartly while declining the bottle of Hennessey he was trying to hand over to me. "You know I don't drink after you, nigga . . . ain't no tellin' where ya mafuckin' mouth been."

B.J.'s face drew tight. Two of the girls he was with laughed as well, staring at B.J. as they did so. Only one of his female guests didn't find much humor in my wisecrack; in fact, she looked somewhat embarrassed. It was easy to figure that she was B.J.'s point of interest for the moment.

Donnie laughed out loud while making his way up the steps to join us on the porch. As if on cue to back me up, he chimed in with a comment of his own; and it was one of the many reasons why I loved him so much.

"Word to my nigga, Lil' Pete down there!" Donnie exclaimed boisterously. "Everybody know you a slimy-ass, nasty-ass nigga, yo!"

The porch erupted with laughter. B.J., along with the one female whom I had seemed to embarrass, didn't find Donnie's comment as amusing. Behind the sharp, measuring gaze in her eyes, I could see her weighing everything B.J. told her against everything she was now seeing. It wasn't taking her long to notice that B.J. wasn't the "hot shot" hustler I'm sure he played himself up to be. Whatever image of himself that he had so cleverly conjured up into the imagination of these young women was slowly being eroded; their attention was gradually focusing more so on Donnie and me.

"Awwwww shit!" said Donnie while looking away from everyone. "There go the mothafuckin' Broad Street Bully, y'all! Deebo is back in the mothafuckin' buildin'!"

I glanced across the street and spotted Moses, formerly known as M, but now known as Musa, exiting from the passenger side of a late-model Buick Regal. Despite the obvious bulk he had put on while in prison, along with the huge beard and clean-shaved head, Moses pretty much looked the same as he did years ago. B.J.

was the only one on the porch who had received Moses so warmly, unwittingly proving to me, again, just how unworthy he was of my trust.

"Yo, Musa!" B.J. exclaimed out loud just as he had greeted me not too long ago. "What's good wit' you, baby?"

Musa only stared at the crowd on the porch while waiting for the Buick to speed off into traffic, and then started across the street. Once across Haddon Avenue, he reached up and accepted the handshake B.J. had extended over the banister of the porch.

"I'm good, 'Al-hamdu-lilla' (Arabic term for 'all praise is due to Allah')," Musa replied with a bright, white-toothed smile. "I can't complain too much about anything."

There was an underlying degree of hardness in Musa's eyes that had starkly betrayed the warmth of his smile. It may be due to the time he spent in prison, or it may be simply because of his personality; either way, I didn't quite like it. I was instinctively warned to guard myself against Musa's false show of subtleness. I watched as he made his way up the steps, shaking hands and greeting everyone on the porch.

And then, it was my turn for him to greet me.

"Assalamu-alaykum (Arabic greeting which means 'peace be unto you')," said Musa with his hand out stretched.

"Wa- alaikum-salam," I replied while extending my own hand and accepting his own.

The grip in Musa's handshake, like the broadness of his back and shoulders, was evidence of him spending a great deal of his prison time on the pull-up bar. Despite me never working out a day in my life, I matched the firmness of his grip with one of my own while at the same time acting as nonchalant as possible. While gauging his eyes for any trace of ill will, I silently wondered if Musa was indulging in the same mental game I was now playing.

"It's 'Wa-alaikumus-Salam,' "aki" (Arabic term for brother)," said Musa while loosening my hand from his grip. "That's the proper way to say it, 'Al-hamdu-lilah'."

I took Musa's correction of my mispronouncing the Arabic term to be somewhat extreme and a bit condescending. Donnie, sharing the same sentiment, moved first to respond.

"Man, go head wit' that shit, good brotha," he barked with a stark mixture of both seriousness and comedy. "You act like you in Arabic class or some shit. Don't start trippin' out here, Muslim! Word up!"

Again, everyone on the porch erupted with laughter. I, on the other hand, acknowledged Donnie's comedy with a guarded smile and a chuckle. Musa, too, seemed to accept Donnie's comment with a measured degree of humor.

"Al-hamdu-lilah, aki," he replied with a smile. "'Inshallah' (Arabic term used when referring to the future meaning, If Allah wills), maybe I'll see you at the masjid one day."

"Who, Donnie?" remarked C-Gutter. "Man, that nigga's a mafuckin' heathen to the heart, homeboy! A million prayers couldn't get his ass through the pearly gates!"

Again, everyone erupted with laughter.

"Oh, shit!" Donnie exclaimed, no longer caring much about our conversation on the porch. "Peace to the God!"

I followed Donnie's glance across the street to see Justice getting out of his late-model Cadillac Deville.

Ever since I could remember, there had always been bad blood between Muslims and Five Percenters. The Five Percenters' concept of them being Gods flew directly in the face of the Muslims' belief of there being only one God. It was a most contentious issue, and it showed in Musa's eyes as Justice drew near.

Justice's dreadlocks were a little more than two inches long, all of them jet-black and twisted extremely thin. They were now styled into two ponytails, each of them tied with camouflage-colored ribbons; it was a bold choice of style that only Justice could have gotten away with.

"Peace," he replied to Donnie while making his way up the steps.

Justice and Musa were never the best of friends, and Donnie's proclamation of 'Peace to the God' only added to their discourse. The air had grown cold between them, but Justice, who is always as cool as a cucumber, remained his usual nonchalant self. In fact, he even moved to dig a bit deeper into Musa's skin, using me as a tool to do so.

"Peace, Don Juan," said Justice. "What . . . all of sudden you ain't tryin' to greet the True and Livin' God an' shit?"

"Man, go 'head wit that shit," I replied while accepting both the handshake and half-a-hug he had offered. "You know I'm down wit' that seven, yo. Peace to the God."

"Actual fact," Justice replied.

He then turned toward Musa.

"Peace, Muslim. Everything all right wit' you?"

Musa's smile seemed etched on his hardened face. There was slight twinge behind his eyes that underlined the true contention between both him and Justice. Donnie, too, recognized the stark sense of hostility between them and was thoroughly amused.

"So I'm a let knowledge be born to a perfection," Donnie began to sing. He was quoting a rap lyric by the legendary rapper, Rakim whose rap lyrics were well known for its ode to the Five Percenters' way of thinking. "All praises due to Allah, and that's a blessin'."

Whether or not Donnie was a hundred percent accurate in his quote was beyond me. What was clear, however, was his attempt to make mischief between Musa and Justice; he loved doing such things.

"Most definitely," Al-hamdu-lilah," Musa replied while smiling in Donnie's direction. "All praise is due to Allah."

"Indeed," said Justice while looking at Moses. "All praise is due to Allah . . . AND the old man . . ."

Besides, Justice and Musa, Donnie and I were the only ones acutely aware of the exact measure of unfriendliness between both the Muslims and Five Percenters. Justice's response was surely an intentional prick against Musa's skin, and both me and Donnie watched on with a sharp sense of curiosity.

Justice allowed his gaze to remain fixed on Musa's eyes for a few more seconds, seeming as if to check to see if there was anything Musa wanted to say. More to Donnie's dissatisfaction than mine, Musa chose to leave the conversation closed, and instead, made an attempt to turn the spotlight on me.

"So, how's uh, uh, uh, Keisha?" Musa asked.

Again, it was Donnie who had beaten me to the response.

"What? You mean you wasn't tryin' to holla at ol' girl while you was in the bing this time?" he asked smartly. "Oh, naw, you couldn't have been, 'cause if you was, you probably would've been out here trippin' like you did last time an' shit."

It was a sharp and pointed statement that had instantly struck a nerve with everyone on the porch. The atmosphere had grown quiet and strangely awkward, all within a matter of seconds. B.J.'s face, along with his female companions', went blank, their eyes watching on with a great deal of anticipation as to what would happen next.

Donnie smiled.

Justice's eyes remained sharply fixed on Musa, who didn't seem the least bit disturbed by what Donnie had just now said. He then turned to me with the same glowing look about his face, seeming to be unfazed by the verbal barbs being spat by both Donnie and Justice.

"Allahu-akbar (Arabic term meaning Allah is the greatest)," Musa declared brightly. "I have a clearer understanding of what's goin' on this time around." No disrespect intended; I was just askin' the young brother how he and his family was doin', aki. That's all."

From a short distance away, I could feel B.J. squirm beneath the weight of the subject at hand. Everyone agreed that B.J. was wrong for not warning me about Lakeisha and Musa's correspondence; moreover, there were even some who had went so far as to suggest that both me and Musa should square off and then take turns dishing B.J. a nice butt-whipping for his part in the entire controversy.

I had too many other fish to fry for me to even waste time thinking about beating up on B.J., and I somewhat sensed that Musa felt the same way. My main concern, for a split second, was more so about what may have been sitting on Musa's mind; and even now, I struggled to see the need for me to find such a thing so important.

"Hey, yo, God," said Justice. "Let me holla at you for a second."

"Let me get another cigarette before you bounce, yo," said Donnie as I fished one out of my pack and placed it between my lips.

I shook another cigarette out its pack and then passed it over to Donnie before making my way down the steps after Justice.

"I need you to take a ride wit' me some time around the wisdom hour," he declared once the two of us were standing a safe distance away from the crowd on the porch. "Me, you an' the God gots to get together and add on about some shit, you know what I'm sayin'?"

"True," I replied, already knowing what he was hinting about. "I'll see you around two."

"All right then, peace," said Justice.

"Peace," I said in return.

And with that, he turned and started back towards his Cadillac.

1:30 p.m.

I watched for a moment as Justice pulled off into traffic and then turned my glance back toward everyone on the porch. They all seemed to be having a good time, and I was all so tempted to return back to the festivities and engage in their smoking and drinking for a short time longer. Nevertheless, I was pressed for time; I still had to go back and see Tamara before reuniting with Justice and heading over to see Peace-Peace. With that being said, I started across Haddon Avenue and began making my way back down Division Street towards the alley which lead to Spruce Street. In a matter of minutes, I was at the back of Tamara's home and on my way inside.

The kitchen was cleaned to perfection; even the smell of breakfast had been done away with and replaced with the sweet smell of potpourri. Tamara was in the living room, seated in the corner of the couch with one leg crossed high over the other. The position in which she was sitting forced her body to shift a bit more onto one of her haunches and show off the ampleness of her thighs and buttocks. While leaning against one arm of the couch with her elbow fixed against it and talking into the telephone, Tamara seemed completely relaxed and totally comfortable; the thick marijuana joint fixed between her manicured fingers verified as much.

Tamara's hair was free of the scarf she'd been wearing earlier and was now uncovered and combed down into a wrap. Blonde and light-brown strands of hair lay sprawled across her forehead, highlighting the reddish-brown freckles and striking brown eyes that accented a smooth, golden-brown complexion.

"Here he is, right here," I heard Tamara say into the phone when noticing that I was making my way towards her. "You wanna talk to him?"

Without bothering to say another word, she took one more drag of her joint, uncrossed her legs, and then leaned over to hand me the telephone. I knew exactly who she speaking with.

Although I was but a child when Sheed was free on the streets and didn't know him personally, we were both such significant parts of Tamara's life that the three of us had somehow managed to meld into one collective unit. Sheed was the unseen, yet audible patriarch; Tamara played her part as the devout sustainer of his law, and I was simply the lost soul who was happy to be a part of both of their lives.

"What's up, big bro?" I asked while taking Tamara's place on the sofa and coyly eyeing the shape of her rear end as she rose up and started towards the kitchen.

"Ain't shit," he replied.

The stark silence in the background of Sheed's end of the phone was an indication of him still being in Administrative Segregation; had he been in regular population, I'd barely be able to hear him above the noise of other inmates on the cellblock.

"I know you ain't still on lock-down an' shit," I remarked with a mixture of both concern and disappointment. "You was supposed to be out that mafucka like a month ago."

"Yeah," Sheed replied. "Some bullshit jumped off in here and they wound up givin' a nigga like two hundred and forty more days an' shit. That's neither here nor there, though. We got some other shit to talk about."

By nature, Sheed was an obscure, no-nonsense type of person who'd always choose his words wisely when speaking. His response had immediately snapped me into full attention.

"What's up?" I asked.

"You know I don't fake no moves an' shit, right?" he began. "Everything is real wit' me."

"True indeed," I concurred while at the same time wondering what this conversation was leading to.

"You know what bein' real is?" he asked. "It's bein' honest. It takes a real mafucka to be honest an' shit. Mafuckas wanna lie an' sugarcoat shit all the time, but

A Day in the Life of A Camden City Drug Dealer

they only be makin' it worse 'cause the whole truth is gon' come out one way or the other, feel me?"

I remained silent while taking every word of Sheed's speech close to heart.

"You got a lot of potential, lil' bro," he went on. "As a matter of fact, you a lot realer than most of the niggas I met in my whole life. Why? 'Cause you tell me what it's really hittin' for out there, you know what I'm sayin'? And you don't gossip or make excuses for the shit niggas be doin' an' what not. It's because of you that I know what's really goin' on out there, and that's what's up."

Sheed's words of praise had left me frozen with pride. If I were on my feet, I'd be standing at full military attention with my chest poked out.

"I already know about the shit that's jumpin' off out there, and it's only gonna get worse," he said. "That shit is no good, yo . . . I'm a need you to fall back from all that shit. You hear me? Don't get mixed up wit' that bullshit, lil' bro . . . that shit is gon' have you on a road that you ain't really tryin' to be on . . . believe me when I tell you."

Sheed is a bona fide legend, both inside my neighborhood and out; so much so, that he was almost a mythical figure so to speak. Needless to say, I was flabbergasted when hearing his demand for me to stay clear of our impending war with the hustlers from Downtown. How could he expect me to do such a thing?

Of all people, I would have thought Sheed could understand my position. I was absolutely speechless.

"Don Juan," Sheed called out. "You there?"

"Yeah," I replied with a tone of indifference. "I'm here."

The feud between MidTown and Downtown had escalated far beyond that of a simple rivalry. My neighborhood has been ripped to shreds by gunfire and someone from our set, a scrawny fifteen year old boy at that, had gotten shot. If Sheed even thinks that I'm going to back away from my 'hood in the midst of such dire and critical times, he was sadly mistaken. There was no way in hell that I would crawl into a hole and allow anyone to enjoy the satisfaction of getting away with such disrespect.

"What's up then?" Sheed asked. "You done got quiet as hell on me, yo. Let a nigga know what's on your mind."

"Listen, big bro," I began squarely. "My love for you an' my love for the 'hood is one an' the same, you know what I'm sayin'? Right or wrong, I'm gon' ride or die wit' y'all niggas, regardless. I couldn't turn my back on the 'hood no more than I could turn my back on you, and that's just what it is. For real, yo . . . I ain't built no other way, Sheed, and that's my word . . . Ijust can't do it like that."

I was now sitting down with my ear to the phone, utterly shocked at the passion that had unintentionally welled up from within my own being; it carried my words in such an authoritative fashion that I was shocked at my own self. Sheed, on the other hand, had remained his usual quiet and seemingly brooding self. His cold, impersonal aura, which I had fought so hard to grow accustomed to, had now emerged, and I was soon beginning to feel somewhat unsettled.

Whatever then, I reasoned to myself. *I said what I said, and I meant every word of it. If this nigga feels some type of way about it, then fuck it. It is what it is.*

"So, that's what it is, lil' bro?" Sheed asked. "That's how it's goin' down?"

"Most definitely, big bro," I replied firmly. "I can't see it no other way."

Just then, a recorded voice had chimed in from out of nowhere to inform us that Sheed's phone time was due to expire in the next thirty seconds. I sat on the couch with the phone still in my hand, absolutely shell-shocked by the conversation we'd just had.

"Everything all right?" Tamara asked from her place across the room.

I inwardly frowned at the thought of me being so absorbed in my conversation with Sheed that Tamara's movements around me went unnoticed. Missing an eyeful of Tamara's beauty isn't what bothered me as much; it was more so my lack of attentiveness that troubled me. I could have been just as easily distracted while on the streets, and on the streets, such unawareness could very well cost me some my most valued possessions: my money, my freedom, and in some cases, even my life.

"Dijuan!" Tamara snapped, this time with her eyes aflame from the thought of being ignored. "I asked you if everything was all right between you and Rasheed!"

"Oh, yeah," I said while placing the phone back on its receiver before checking the time on my wristwatch. "Everything is cool . . . it's all good."

Tamara was sitting across the room in a sofa chair with her legs curled beneath her; an apple was in one hand, and a paring knife in the other. The anger she once held in her eyes was now mixed with a look of disgust.

"Oh, so now you gon' start lyin' to me an' shit?" she remarked with a genuine tone of disdain. "You gon' sit there and act like I don't know you, Dijuan? Is that how you're tryin' to play me? Tell me what happened between y'all."

Tamara was getting herself worked up by the second, punctuating each one of her questions with a sharp jab of the knife she was holding.

"Answer it," she snapped with the knife pointing at the phone that had just now begun to ring. "See who it is."

The thirty minutes I had to spare before seeing O.J. had now dwindled to fifteen.

"Tammy, listen," I began. "I . . ."

"I swear to God, Dijuan," Tamara interrupted. "Answer the fucking phone."

Tamara's feet were planted firmly on the carpet, her body upright and seemingly ready to spring out of the chair and strike me if necessary. Her face was blank, yet her eyes held a stark combination of being prepared to stab me with the paring knife while simultaneous pleading with me not to force her into doing so.

Never in my life would I have believed that Tamara would try to harm me, but at this precise moment, I was utterly convinced. With tinged feelings and an aching heart, I answered the phone on its fourth ring.

After accepting the call, I turned my sight away from Tamara while preparing myself to continue talking with Sheed.

"What up, big bro'?" I asked while trying as best I could to mask my wounded feelings.

"Listen, lil' homie," he began. "I see that you got your mind made up, and there ain't no turnin' back for you."

"That's my word," I replied coolly while still trying to collect my thoughts.

"That's what it's all about, my nigga," Sheed went on. "Not compromisin' your goals for another mafucka is one of the things that makes a man who he is. It's the degree of honesty you use, though, that determines what kind man you are; and that, lil' bro, is the definition of love. Believe me when I tell you that love and loyalty are one and the same."

It wasn't until I had witnessed Tamara act out Sheed's concept of love and loyalty that I had began to notice just how smooth a talker he really was, and I suddenly found myself becoming somewhat disenchanted with my neighborhood hero.

"I got a question to ask you," he went on to say. "I been wantin' to ask you this shit for a minute, but I ain't really know how. But seeing the type of nigga you turned out to be, I know you gon' keep it real wit' me, regardless."

After hearing what Sheed had just now said, I quickly went from disgruntled to guardedly curious.

"What's up, yo?"

"You fuckin' Tamara?" he asked.

I was shocked.

"Wh-what?" I managed to utter out loud. "What the fuck did you just ask me?"

"Relax, yo," Sheed went on to say. "Don't get all emotional or go off an' make a scene an' shit. I'll explain everything to you in a hot minute. Right now, I just gotta know if you fuckin' her or not."

"No, all right?" I answered coldly. "Fuck no."

"Okay, okay," Sheed remarked. "All right, listen. I'm gonna tell you somethin' that I ain't even tell Tamara yet."

There was a short pause that felt like an eternity. I glanced at my wristwatch once more and damned the fact that I was going to be late.

"My Motion for Reconsideration's been approved," said Sheed. "And I'm waitin' to go back to court so I can give some of this time back."

Mindful of Tamara's presence, I did my best to keep my composure in check. "You serious?" was all I could manage to say, and it was a rather thoughtless remark at that.

Serious? I thought wildly to myself. Of course, he was serious. Sheed was ALWAYS serious. Serious could have easily been his middle name.

"That's why I had to ask you," Sheed went on to explain. "I'm gon' be comin' home a lot sooner than mafuckas think, and I don't wanna be comin' home to no complications or no surprises, feel me?

"If you ain't fucked her by now, you'll probably fuck her sometime before I come home; or at least you'll end up in a situation similar to what I'm talkin' about. Whichever way the ball bounces, it's all good. She's human, lil' bro', and I gotta keep it real about me an' her situation. I just don't want you to get too attached to whatever might've been goin' on between y'all. As long as you understand that, everything is everything . . . feel me?"

My silent celebration of learning about Sheed's great legal victory had been utterly hampered by him entertaining the possibility of Tamara and me sleeping with each other. Of course I would ogle Tamara behind her back and somewhat wonder what she'd be like in bed, but it would definitely go no farther than that.

Tamara was like my older sister, and as far as my mind's eye could see, she was his faithful and ever dutiful wife. Why would Sheed dare to think I would even attempt to disrupt such a thing? Did he think that low of me? Did he think that low of her? Whatever the reason that could lead Sheed into believing such a thing, there would be no smoothing over what he had just now said to me. I was completely offended.

"Aye, yo," I began. "Why would you even come at me wit' some bullshit like that?"

"What?" he asked. "You trippin' over what I said about you fuckin' Tamara?"

I nearly winced at the ease in which Sheed had spoken so crudely of Tamara. Even if such an unforeseeable thing like that were to happen, still, I wouldn't be able to just *fuck* Tamara; and had such an impossible thing was to happen, I'm sure that Tamara would fuck me instead of me fucking her. Nonetheless, Tamara deserved much more than being spoken of in such a crude and thoughtless manner, and I quickly felt myself growing to dislike the notion of thinking of her this way.

Sheed had cut into my pondering this forbidden idea by continuing on with his conversation.

"I know the type of chick Tamara is, just like I know what type of dude you are," Sheed said. "I . . ."

"Hold on, Sheed," I tried to interrupt. "I . . ."

"Listen, dawg," Sheed snapped. "Let me say what I gotta say before this phone hangs up. This shit is mad important, my nigga, so let me hurry up and say what I gotta say."

Sheed's words and tone of voice reminded me of the short temper and vicious nature that had made him infamous. His release to the streets will no doubt be a pivotal event in Mid Town's history, and I was now beginning to question whether or not the 'hood would be ready for him.

"I know Tamara like the back of my hand, an' there ain't no secrets between the two of us," Sheed went on to explain. "It's only due to the order of operations that you know about my situation before she does. Anyway, Tamara's feelin' you, and I ain't talkin' about feelin' you like on some brother-sister shit, either. "

I shook my head with disbelief.

Prison done made this nigga crazy, I thought sadly to myself. *He's fuckin' bonkers.*

"That's the only reason why she lets you get away wit' the shit you do and still be where you be. (It was the best way Sheed can speak to me about Tamara allowing me to use her home as a stash house without saying anything incriminating.) Ain't no way in hell she just gon' let you get that off on her like that. Tamara's got principles, an' she don't break 'em for nobody.

"Shit, I wouldn't even be able to come home an' do half the shit you're doin, "Sheed went on to explain. "Man, she even disowned Marquis for fuckin' wit' those homos in here . . . and you how much she loves that nigga."

Again, I was speechless.

Marquis? A homosexual?

Since the very moment I began talking to Sheed, my mind had been constantly assaulted with one vicious revelation after another. Through it all, I remained silent while struggling not to succumb to some sort of mental breakdown.

"You quiet as hell, lil' bro . . ." said Sheed. "What? You still wrestlin' wit' what I said about you an' Tamara? Let me show an' prove just how much I know the both of y'all."

"I'm listenin'," I said while rising up and heading toward the kitchen for another beer.

"You stay on the move like a mafucka, so you was probably on ya way out the door when Tamara gave you the phone," Sheed commented. "It was either on the strength of me or on the strength of Tamara that you slowed down to get on the phone wit' me. Honestly, it was probably a little bit of both. Anyway, I think you felt some type of way when I told you to fall back from that little situation, and you probably wouldn't have got back on the phone if Tamara ain't make you."

I didn't like the way Sheed stressed the phrase "make me." The thought of someone, especially a woman, making me do anything was a definite thorn in my ego. The fact that he was absolutely right only made things worse.

"Tamara loves you just as much as she loves me, probably more. She'd rather die before letting you walk away without settling a dispute between the two of us."

Despite Sheed dealing with a handful of "maybes" and "probablies," he was pretty much right on the mark. His judge of character was striking, yet he was very much mistaken when claiming that Tamara may love me more than she loves him; after all, he wasn't here to witness her forcing me to answer the phone by way of a paring knife. It was a stinging memory.

"Tamara ain't had no dick in like three years," Sheed went on to say. "And the last nigga she fucked was so fuckin' lame that she was like fuck it, and started fuckin' with them toys an' shit. Now you're all grown up an' shit, and she sees my ways and actions all inside of you like a mafucka; and it's like she's watchin' her first love grow up all over again."

Again, I found myself struggling to withstand the bombardment of what Sheed was saying. I didn't know which accusation to counterattack first. I have never, and I mean never, seen Tamara with another man, and the idea of her fiddling around with sex toys was just too much for me to imagine.

"Listen, my nigga," said Sheed. "I ran wit' your brother a few times on the streets, and y'all might've come from the same pussy, but y'all niggas are definitely cut from a different cloth. Y'all mafuckasis different as hell by a long shot . . . trust me. On the other hand, though, you an' me is somethin' different. The two of us are pretty much cut from the same cloth; you're just a younger, smarter version of me. You'll see it sooner or later, but that ain't the point right now. The fact of the matter is that I see it, and Tamara definitely sees it, too.

"A thorough bitch and a thorough nigga is bound to connect . . . it's a muthafuckin' force of nature, yo, so don't think you're crossin' me if you "smash" (slang term for having sexual intercourse) or think that I would feel some type of way if you did. You're out there, and I'm in here. I know she got needs an' shit, and she is gon' fulfill them shits. All I ask is that you respect the fact that I'll be outta here sometime soon . . . and on the strength of that, you don't try and "wife" her (slang term for having an exclusive relationship with a female). We all have feelings an' emotions an' shit, but we can't let them determine how we handle our handle; you dig what I'm sayin'?"

Suddenly, the pre-recorded voice had appeared once more to warn us before terminating our conversation; and with that, we both said our goodbyes before hanging up the phone.

I walked back into the living room where Tamara was sitting in the corner of the couch with her legs curled beneath her.

"What's up wit' y'all?" she asked with a bit more curiosity than I cared to recognize.

Although clad in a white tank top and black jogging pants, in the back of my mind, Tamara was naked. She was naked, sweaty, and feverishly panting while engrossed in a number of lewd acts that I'd only seen on adult films as a young adolescent. Almost instantly, I blinked away such disgraceful thoughts while swallowing a mouthful of beer. The remembrance of her being braced to attack me with a knife helped substitute my impending lust with a great deal of pain and anger.

"Yeah," I answered while placing the phone back on its receiver. "We had a lil' heart-to-heart conversation. Everything is good."

"A heart-to-heart conversation, huh?" she remarked. It was a sharp, almost sarcastic retort. Her eyes went narrow and inquisitive all within an instant. One of Tamara's eyebrows was now arched up into the flurry of blonde and light-brown strands of hair that lie swept across her forehead. "What y'all have a heart-to-heart conversation about?"

"Gangsta shit," I replied while checking the time on my wristwatch. I was ten minutes late and terribly pissed.

"Gangsta shit, huh?" she remarked with her eyes now registering a look of suspicion. "And what gangsta shit were y'all talkin' about?"

"Listen," I said, fighting not to show just aggravated I was getting with Tamara and her relentless line of questioning. "I'm late as hell for an appointment, yo, and I really gotta bounce. We can talk about this later."

"Dijuan . . ."

"Not now, Tamara," I snapped. "I got somethin' to do, all right? Stop puttin' me through this bullshit every time I leave the fuckin' house. "You act like we on ol' husband an' wife type shit!"

Tamara's face went stiff, her eyes narrowing before turning cool and relaxed.

"Ain't nobody treatin' you like you're their fuckin' husband," she replied with a voice that was now barely above a hiss. "But YOU ARE my fuckin' family, nigga, and I was just bein' concerned about your selfish fuckin' ass."

"Yeah, ok," I replied hotly. "You wasn't talkin' that family shit when you was over there actin' like you was gon' stab me if I ain't get back on the phone wit' Sheed, though!"

Tamara's jaw fell open and then snapped shut just as fast. It wasn't so much as what I had said, but more so the emotion behind my words that had made such a striking impact. I was terribly hurt by what had just happened between us, and it showed. I was instantly struck with an overtone of embarrassment for appearing what I thought to be tender and woman-like.

"Dijuan," Tamara began. "I . . ."

"I gotta go, yo," I said while starting toward the backdoor. "I'll holla at you later."

And with that, I proceeded to make my exit, and never before had I been happier to be in such a rush to get somewhere.

2:30 p.m.

Despite the many times I've traveled with Justice, I was always struck with an overwhelming sense of comfort when riding in his car; no one can truly appreciate the luxury of a Cadillac until riding in one. The interior was meticulously clean, the leather seats were plush and the faint scent of a Muslim fragrance lingered all throughout the vehicle. In fact, I felt more like a potential customer set to test drive a brand new car rather than a passenger. The soulful sounds of an oldies song filled the car, and I, while watching the streets of Camden from behind tinted car windows, made myself comfortable and moved to fish a cigarette from the pack inside my pants pocket.

"Hold up, sun," said Justice. "Don't light that cigarette just yet. We got a quick chore to do first."

A quick chore to do?

I looked quizzically at Justice as he navigated his car into an open parking spot in front of Washington Park Apartments, an apartment complex in the East Camden section of Camden. I exited the car with Justice and followed his lead by grabbing a bag of groceries from the back seat and proceeded up the steps to a second floor apartment.

"Here's where Peace-Peace's 'grand-Earth' (Five Percenter term for grandmother) lives," said Justice as he proceeded to knock on the door.

"Adam, is that you?" asked the voice of an elderly woman from inside.

"Yes, ma'am," he replied with a great measure of charm.

"Adam?" I whispered with what I'm sure was a most befuddled facial expression.

"Peter had to work overtime, so he asked me to drop these groceries off at your house before I headed home," Justice so pleasantly replied.

Peter? I thought shockingly to myself. *Was that Peace-Peace's real name? And what's up with Justice callin' his self Adam? What the fuck is goin' on here?*

Justice acknowledged my expression of utter shock and surprise with a genuine look of annoyance before switching back to an award-winning "boy next door" impersonation as the door began to unlock and open. After a short series of metallic clicks, which was then followed by the jingling sound of a chain-lock being unfastened, a short elderly woman with sharp eyes and gray hair had appeared from behind a slim opening between the door and the doorway. Despite the obvious difference in size and weight, the resemblance between Peace-Peace and his grandmother was uncanny.

Her complexion was a dull-yellowed color with freckles sprinkled beneath her eyes and across her cheeks. Her lips, full and shaded a light tannish-brown, were the same as her grandson's. In spite of the tiredness in her eyes, they still proved sharp and cautious. Peace-Peace's subtle, yet guarded nature was undoubtedly a hereditary trait. Not yet welcoming us inside, she paused long enough to hint around for Justice to explain who I was.

"Oh, I'm sorry," he said rather apologetically. "Marcus, this is Mrs. Chambers. Mrs. Chambers, this is Marcus Graham. The three of us work together at the Johnson and Milford Recycling Plant in Pennsauken. Not only am I at fault for bringing him to your home unannounced, but please pardon me for not introducing the two of you from the very beginning. That was rude. I hope you accept my apology."

With fine-tuned ears, I listened carefully to Justice as he so smoothly spun his tale of deceit. Knowing Justice to have always been a man of few words, I found it quite disturbing to witness him break his character while lying to an elderly woman; moreover, to witness him do such a thing so efficiently and without hesitance was also a bit unnerving.

"Well, it don't make much difference now," she brusquely replied while widening the door and allowing us to enter inside. It was also obvious that Peace-Peace's gruff demeanor was also a hereditary trait that had come from her side of the family. "The boy's already here, Adam; besides, this old woman ain't got nothin' worth takin' anyway. Y'all go on ahead and set them bags in the kitchen."

I followed closely behind Justice, observing her tiny apartment as I went. It was the typical set-up for an elderly person who lived alone. A modest-sized television was set on top of an old-fashioned wooden TV stand. Two couches, both of them covered in plastic, sat across from one another with a small coffee table set in between the two. A rocking chair was at the front of the living room and facing the television; its hand-knit cushions told of it being Mrs. Chambers' preferred comfort zone.

Scores of photographs were situated all throughout the apartment; they covered the walls and cluttered all of the nightstands. Framed photographs of all shapes and sizes were perched on top of the television set, and they also filled the little table that lie between the two couches. One set of photos in particular, which were situated amongst a huge collage of pictures in a giant frame set on a wall in the dining room quarters, caught my attention.

Among the dozens of photos set within this huge frame were pictures of Peace-Peace at various stages in his life. Never before did I have such an intimate glimpse of this mysterious man, and I was soon struck with an odd feeling of discomfort when noticing that he wore the same despondent expression in each of his pictures.

Even as a child, Peace-Peace held a blank and disturbing stare; he seemed to be born with it.

After setting the groceries atop the kitchen counter, Mrs. Chambers thanked both me and Justice while abruptly ushering the two of us towards the door. "One of you boys brought the smell of weed and liquor into this apartment, and I really don't appreciate it," she said while handing us both a peppermint. "You can't bring those types of habits into a person's home; it's disrespectful and shows no class, you understand?"

"Yes, ma'am," the two of us said, almost in unison.

Being the one guilty of this transgression, I silently burned with guilt as I placed the candy into my mouth. With that, I shamefully remained quiet and meekly followed Justice down stairs to the car.

Now on Route 295 South, Justice remained silent while driving down the highway. He sat leaning to the left with his right hand gripping the steering wheel, seemingly absorbed in the harmonious tunes of a classic Bobby Womack song. The silence between the two of us, along with the sad, bluesy feel of the music booming from his car speakers, was beginning to drive me insane.

"Yo," I began in my attempt to break the monotony. "What's up with that 'Adam and Marcus shit?' Why is we shootin' aliases to Peter's grandmom an' shit?"

"First of all, don't be playin' wit' the God's honorable name like that," Justice went on to lecture. "That shit ain't what's happenin'. As far as the aliases are concerned, we'll born the science about all of that once we get to the God's rest (one of the many Five Percenter terms with a dual meaning. In this case, "rest" means the place where a Five Percenter lives).

With that, Justice fell back into silent mode, leaving me with nothing else left to say. We remained that way for the next twenty or so minutes until he turned onto an exit ramp that would soon lead us into a small town in Gloucester County.

Paulsboro is a small town consisting mainly of one road that stretched from one end of town to the other. Every other street branched off of this main road, and in turn, splintered off into several other streets. Aside from the size of the town, its homes were mostly spread apart, giving each residential section a slightly rural appearance.

After turning off the exit, we drove across a drawbridge which lead us into Paulsboro and then made a sharp turn just before heading into town. From behind tinted windows, I watched the scenery as we cruised by, noticing the elements of inner-city life within Paulsboro's interior. The streets were littered with both garbage and local inhabitants; some of them huddled together in circles while standing on the curb. A near-abandoned public basketball court stood across the street from a public housing complex which, despite the cold wintry weather, was congested with what I guessed to be more criminal activity. It was then that I noticed the chorus of an oldies song now booming from the car's stereo system speakers singing about the world being a ghetto. While observing the vicinity as we zoomed by, I couldn't have agreed more.

We continued down the street until the scenery changed from fussy and cluttered to peaceful and serene. After turning onto a side street, which in turn, led to another series of streets, we soon found ourselves in a rather aristocratic-looking neighborhood that appeared to be on the very outskirts of town. The sidewalks were clean and lined with huge leafless trees; either side yards or driveways worked to separate the houses apart from one another, and the streets were both spacious and clean.

Spying the familiar late-model Jeep Cherokee parked amongst a group of automobiles in a nearby driveway, I assumed that the large, white-painted porch house with gray trimming is where Peace-Peace lived. It was a huge house with a spacious driveway and a two-car garage to match. A small wooden gate surrounded an impressive and roomy front yard giving his home an all around feel of the American dream being realized. I found it hard to believe that Peace-Peace lived in such a suburban-looking environment.

Because of the crowd of vehicles in Peace-Peace's driveway, Justice opted to park in front of the house. We exited the car and started up the steps where Justice stopped at the door of the closed-in porch to ring the doorbell. A slim, brown-skinned man with a clean shaven face and heavy-lidded eyes answered the door. He and Justice greeted each other warmly.

"Peace, True and Livin'," the man said cheerfully.

"Peace, God," Justice replied before introducing the two of us to one another. "This is the God, Infinite Truth."

Justice then paused to place his hand on my shoulder.

"And this is my main man, Don Juan."

Infinite Truth and I both greeted each other with "Peace" and a handshake before he led both me and Justice inside the house.

In Harlem, during the early sixties, a group of men formed the Five Percent Nation, its members aptly dubbing themselves "Five Percenters." It was a movement spurred by Clarence Smith, a one-time member of the Nation of Islam, and his ideology had taken the ghettos of New York by storm. As time passed on and the movement expanded, its followers changed the name of their organization from the Five Percent Nation to the Nation of Gods and Earths, its male followers now being referred to as "Gods" and its female followers now being referred to as "Earths."

Some of the members of this organization were strict as to not allowing others to refer to them as Five Percenters, while others were a bit more forgiving. Those whom were firm on what they were to be called normally seemed rigid and unyielding, much like that of a member of the military, their attitudes mostly cold and indifferent. Such was the aura of the Five Percenters now crowded in Peace-Peace's living room. From both the men and women alike, there was a concentrated force of solidarity. I could sense a bleak air of disdain and the hidden element of aggression that radiated from their cool, disconnected gazes. Maybe it was more so my insecurity; regardless of that fact, their overall tone, to me, was quite unfriendly.

The first decree I had silently made to myself while removing my boots was to address each one of them as the Gods and Earths they proclaimed to be. I wasn't raised in a religious household, nor was my belief in God rock-solid; therefore, I had no hang-ups with referring to them as such. Secondly, I planned to appear humble and not as some begrudging "know-it-all" scholar with something to prove.

The knowledge held by the average Five Percenter was, by far, very impressive; the intelligence and spirituality possessed by those truly in tune with their lessons was even greater, and in some cases, downright intimidating. The last thing I'd want to do is spark some sort of debate. Most Five Percenters were exceedingly book smart and possessed an incisive ability to produce a most formidable argument, no matter what the topic. My intentions for being here were to see Peace-Peace and not "building" (a Five Percenter term for learning and teaching). I wanted to see Peace-Peace, discuss whatever there was to be discussed, and then head back home to prepare for my trip to the mall.

With my boots now placed on a shoe rack, I followed closely behind Justice as he made his way through the living room, all the while exchanging greetings with all of his "brothers" and "sisters." The man named Infinite Truth rejoined his female companion who was sharing a couch with another couple. In a plush sofa chair which lay angled against the wall and in front of a huge flat-screened television sat a kid no more than fifteen or sixteen years old. His greeting of "peace" appeared strained, almost begrudging. They all seemed to sense that I wasn't "one of them" and acknowledged me with a nod and a neutral "what's up" or "peace." The teenage boy held his glance a bit longer than the others, his eyes reflecting a curiosity as to what business I may be having with his "brother," Peace-Peace.

A huge poster-sized picture was perched on the wall above the boy's head. It was an enlarged black and white photograph of a man standing in front of some type of mom-and-pop shop dressed in a dark pair of slacks, a white button-up shirt, and a light-colored trench coat, the words "Father Allah" lay engraved at the bottom of its metal frame. Taking a moment to stare at the photo a bit longer, I figured it to be of Clarence Smith, the nation's founder. He wasn't a particularly large man; still, the faint smile beneath his full-grown moustache suggested a smooth, easy-going, and humble nature. I found it incredible for a man of his build to have survived some of the situations that a lot of Five Percenters claim that he had done.

I followed closely behind Justice, all the while still sensing the vibe of Peace-Peace's houseguests which felt as cool as the balls of my feet when stepping into the plush, cushiony carpet. I couldn't help but to marvel at not only the size of Peace-Peace's home, but the furniture and interior decoration of it all. The walls were eggshell white; the living room furniture was leather and matched perfectly with the black wall-to-wall carpeting that stretched along the entire length of both the living room and dining room.

Across the kitchen and beyond itssliding glass door, I could see Peace-Peace seated by the windows of his closed-in patio. A tall, black-skinned woman stood behind him, dutifully braiding the rest of his hair. To say that she was attractive would clearly have been an understatement. Never before had I seen a woman whose complexion was so black and yet, so beautiful.

The gloss of her coal-black skin was a shining sign of her living well and eating healthy. Her face was slender, each one of her features being sharp and well-defined. Her hair was styled in a looping and decorative array of braids; and that, along with the metallic earrings I saw dangling from her earlobes, helped contribute to her resemblance of a delicate African sculpture.

Much like the front porch, Peace-Peace's patio was closed-in and well furnished. There was a wicker table and two matching chairs, one of them which he was currently sitting in, placed by the windows of the patio. The view of his backyard and its evergreen scenery was a sight to behold. A sofa was placed against the rear of the room and facing the window; and a weight bench, along with a variety of dumbbells and free weights, sat far in the corner.

A young girl, no more than ten or eleven years old, sat perched atop the weight bench watching as Justice and I entered. She was a short, rather petite little girl with the genetic features of both Peace-Peace and the woman standing behind him who was still busying herself with braiding his hair. Although sharing her mother's build and dark-skinned complexion, the little girl's sharp and pronounced features undoubtedly belonged to Peace-Peace.

Not bothering to turn his head, Peace-Peace strained his one healthy eye in Justice and my direction.

"Peace, God," said Justice.

"Peace to the God," Peace-Peace replied.

After being addressed by Peace-Peace, Justice then greeted the woman whom was still braiding Peace-Peace's hair.

"Peace, Earth."

"Peace, Justice," the woman replied with her eyes quickly shifting from Justice to me and then back to the task of finishing Peace-Peace's braids.

The child who was once seated in the far corner of the patio had now began to make her way beside her parents as Peace-Peace began to introduce me to his family.

"Don Juan," he said while using his thumb to point at the woman behind him. "This is my Earth, Sha' Asia Mecca." He then pointed his finger over to the cute little girl. "And that's my young queen, over there, Princess Medina. You can call her Princess or Medina . . . it's up to you."

"Peace, Don Juan," said Sha' Asia Mecca. Her eye contact was brief but direct, which left me with the impression of Peace-Peace's braids being far more important than me being here. Still, it was my first time ever seeing a more intimate side of Peace-Peace; and I enjoyed it.

"Peace, Earth," I said, feeling a bit caught up in the positive vibes of everyone in the patio room. I then turned to the cute little girl standing beside her father. "And peace to you, lil' Earth."

"I'm not an Earth, yet," Medina replied. "I'm too young, and more importantly, I don't have no babies yet."

She then fixed a most inquisitive glance upon my own.

"Do you know the science of the universe?" she asked.

Not only was I taken aback by the surprising amount of intelligence Princess Medina possessed, but the conviction in which she spoke was like that of a young college student; it was a very sobering experience. Peace-Peace was sitting with his head bowed as Sha' Asia, who appeared oblivious to my conversation with her daughter, continued on with putting the finishing touches on Peace-Peace's hairstyle. Justice took a seat on the sofa couch and was curiously observing our exchange. Medina remained standing before me, shrewdly awaiting my response; her gaze was eerily similar to the dead-serious stare of her father's.

Much to my relief, Sha' Asia moved swiftly to interrupt our conversation.

"Princess Medina, that's enough."

Princess Medina turned to her mother with a facial expression like that of a child being caught in the midst of making mischief. "But mom," she explained. "I'm just buildin' with the God."

"He's not the God, Medina," Sha' Asia replied with a practiced tone of patience. "He doesn't have knowledge of self."

Not having "the knowledge" or "knowledge of self" meant not conceding to the Five Percents' concept of the Blackman being God. Five Percenters didn't perceive God as being some invisible, supernatural force, nor did they believe in life after death. As weak as my faith in God may have been, there was still something inside my being that kept me from forsaking the concept of there being an invisible but almighty God, and for that, I was considered an "eighty-fiver" (one who was ignorant to the truth of the Blackman being God and a mental slave to the powers that be).

I felt my face grow tight when hearing Sha' Asia's blunt remark about me "not being the God." I may not have been a part of their "nation" and I may not agree that the Blackman is the one and only, almighty being, but there were many, many other talking points that I saw eye-to-eye with them about. Because of that, I was usually recognized as not being a part of the Nation, but still credited for dealing with some sort of self-awareness.

Such wasn't the case in this particular instant. Sha' Asia spoke to her daughter about me in the same manner as one would an indigent or a homeless person; it was both matter-of-fact and indifferent. A part of me was happy to see Sha' Asia preparing to leave while the other side of me wanted her to stay and receive a piece of mind.

"Do me a favor and twist somethin' up for me an' brothers," said Peace-Peace to Sha' Asia as she and Medina began making their way to the kitchen.

I, in turn, found a seat on the sofa beside Justice. Peace-Peace rose from off the chair and took a moment to stretch his body.

"Oh, no," he said as I placed a cigarette between my lips. "Nobody smokes cigarettes in this house. If you gon' burn that poison, you gon' have to do that shit outside."

"You might as well wait," Justice reasoned. "Sha' Asia's about to bring back some herb, and I know you gon' wanna smoke a cigarette after you're done, so you might as well relax for a second and be easy."

Seeing no need to argue, I proceeded to make myself comfortable by slipping out of my coat and then asked Justice and Peace-Peace about the show that had been put on for Peace-Peace's grandmother back in Camden.

"So, y'all stopped at the house?" Peace-Peace inquired.

"Yeah," I replied. "She's a nice lady."

Peace-Peace rose from out of his seat on the wicker chair and found a space on the sofa beside me. I was thankful that he had chosen to sit with his glass eye on the other side of me; I hate having to look at the damned thing.

"If the police were to ever question my family about me or anybody associated wit' me, your real name would never come up, not even by accident," Peace-Peace began. "Imagine me bein' locked up for the shit we about to get into tonight and my grandmom's talkin' to the cops about how nice it was for Dijuan and Justice to deliver her groceries on the same day it happened. Next thing you know, Homicide'll be chasin' you down, and you'll fuck around an' be trapped off in the county jail an' shit. If somethin' goes wrong, the last thing any of us needs is a fuckin' co-defendant."

"Well, if that's the case," I asked. "Then why introduce me to her in the first place?"

"I got insurance on you, so it's only right for you to have it on me," Peace-Peace answered.

I eyed Peace-Peace quizzically.

Insurance?

It took less than a few seconds for me to understand what he meant by insurance, but still, I had to press further.

"Insurance?" I asked, although already knowing the answer. "What the fuck do you mean by that?"

Before Peace-Peace could respond, Sha' Asia returned with two blunts.

Everyone fell quiet, our moods instinctively relaxed as she entered and handed the freshly rolled blunts to Peace-Peace; it was as if the three of us were never discussing plans for murder. Yet and still, there was something about Sha' Asia that gave hint of her having some idea about her God's doings. She was quiet and accommodating, but very observant, both observant and intelligent.

"The Gods are getting ready to leave," she dutifully announced.

"Thank you, Earth," Peace-Peace replied. "Give 'em the peace for me, and tell 'em that'll I'll build with 'em later."

With that, Sha' Asia turned and left.

Peace-Peace tucked one blunt behind his ear and then took his time setting fire to the one he held firmly between his fingertips. I sat beside him in silence, all the while replaying his reference to both his and my own family as "insurance" over and over again in my mind.

Satisfied to see the blunt was lit evenly all the way around, Peace-Peace inhaled the reefer deeply before continuing.

"If you was to ever get locked up and snitch on me or Justice, then you or your family will pay the price for it. The mafucka that turns around and sells his own people out to the police is really the one who deserves to die; however, I'm more so aware that there are some things that hurt a lot worse and are far more punishing than a physical death."

Peace-Peace looked me square in the eyes while speaking, his tone of voice being every bit as blank and as unfeeling as the marble fixture in his grim, expressionless face. As stunned and as outraged as I may have felt about what Peace-Peace had just now said, still, I fully understood his point. Countless criminals have been betrayed and sent away for the rest of their lives, not only because of their trust in a weaker link, but more so because of the lack of repercussions dealt to those guilty of breaking the sacred street code of never ratting out their friends. Peace-Peace took a moment to smoke a bit more of the blunt before continuing.

"Hey, man, don't take this shit personal," he remarked quite candidly. "I expect you to handle shit the same way."

"Listen, my nigga," Justice smoothly interjected. "If you don't snitch, then you ain't got nothin' to worry about. It's as simple as that."

Peace-Peace handed me the blunt before continuing on with what he was saying.

"If we thought you some shaky, sucka duck-ass nigga, we wouldn't be fuckin' wit' you in the first place; and you know that; however, everything is real. If you feel some type of way about how things is set up, you gotta let niggas know right the fuck now, 'cause there ain't no turnin' back after tonight."

Peace-Peace took one more drag of the blunt before passing it over to me. While accepting the weed, I couldn't help but to realize that Peace-Peace's most recent remark was actually a way of him acknowledging me as a stand-up guy; such praise from him was normally far and in between. In light of our conversation, however, Peace-Peace's words of appraisal were far from heartwarming. I tapped a long stick of blunt ash into the ashtray and then helped myself to a healthy drag of the marijuana. By nature, Peace-Peace was a gruff individual. I had long grown accustomed to his blunt manner of speaking; moreover, I respected him for it.

I tried to convince myself that anyone willing to place their own grandmother in harm's way was unworthy of such high regard, but the sad truth of the matter is that not only did I respect him for it, I slightly feared him for it as well. It wasn't the fear commonly felt by a coward when facing the school bully after school, nor was it the gnawing dread one felt when staring point blank down the barrel of a gun. This type of fear was nothing like the apprehension or trepidation brought about by normal circumstance; it was more so the heightening of one's senses when involved in a life or death situation.

At this particular moment, Peace-Peace very much personified the extremes to which our situation could very well lead. If a man was willing to sacrifice his own flesh and blood for a particular cause, there was no telling what more he was capable of doing. The same went for Justice, a man who could entertain the thought of murdering an elderly woman while charming and befriending her at the same time.

Both Peace-Peace and Justice are two very dangerous men, and I was very much aware that our relationship could prove fatal at any given moment; still, I wouldn't want to form an alliance with anyone else. The three of us shared a genuine love for our neighborhood, and we were determined to do right by it and succeed at any cost. We were men of principle; our pedigree and aspirations are what drew us together, and tonight's course of events would solidify such a bond.

I took another long drag of the blunt; its thick, billowy marijuana smoke filled my lungs, and forced me into a brief moment of thought. The weight of what Peace-Peace and Justice had just now said to me was increasing by the second. I took one more pull, this one a short concentrated toke, and then let the smoke settle deep into my lungs before exhaling. My euphoria came almost instantly. I repeated the process once more before passing the blunt over to Justice.

One by one, Peace-Peace's houseguests showed up to announce their departure. I sat back against the couch and allowed myself to give into the feeling of being free, high, and relaxed. While silently enjoying my high, I learned through Peace-Peace's departing company that his righteous name was actually Eternal Peace Love Allah, and I found it quite ironic that someone with such a serene sounding name could be so willing and so very capable of administering a most severe measure of death and destruction.

Seeing that everyone had now went on about their way, I moved to speak my mind.

"What do y'all mean, let y'all know now 'cause there ain't no turnin' back after tonight?" I asked, sounding a bit more relaxed than I really was. "At this point, it's too late for niggas to be talkin' all of that 'no turnin' back' shit anyway, you know what I'm sayin'? We're in this shit together, son, so enough wit' the bullshit . . . ain't nothin' to it but to do it."

Justice cracked a smiled while passing the blunt to Peace-Peace, whose reaction surfaced as nothing more than an absent purse of the lips. I was sure that beneath his cool, poker-faced demeanor, Peace-Peace was more than satisfied with my response than he let on.

"In it to win it?" he asked.

"In it to win it, my nigga" I remarked. "We gon' ride this bitch till the wheels fall off."

This time, it was Peace-Peace who smiled.

"All right, then," he said after taking a long drag of the blunt. "Till death do us part, my niggas."

"Till death do us part," both Justice and I replied.

And just like that, I thought to myself. *It's on and poppin.'*

4:30 p.m.

After the three of us spent nearly an hour reviewing our plan to retaliate against Jay-Dollar, I was more than ready to return back to the 'hood. Justice, Peace-Peace and I had gone over the plan repeatedly, each one of us scrutinizing what was to be done down to the finest detail. Both Peace-Peace and Justice were exceedingly anal about the entire scheme, and as frustrating and as irritating as they may have seemed, I completely understood.

This time, while on our way back to Camden, Justice and my roles were now the complete opposite to what they'd been on our way to Paulsboro; Justice was the energetic and chatty one while I, on the other hand, had grown quiet and terribly reclusive. The fact that I had left my gun and drugs in Mannie's possession for such an overextended period of time was haunting me greatly. Despite the abundance of trust that I indeed held for Mannie, I had little faith in his measure of responsibility. As seconds turned to minutes, I began to grow more and more anxious. Looking to somehow escape these negative and seemingly soon-to-be nervous thoughts, I chose to reflect more so upon the thoughts and ideas exchanged between Peace-Peace, Justice and myself.

I was once told that human beings are creatures of habit, but it wasn't until thoroughly conspiring to commit murder that I was able to realize just how surprisingly predictable a person really can be. The daily schedule of a drug dealer is surprisingly routine. From a safe distance away, one could easily observe the enemy in his own territory and learn all there is to know in order to commit the perfect murder: where he lives, where he hangs out, where he goes to eat, who he hangs out with and so on. If one didn't know where his enemy lives, then he was sure to know someone else that does. Such information, along with the address and whereabouts of relatives and love interests, are far more accessible than many would dare to imagine.

The daily activities of a drug dealer, aside from the obvious bustle of drug dealing, normally involves an overindulgence in drugs and alcohol. This, in itself, makes it all the more easier for him to fall victim to a premeditated killing. Their judgment is normally clouded, their inhibitions lowered, and most of all, their ability to react effectively in a "think-fast" situation is seriously impeded. To exact a perfect murder, as Peace-Peace explained, all one needs is patience and practice - the target himself will unwittingly lend the greatest hand in getting the job done.

By taking turns staking out all of Jay-Dollar's movements, Peace-Peace and Justice were able to produce an accurate account of his schedule from nine o'clock in the morning until whatever time he retires. They even managed to convince Tamika Barlow, a woman who was not only a best friend to Jay-Dollar's "baby-momma" but his secret lover as well, to make sure he was at the right place at the right time for us to exact our revenge. She was somehow beguiled into thinking that Jay-Dollar would be set-up for an armed robbery instead of him being murdered, to which she'd then receive a sizable portion of the spoils as a result of her betraying him.

Although I didn't see Tamika as an innocent victim, I wasn't the least bit fond of her having to be killed along with Jay-Dollar; moreover, me being the one designated to murder her only sickened the idea even more. Nevertheless, I fully understood the risk of us leaving her alive. Despite it being the most logical means to an end, however, I just wasn't comfortable with the notion of murdering her. In my mind, I did my best to justify such an act as best I could, yet, there was no comfort to be found.

Above all, it was Peace-Peace and Justice's indifference to the lives of innocent people that disturbed me most. In the midst of realizing their own ambitions, anyone one could be murdered. These two friends of mine were willing to murder anyone who stood in their path, and I completely understood why. Moreover, I could honestly admit that I felt the same exact way. The compassion and reverence for life that I've come to learn and exhibit since childhood held no merit when compared to the success I was seeking in the streets. If I was willing to forfeit my own life for the sake of my neighborhood, how much compassion should I exhibit for the sake of someone else's?

At my request, Justice pulled the car over and dropped me off on the corner of Mt. Ephraim and Kaighns Avenue, which was roughly five hundred or so yards away from my neighborhood. The sun had already begun to set, darkening the once bright blue sky to a dark, pallid shade of gray. The gusts of wind had grown thick and full and were now beginning to whip about more often, numbing my fingers as I smoked a cigarette while in route to Mid Town.

Countless thoughts whirled about my mind, at times disappearing as quickly as they appeared, all in unison with the short, brisk steps I took while hurrying down the street. I was due to rendezvous with Peace-Peace and Justice at eleven o'clock tonight; and with the evening fast approaching, I felt as if the day was swiftly passing about without me completing my ever- looming list of my daily objectives to get done. While reflecting on my list of "things to do," I was fiercely debating with myself as to which chore I should tackle first, either go to the mall or visit my mother. After much scrutiny, I concluded that shopping at the mall would be the most time consuming task; therefore, I'd visit her afterwards.

Branded as the reason for an increase of crime in surrounding boroughs and townships, a series of checkpoints were erected along Camden City's borders; and, consequently, they were rigorously guarded by the police departments of our neighboring towns. It was a program supposedly designed to curb residential drug trafficking by way of targeting vehicles in violation of some type of DMV regulation; but the seemingly countless unlawful stops had made it painfully obvious to those living in Camden that it was nothing more than a guise for racial profiling.

Whatever the case may be, the bottom line was that I didn't have a drivers' license, and I couldn't afford to gamble my precious time against the hawk-eyes of suburban police. My only other option would be to catch the bus. Anyone else in possession of fifteen hundred dollars to spend probably wouldn't mind spending thirty or forty dollars for a taxi, but I was also a man of principle, counting my pennies even while splurging. The need for a hustler to be as frugal as humanly possible is a principal that has been branded into my brain for many years now. When handling any amount of money, there was always an impulse for me to save some of it; and it was this way of thinking that had helped me acquire nearly ten thousand dollars in cash.

The time spent traveling by bus may take much longer than traveling by car, but I was staying clear of the unnecessary risk of being pulled over and having my car, which was uninsured as well as unregistered, towed away. Again, it was all about the money - how much I can make and how much I can save.

While crossing the corners of Spruce Street and Mt. Ephraim Avenue, I took a brief moment to glance down the street and recognized my mother's gray Ford Cavalier parked in front of the house. The time on my wristwatch read four-forty p.m., which told me that she'd been home from work for at least twenty minutes now. I imagined my mother sitting on the sofa with her feet resting on a foot stool as she watched the evening news, all the while boiling with contempt not only for this cruel and unjust world, but also for a stiff-necked and rebellious son whom refuses to do anything positive for himself.

Ever since the beginning of my career in the streets, the relationship between my mother and I has been nothing short of a strained acquaintance; and it has only grown worse over the years. Because of the lifestyle I've chosen for myself, my mother had refused to see me as anything but less than a man, and at any given moment, she would make it her business to tell me so. In her eyes, it wasn't enough for her to have a son that loves and respects his mother; for Lorraine Martha Ingles, there was never such a thing as unconditional love. In my mother's eyes, it will be either her way or the highway, and a most serious contention between us now existed because of it. Her calling me a "jigaboo" and labeling me the worst thing that has happened to Black people since the A.I.D.S. epidemic was just some of the ammunition she'd so effectively use to wound my pride.

It has been almost three weeks since we've seen or spoken to one another, yet I doubt that her request to see me was one of sentimental value. My mother was, and always has been, a tough, unapologetic woman. If anything, she was planning to make some form of reconciliation, if only for the sake of her two-year-old grandson. Dijuan Jr. was the only chink in my mother's armor, and he was probably the only reason why she hadn't moved to completely disown me by now.

Satisfied to find that my car hadn't been ticketed, stolen or towed away, I began making my way onto Haddon Avenue, which by now was abandoned and clear of all activity. The porch houses that normally served as hangout posts for its neighborhood thugs, both condemned as well as occupied, were all clear. The emptiness of Haddon Avenue, along with the dark, gusty feel of the cold winter winds, combined to emit a most haunting sense of vacancy.

Although pressed for time and unable to conduct business, I took a brief moment to remain still and enjoy the desolate and lonely atmosphere. I was totally at peace with the creepy, ghost-like environment and took a moment more to further indulge in the lonely feeling of the streets. Content that I had taken in enough of the gloomy ambiance, I started across Haddon Avenue and entered inside the abandoned house where Mannie had stashed both my product and my pistol, only to frown when finding that both of them were missing.

I took a moment to light my cigarette before exiting off the porch where I spied Mannie up the street standing in front of the grocery store at the corner of Haddon Avenue and Pine Street. Recognizing me as I threw up both my hands, he proceeded to meet me halfway.

"The cops raided right after y'all left," Mannie said after we greeted one another.

"Word?" I replied, hoping that his story of our neighborhood being raided wouldn't lead to the reason why my gun and thousand dollars' worth of base cocaine were missing.

"Yeah," Mannie said in confirmation. "They locked up Donnie and C-Gutter, too."

My eyes widened at the news.

"Word?" I remarked, genuinely taken aback. "Donnie AND C-Gutter? What the fuck for?"

"C-Gutter got locked up for warrants or some shit," said Mannie. "And Donnie got locked up for like two pounds of weed and a burner (slang term for a firearm).

I fell silent for a brief minute, and after a moment or two of reflection, I then moved to comment.

"Two pounds, huh?" I remarked with measured surprise. "That's a nice amount of weed."

"Yeah," Mannie concurred, his abrupt state of silence leading me to believe that he was now contemplating the thought of buying a few bags of weed for himself.

"So, what's up wit' Donnie?" I asked. "How'd he get knocked wit' all that shit?"

"Some dummy-man shit," Mannie replied with a sneer. "Donnie was sittin' on the hood of his car talkin' mad shit to the cops while they was raidin' an' shit. They asked the nigga if he had a license, an' he wasn't even legal!"

Mannie took a moment to laugh out loud when speaking of Donnie and C-Gutter's misfortune; I found myself growing more peeved with his attitude by the second.

"They checked his car an' found mad mafuckin' weed an' shit," Mannie continued. "Man, they straight locked his ass up. He's a stupid mafucka, yo. Word up."

Although I, too, found a great deal of Donnie's choices to be extremely foolish, I more so didn't approve of Mannie speaking so disrespectful about him. The fact that Mannie would never, ever speak like that in Donnie's presence had begun to kindle certain hostilities within me. Choosing not to indulge, I switched our point of conversation to a more relevant issue.

"It looks dead as hell out her," I remarked with an overt mixture of scrutiny and curiosity. Ain't no money comin' through?"

"Nah, not really," he replied. "The cops got niggas scared as hell to move out this bitch."

"Where the stash at?" I asked while taking a brief look up and down Haddon Avenue.

"Oh, I put all that shit in the trash can in back of your mom's crib," Mannie answered.

"What?!?" I nearly exclaimed. "You stashed a G-pack and a fuckin' burner in the back of my mom's crib?"

The thought of Mannie stashing anything illegal so close to my mother's home was infuriating. Words couldn't describe how fast I had become angry.

"The fuck was on your mind, stashin' that bullshit in the back of my mom's spot, nigga?" I asked quite forcefully. "You done lost your mafuckin' mind wit' that shit, nigga . . . for real, yo. You really fuckin' bugged out wit' that one."

At that very moment, I wanted nothing more than to grab Mannie by the throat and squeeze the life out of him; and by the look on Mannie's face, it seemed as if he could read my mind. His reaction was that of genuine shock at how angry I had become; subsequently, his authentic look of shock and concern was soon transforming into a mixture of both worry and uncertainty. Fear was now beginning to seep from behind Mannie's mask of concern, and it was his involuntary show of cowardice which only aggravated me more.

"I'm sayin' though," Mannie began to plead. "It was the only place I knew where nobody would find it. Where the fuck was I supposed to put it at, yo?"

Seconds passed by as I stared squarely into Mannie's eyes without saying a word. In less than a minute's time, though, I had completely regained my composure. In all reality, what's done is done, and fussing about what had happened would be nothing more than a waste of time. I stepped back while calming the breaths I had been taking; then I looked up and down Haddon Avenue once more for any signs of the police. There weren't any.

"Fuck it, yo," I said while making a mental note to never again leave Mannie alone with anything of mine that was illegal. "You did the right thing."

Mannie was visibly relieved. He flashed a broad smile while pulling a half-empty bottle of brandy from inside of his goose-down coat. Glancing at my wristwatch, I figured it best to get going. There was still much that had to be done.

5:30 p.m.

Back in my younger years, shopping malls were nothing more than social hunting grounds for both young thugs and hoodlums alike; there were many young inner-city street goers who, like I had once been, just couldn't resist preying on the innocence of young suburban girls who were curious about the "bad boys" who live in the 'hood. The players may grow old and the rules may change a bit, but the game itself always remains the same. Even now, while Christmas shopping for the faithful woman I had waiting at home for me, the "thrill of the hunt" still coursed uncontrollably through my veins.

With my coat open and the glistening charm of my necklace swinging from side to side like a pendulum, I traded glances with everyone around me while boldly striding past them. Due to a heavy dose of self-confidence, which was mixed with the euphoric effects of the weed I'd been smoking earlier, I was marvelously in tune with the vibes of those bustling around me.

In the eyes of the men, boys, and wannabe gangsters I passed in my travels, I was everything they wanted to be and more: a bona fide street hustler. To the ladies, I was a flawless representation of what it meant to succeed in the street life: my hair was cut and freshly trimmed, my clothes were clean and well put together, my jewelry was shining, and most of all, I had three months' worth of rent money in my pocket that I could very well squander if I truly wanted to.

The mall was filled with females, some of whom were shopping without the company of a significant other. I took my time to measure them all with a sharp, studious eye while strolling so coolly about. There was an enormous variety of women, all of them ranging from "chicken heads" to sophisticated business women. Regardless of the assumed lifestyle, all that mattered to me was how good they looked while walking about.

I was thoroughly enjoying the smorgasbord of skin tones, facial features and hairstyles of all these women in my midst; it was a feeling very much equivalent to that of me being a food critic at an exotic buffet table. I wallowed in this myriad of sensations that swirled about the mall and fed from it like a shark in a feeding frenzy.

One of the many aspects of being a "true player" entails a man never having to lie to the woman he is courting, and although a great deal of the women I approached may have wrinkled their noses at my admission to having a family at home, only a few of them were disinclined to get to know me better; we'd speak only for a brief moment or two before exchanging phone numbers. Mine would usually be a fake, and I'd more times than not tear theirs up as soon as we parted ways.

I already had a few ladies on the side and wasn't really looking for any more. For me, it was more so the thrill of the hunt that had enticed me so. Moreover, it was a great feeling to know that I was more than able to still play the field.

Despite not having a preference as to what type of female I preferred to court, there was, however, one particular sort that I tried my best to avoid: Camden women. Like me, most Camden women were complicated and ambitious people with more than a hand full of issues, some of which may prove quite dangerous, and at times, even fatal. There was always the possibility of them being romantically involved with, related to, or simply acquainted with an individual whom was always more than willing to express their criminal and sometimes violent tendencies.

For the Average Joe, these elements were no more than a threat of him being a potential victim; I, on the other hand, was not only a fellow Camden resident, but a drug dealer as well, which made it quite easy for a simple altercation to escalate into something far worse than a measly scuffle or robbery.

With these factors in mind, I searched for characteristics in any woman that I came across that would appear "Camdenesque," or in other words, traits that were anything reminiscent of a typical Camden resident. Life in the 'hood is hard, and their will to survive is often displayed through their demeanor, no matter how subtle the personality.   There is usually a dark, yet inviting aura about these women that only magnifies their actions, consequently separating them from any other female.   More than anything, there is normally a certain air of toughness that resonates in the eyes of these women, which is nothing more than a reflection of their truest nature. When spoken to, these females will usually respond with a sharp look of appraisal, seeming as if to measure one's potential value while speaking back. When two people are cut too much from the same cloth, it never takes long for one to figure out the other. And once recognizing these types of women and their hustlers' persona, I'd immediately switch gears and leave them behind.

I spent the next thirty or so minutes strolling about the mall, carefully screening each female I'd meet while perusing through certain retail stores. I was in Foot Locker, purchasing sneakers for the entire family, when I noticed a distinct looking female making her exit from a women's clothing store just across the walkway. She was barely five feet tall, brown-skinned, and possessed a physical build similar to that of a track and field athlete. She wore a short, sleeveless dress that exposed thick, well-defined legs that complimented an ample buttocks and a firm set of breasts which pressed ever so snugly against the fabric of her outfit. Her hair was combed and pinned to the back of her head, the rest of it spilling past her shoulders and streaming down along her spine. In short, she was absolutely exquisite.

Adding to my attraction was the fact that she actually took a second to slow down and deliberately glance in my direction before going on about her way, and it was at that exact moment in which I decided to make her my "big game prey." Yes, she'd be the one that I'd fight not to accept rejection from. I took an extra moment to admire her physical stature as she walked away, and then I paid for all our sneakers before leaving out of the store.

While making my exit, the pangs in my stomach were a staunch reminder that my hunger for food far outweighed my hunger for women. I started towards the food court, this time oblivious to the stares coming from the females I passed in my travels. My mind was already set on courting one particular woman, and nothing short of a video vixen would cause me to deviate from my plans to do so. I stood in line at a Chick-Fil-A restaurant and noticed that it, too, was filled with beautiful women. These women were not only beautiful, but the majority of them were professionally dressed and appeared classy as well.

Some of them had apparently lost interest in me and turned their attention elsewhere; others took a moment to stare a bit longer, indicating the possibility of them being available if I played my cards right. My own attention, however, was held by the pager now vibrating against my waist. It was Scrappy Shine's address with no further numbers behind it which meant that he was merely reminding me of my promise to reward him for his prior patronage. As much as I wanted to honor my promise to Scrappy Shine, my schedule, unfortunately, wouldn't allow me to do so . . . at least, not tonight.

While clipping the pager back to the waistband of my jeans, I noticed the mystery girl once more, this time, walking in the opposite direction. We locked eyes once again as she passed by, and at that moment, nothing else mattered. With bags in hand, I left my place in line to pursue her.

"Excuse me," I said while walking behind her. "Excuse me, Miss. Can I please have a word wit' you?"

She half-turned her head while slowing her pace.

"Are you talking to me?"

A French accent!

She not only looked exotic, but sounded it as well!

We were now standing still, forcing the stream of Christmas shoppers to split rank and travel around us. I suddenly and without warning began to feel a bit overwhelmed, for this particular female was far more beautiful than I imagined when first seeing her from a distance. Her facial features were delicate, yet sharp and well-pronounced. Her lips were full and shimmered with a modest application of lip gloss; her complexion was blemish free and the soft color of cinnamon. Quick, intelligent eyes peered out from behind a pair of silver-framed eyeglasses which rested on the bridge of a short, button-shaped nose. She was indeed an image of perfection.

"Yes," I earnestly replied. "After crossin' paths with you more than once in the same night, I had to at least get your name."

Careful of roaming thieves, I placed my bags between the two of us while extending my hand. "My name's Don Juan."

She gave me her hand, and I couldn't help but to place my lips on the skin of her knuckles. The sweet smell of scented lotion filled my nostrils as I kissed her; it was an impulsive gesture on my behalf that had shocked me every bit as much as it did her. Despite the abrupt show of caution, her eyes brightened and began to dance as she smiled.

"Don Juan?" she remarked with a hint of curiosity. The sound of my name rolling so smoothly from off of her tongue was all too sensual. "You mean like the Casanova?"

"True," I replied a bit guardedly. "But I ain't no Casanova, though."

I fought not to snicker when noticing that I had just quoted a verse from the Levert song, Casanova. My inward giggle threatened to surface upon my face as an all-too goofy-looking smile. Aware of my need to remain focused on the task at hand, I went on to finish my introduction.

"I'm just somebody tryin' to meet somebody else, you know what I'm sayin', ma?" I continued on. "Now, wit' all that bein' said and done, may I please know your name?"

"Michelle," she replied with her eyes never leaving mine; it seemed as if she was every bit as interested in me as I was in her.

As enraptured as I may have been by Michelle's beauty, however, I was still terribly hungry. The overwhelming urge which was driving me to court Michelle was every bit as fierce as my urge to satisfy the hunger now gnawing at my stomach, so I felt it best to try and kill two birds with one stone.

"I was just about to get somethin' to eat," I remarked. "Would you like to join me?"

"Sure," she replied. "That is, if your wife doesn't mind."

My wife?

Michelle's reply had caught me completely off guard. I imagined my attempt to appear unfazed by her remark to resemble something more like a pained grimace rather than a smile. From the mixture of both humor and curiosity that I read in Michelle's eyes, I saw that not only was she testing me, but enjoying the sight of my unease as well. It was definitely a strike against my ego. The giddy, almost child-like infatuation I had once felt for her was now beginning to fade within a matter of minutes.

"All right, all right," I replied firmly, but lightly. "That joke was far from funny. Let's get somethin' to eat. I'm starvin'."

Michelle agreed, and the two of us started back toward the food court where I found a table near the rear of the mall's dining area. It was close to a side exit and a great distance from the traffic of other Christmas shoppers, a rather incognito location. Michelle took a seat at the table and nodded as I promised to return with both her and my order. After a few short minutes, I was back from one of the food stands with a cheese burger and fries for myself and a small fruit salad for Michelle.

"Why does it feel like we're hiding?" she asked.

Again, I thought Michelle's French accent was absolutely mesmerizing, but this time, I was far from being enchanted. Her detective style of questioning was beginning to annoy me; she was proving a bit too observant and inquisitive for my liking.

"First of all," I said in between bites. "I don't hide from nobody. I just try my best to avoid crowds and stuff like that, you know what I'm sayin'? I got a thing about bein' around too many people."

"Is it because of your occupation?" Michelle asked.

I couldn't help but to raise an eyebrow.

"My occupation?" I asked with genuine curiosity.

"Yes," she replied. "Aren't you a thug?"

I fought not to burst with laughter.

"A thug?" I remarked comically. "What do you know about bein' a thug?"

"Nothing much," she replied rather plainly before munching down on a sliced pineapple. "Just from what I see on the news and on rap videos, that's all. A lot of people imitate them . . . you know . . . with the slang, the jewelry, the clothes and everything."

Her voice was soft and with a pitch of excitement, almost as if sharing a juicy secret of some sort.

"Although I knew of the hardships that African-Americans face in this country, I had no idea that the violence is really as prevalent as it is portrayed. I thought that rap artists were merely exaggerating for the sake of selling their records, but your people really do kill each other over the most trivial of things . . . it is truly a shame."

I was shocked by Michelle's estrangement from African-Americans. Her usage of the term "your people" made her sound more like some "high and mighty" white person speaking about the poor, ignorant Negroes in the ghettos of North America. In my eyes, black folks were black folks, no matter what the nationality, and I was offended by her mild disassociation from my people and our issues.

I now began to see Michelle in a different light. On face value, she would undoubtedly prove to be a most remarkable catch, but my unconscious urge to break the "player rules" and say whatever it took to win her over was now dashed to pieces. My burning passion to court her had cooled and was now being replaced with a feeling of indifference as to whether I succeeded or not. Careful not to let such personal feelings dictate my original course of action, I separated myself from any misgivings and continued the pursuit.

"So," I began, this time trying to change the subject before things took a turn for the worse. "What made you come at me with all this talk about havin' a wife?"

"With all of those bags, it's easy to assume that you are shopping for more than just one person," she answered. "I figured that you are either shopping for all of your children or all of someone else's children. The woman you're with, whoever she is, is truly a fortunate woman."

I almost smirked at the stereotypical view of blacks and illegitimate children that Michelle had coupled me with. I also recognized how well she had tied a compliment into the end of her negative observation; it was smooth, but not smooth enough. I received what she had just said with a guarded measure of amenity. In my case, both of Michelle's remarks proved true, and it irked me.

"Well, you're half-right," I replied matter-of-factly. "I got a baby-mom, not a wife."

"Is there really a difference?" she remarked.

The melodic flow of Michelle's accent was quite effective in cushioning the blow of her rather pointed response. I matched her smile with a slight grin of my own.

"So, you're sayin' that you ain't bothered by the fact that I got a chick at home?"

"Why should I be bothered by your infidelity?" she asked with the eyes of a mischievous child. "Would I not be the other woman? What does the other woman have to be bothered by?"

A vindictive common-law housewife with the fighting skills of a professional boxer, I said to no one but myself while answering the cell phone that had just now began to ring.

I answered the phone with a "yo" and soon found myself being scolded by the caller on the other end.

"Don't 'yo' me, mafucka," Tamara hissed. "Where you at?"

"I'm at the mall," I answered. "Why, what's up?"

"You, nigga!" she rasped. "How come you ain't seen your mom yet?"

This time, it was Tamara's rush for me to see my mother, and not her usual pushiness, that had begun to vex me.

"Who the fuck are you supposed to be, Matlock or some fuckin' body?" I remarked rather sharply. "God damn!"

From the corner of my eye, I spied Michelle watching my exchange with an acute interest.

"You'd better watch your fuckin' mouth, boy," Tamara retorted.

"Stop bein' a bitch then," I replied.

"That's Miss Bitch to you," Tamara shot back. "And don't you forget that shit."

Tamara's snappy comeback, as usual, had managed to penetrate and dismantle my crabby attitude. A soft giggle escaped from my lips as I broke into a smile.

"All right, all right," I finally resigned. "I got a couple more things to get, and then I'll be straight over. Is that all right with you?"

"Don't ask me, goofy," she replied indignantly. "I can't answer for your mom."

"All right then," I replied sharply. "Stop actin' like her. Later."

"Whatever," she jovially replied. "Goodbye."

With that, I closed the phone and slipped it back into my coat pocket.

"Was that the Misses?" asked Michelle.

"Nah," I answered back, trying as best I could to mask my growing impatience with Michelle and all of her prying. "That was my big sis'."

Michelle's eyes went narrow, her smile now tainted with a light mixture of both jealousy and disbelief. "Your sister?"

Michelle's response was ordinary, the vibe behind her words, however, was prickly. I suddenly began to notice that her interest in me had heightened rather quickly since my conversation with Tamara; now seemed the perfect time to reaffirm my position.

"You act like I'm lyin' to you or somethin'," I remarked pointedly. "You tryin' to play me like I'm some kind of coward that has to lie to a woman an' shit?"

Michelle's eyes wavered a bit beneath my stone-cold facial expression. Her attempt to appear cool and in control was failing fast.

"I didn't accuse you of anything," she replied somewhat firmly. "It must be your conscience that's bothering you."

Seeing Michelle's reply as nothing more than a poor attempt to surrender while saving face at the same time, I simply acknowledged my victory with a warm smile.

"I just want you to understand that I'm a truth-tellin' type of dude, know what I'm sayin'? Liars and cowards are one and the same, and I ain't neither one, feel me?"

Michelle smiled and replied, "I'd expect nothing less."

The grand feeling of accomplishing my goal to successfully court Michelle had abruptly disappeared as I glanced over her shoulder to recognize the female fast approaching us.

"There's a stalker on her way over here," I declared with a soft but pointed touch of urgency. "Just be cool and let me handle this. I don't want her to make a scene an' shit."

It was now Michelle's turn to raise an eyebrow. From the movement of her lips, I could tell that she was set to respond, but Shakira had emerged from the crowd and taken a seat between both me and Michelle before another word could have been spoken. A fearsome, war-like expression was etched across the face of my newly emerged party crasher, which had all but eclipsed the God-given beauty that she'd been blessed with. The brilliance of Shakira's hazel-green eyes was darkened with scorn; and rage was now boiling from beneath her smooth, honey-brown complexion.

Shakira hadn't been seated for a solid five seconds before Michelle took the initiative and introduced herself.

"Hello," she said with a sharp, sarcastic degree of spunk. "I'm Michelle."

Shakira recoiled from Michelle's greeting as one would a repugnant odor.

"Oh, what the fuck are you supposed to be, French or somethin'?" Shakira remarked with an overtone of sarcasm. "Bitch, please!"

Shakira was visibly teeming with anger; careful not to provoke her into doing something crazy, Michelle didn't bother to reply and instead, chose to remain seated in silence.

There was only one time in my life, prior to this moment, when I had found myself trapped in between two warring women. The end result of that situation being both women pressing charges on one another while simultaneously agreeing that I wasn't shit. My present situation was jarringly similar to the last. While Shakira sat with her back to Michelle and her eyes fixed firmly on me, Michelle remained quiet while staring intently at both me and Shakira. I, too, remained quiet, silently fighting to help my mind discover a way to defuse this current dilemma. Shakira turned and was now fixing her stare on Michelle, and I was now speeding to somehow keep her wrath from falling down upon the girl I had just met.

"Shakira!"

The sharp, commanding tone of my voice had immediately grabbed her attention.

Shakira then turned her gaze from Michelle and back onto me. The feral, vexatious glint in her eyes was now threatening to unravel the cool, unfettered exterior I was struggling to maintain. And at that very moment, probably more so from a mere reflex for survival than anything, I switched my attitude from one of nonchalance to genuine disgust.

"After all that talk about how civilized you are, you come in here actin' more ghetto than a mafucka," I remarked pointedly. "What the fuck is wrong wit' you?"

"Nigga please," she spat. "You just . . ."

"Man, I ain't tryin' to hear that shit," I interrupted with a mixture of both anger and impatience. "Just be quiet for a minute and hear what the fuck I got to say."

All of the anger, frustration and rage that I had been dealing with throughout the entire day was now beginning to ebb out to the surface. It hardened my demeanor and put an edge to the words I spoke. Never before had Shakira seen the cold, more threatening side of my personality, and I could tell that she was very much captivated by my semi-aggressive demeanor. She remained quiet with her lips pressed tightly together; the broiling look of rage was ever so vibrant in her eyes and I could tell it was a struggle for her to remain civil.

Recognizing that I now had a chance to settle things without making a scene, I moved quickly to capitalize on the potential power move she had afforded me.

"Listen," I began swiftly and firmly. "Of all the times we've been out together, I ain't never disrespect you . . . I ain't never disrespect you, and I ain't never let nobody else disrespect you, either. Right now, all a mafucka wants from you is to do the same, you know what I'm sayin'? Now ain't the time for you to be comin' out of nowhere actin' like a mafuckin' crazy person. That'll be a fucked up way to end a good friendship, yo . . . especially over some bullshit."

Ever the perceptive type, Shakira could sense the true measure of my aggravation and chose not to antagonize me any further. She ran the tip of her tongue across the top of her lip before standing up to straighten the bottom of her button-up blouse. Michelle remained seated; her posture was totally relaxed and at ease, almost as if Shakira's presence was of little to no significance at all.

Now, it was Shakira's turn to save face.

"You'd better stop actin' like that phone is just for business and call me back when I page you, Don Juan," she threatened. "You understand me? Stop with the games, baby, for real."

Never being the one to allow anyone to escape after speaking to me in such an unfashionable manner, I found it a struggle not to admonish Shakira for her scorn. Still, I had to admit that she was leaving without incident, and for me, that was a victory within itself.

"I got you, Shakira," I grumbled. "I got you. Just go somewhere and cool the fuck off."

"You'd better call a bitch back, Don Juan," she threatened. "I swear to God, you'd fucking better."

With that, Shakira turned and stormed off, leaving both Michelle and I alone; this time,there was an air of unease left hanging between the two of us.

"My," Michelle remarked rather cheerfully. "You sure have the greatest effect on women. I think you need to be a bit more careful with whom you choose to bless with your presence, though."

By now, my level of aggravation was at its peak, and I was far from in the mood to be on the receiving end of anyone's sharp sense of humor. I figured it best to cut straight to the chase.

"I got a lil' bit more shopping to do. You wanna roll wit' me, or do you just wanna trade numbers and part ways?"

Michelle clucked her tongue and smiled.

"It may not be safe for me to be seen strolling around the mall with a hot item such as yourself, Don Juan," she remarked with a slight air of humor. "There's no telling who may come from out of nowhere and attack me."

Behind the innocence in Michelle's eyes, I could now easily see the attraction that she held for me. She was a "good girl" lured by the element of danger, the element of danger bought on by her association with "bad boys," and I didn't like it. People who were thrilled by chance and the consequence of peril were usually the same people who caused it.

"You'd better call this number, Don Juan," Michelle laughed, mocking Shakira's threat while scribbling her phone number onto a piece of paper.

Not bothering to comment, I forced a half-smile to my lips while jotting down my phone number as well. After an exchange of information, Michelle rose to her feet with a most intense measure of seduction blazing in her eyes.

"Goodbye . . . for now," she said before parting. "Do us both a favor and be careful of the women you choose to bewitch."

And with that, Michelle turned and made her way back into the stream of holiday shoppers.

Watching as she disappeared into the flux of mall patrons, I couldn't help but to ponder the nature of the woman I had just met. Michelle may have been one of the most beautiful women I had ever seen in the flesh, but deep down, I could tell that she wasn't too much different from Shakira.   While tearing up the paper with Michelle's phone number written on it, I vowed that if by chance she were to ever give me a call, I'd definitely adhere to her astute words of advice.

Keeping in mind the busy schedule which lie ahead, I hurried into a department store and purchased an outfit for each one of the children; then, I decided to stop at one of Lakeisha's favorite clothing stores for one final purchase.

The Liaison was a newly erected clothing store for women which sold only the latest, most expensive fashions to date. To me, The Liaison was no more than a snobby boutique that sold fancy clothes at some of the most outrageous prices, but for the women who shopped there, The Liaison was nothing short of the new Mecca of fashion.

Who in their right mind would pay more than three hundred dollars for a measly blouse or a pair of shoes? *Me, of course,* I thought dejectedly to myself while hustling through the mall and trying not to recant my resolve to buy something from this larger-than-life department store. Lakeisha was planning to attend a family reunion next month and would love nothing more than to flaunt a fancy designer outfit to the event. She'd be every bit as happy and just as giddy as the children when discovering the expensive gift I'd bought her for Christmas, and that alone would be a sight to behold.

Yes, there is absolutely no amount of money that could equal the joy I'd feel when seeing how happy Lakeisha would be. Standing firm on my decision to purchase something special from this extravagant store, I entered into The Liaison with my mind set on bringing home something nice for the mother of my only child.

It was a large and roomy establishment. The overall feel of the place was high-priced and dreadfully expensive. There were nearly a dozen mannequins, every one of them placed on top of a platform and spread all throughout the store. Each model was dressed in a certain fashion and surrounded by wooden shelves which contained the articles of clothing so grandly displayed by these large, life-like statues. A wide variety of saleswomen, all of them well-dressed and appearing as high maintenance as the female shoppers, skittered and buzzed about while potential customers examined and scrutinized the merchandise. I was the only male in sight and felt terribly out of place.

"Shopping for the Misses?" asked a familiar voice from behind.

Without turning around, I knew it was Michelle; not too many women strolled about with a French accent. The first notion I had of my newly acquired friend being a stalker was immediately negated by my turning around to see a company name tag pinned to the front of her dress.

"You work here?" I asked.

"Sort of," Michelle replied. "I'm a Regional Quality Control Manager."

"A Regional Quality Control Manager?" I laughed. "What's wit' the long 'regional quality control manager' line? You still a manager, right? Why the fancy title?"

"The function of a store manager is to maintain the order of company policy on a local level; whereas a regional manager travels from store to store, overseeing procedures and making sure that all local managers are performing their duties efficiently. A regional quality control manager makes sure that they all are doing their jobs."

I fought not to laugh at Michelle's attempt to sound all so educated about being some sort of a "super manager." "I'm impressed" were the only words I could muster.

"No, you're not," Michelle said with a laugh. "But I appreciate you being nice. Now, would you mind answering my question now?"

"And what question was that?" I asked rather pointedly.

"The question of whether or not you are shopping for the Misses," she answered.

Again, I was beginning to get annoyed.

"Yeah," I answered smugly. "I'm shopping for the Misses. Why? You gon' give me a discount or something?"

"No," Michelle replied, half-laughing. "I will, however, assist you in buying something nice. Men have such a hard time shopping for their significant others."

I found the choice of Michelle's term "significant other" as a sign of her still feeling a bit bothered by the notion of me being taken.

"First, we must check your bags," said Michelle.

"Check my bags?" I remarked with a touch of repugnance. "What do you mean check my bags? What kind of shit is that?"

"It's store policy, Don Juan," replied Michelle while leading me to the counter. "There's no reason for you to take offense."

I handed my bags to the clerk behind the counter and received a laminated card in return; then, I began making my way to the ladies' suit section where Michelle was following close behind.

"Is she a businesswoman?" Michelle asked out of curiosity.

"Never mind all of that," I replied, totally ignoring Michelle's question. "I just need something classy. Can you find me somethin' classy, Madame Butterfly?"

From experience, I learned that most women could handle a man's sarcasm, so long as it was delivered softly and topped with a delicate moniker. Michelle proved to be no different. She was beaming at the mention of her newly acquired nickname.

"Of course, I can," Michelle said with a smile. "I don't how much you have to spend, but I recommend the pant suit designed by Estelle Delancey."

I now recognized a measure of desire in Michelle's eyes that had been heightened even more since I had last seen her. How could a woman such as herself fall for someone like me so quickly? There was definitely more to my little French butterfly than meets the eye. I shrugged off this sudden feeling of excitement and smiled affably.

"All right, cool," I replied. "Gimme this suit wit' a matchin' blouse and a pair of shoes, too."

"Are you sure, Don Juan?" she remarked. "This outfit is a bit . . ."

"A bit what?" I interrupted with an exaggerated tone of nonchalance. "Expensive? Gimme this navy-blue Estelle Delancey joint wit' a matchin' blouse and a pair of shoes. Is my money good here, or what?"

"Yes," Michelle replied dryly. "Everyone's money is good at The Liaison."

"Good," I remarked curtly. "Size six in shoes, ten in pants, and a blouse that looks good in a thirty-six C cup. I just hope I got her measurements right, that's all."

Judging from Michelle's reaction, it wasn't hard to see that she wasn't used to being spoken to in such a short, abrupt manner. She stood silent for a moment, allowing her eyes to travel back and forth from the large wad of cash I was now holding in my hand to the cold, unfeeling look I was now successfully projecting from my eyes.

Despite her undeniable attraction to me, Michelle seemed torn between accepting my patronage and telling me to go straight to Hell. Just as I had figured though, business held the higher principle. Michelle flashed a most brilliant smile before sending one of the saleswomen to materialize my request.

"Size ten in the waist?" she mentioned while leading me back towards the counter. "You never struck me as one who likes their women plump."

I answered Michelle's comment with nothing more than a slight smirk as the saleswoman placed the newly packaged merchandise on the glass shelf which now stood between us. I was more focused on trying to estimate the impending damage about to be done to my bankroll as the cashier flashed an ominous glance in my direction while ringing up the total price.

Oh, yeah, I said only in my head. *This is gon' cost me a pretty penny.*

As if reading my mind, the cashier announced the grand total.

"Six hundred thirty-five dollars and sixty-five cents."

Sixty hundred and thirty-five dollars! I screamed out loud in my head. *Six hundred and thirty-five dollars for a fucking outfit?!?*

I wanted to explode!

Conscious of both Michelle and the cashier's anticipation as to how I'd react, I merely clucked my tongue as if I were the coolest man on Earth; then, I smoothly and very nonchalantly counted out sixty hundred and forty dollars in both fifty and twenty dollar bills.

On the inside, however, I was seething. Words couldn't describe the anger I felt for allowing myself to be swept into spending such a large amount of money on one single purchase. I tried to focus on Lakeisha's reaction when discovering what I had just now bought for her, but it was of no consolation. The very thought of burning over a thousand dollars in just one night made me sick to my stomach.

To make matters worse, I felt as if I had allowed Michelle to hustle me into making a high-priced purchase to which she may probably receive a bountiful commission. I would undoubtedly have to hit the streets with a vengeance in order to make up for the huge dent I had just now put into my wallet. I pocketed my change, grabbed my bags, and then started my way outside the store. The sound of Michelle's voice had momentarily distracted me from my period of self-loathing.

"Six hundred and forty dollars for an outfit?" she remarked as we both approached the edge of the store. "You must really love your wife."

Even while in the midst of hating and cursing myself, I still managed to project a smooth, unfettered persona. In short, it was now my turn to save face.

"Life ain't about love, Michelle," I replied coolly. "It's about mafuckas playin' their positions. You play your position, I play my position, and everybody's happy in the end."

Michelle took a moment to look away, seeming as if to take what I had just now said into serious consideration before turning her attention back into my direction.

"Goodbye, Don Juan," she said while staring me intently in the eyes. "I hope we get to see each other again. Call me."

After witnessing me spend more than half a thousand dollars on one single outfit, I was quite sure of just how sincere Michelle was about what she had just said.

"Likewise, Madame Butterfly," I said before turning around and starting home. "Likewise."

7:30 p.m.

After catching the bus back to Camden then reaching my neighborhood by taxi, I transferred my bags from the backseat of the cab to the trunk of my car; then, I retrieved my G-pack before driving to the liquor store. I pounced at my pager when it had begun to vibrate; the thought of spending nearly twelve hundred dollars in one night before paying my rent, or any other bill for that matter, was more than enough motivation for me to jump at a customer's request to buy base. Before making my delivery, however, I sought to quench my thirst for liquor with a taste of cognac. At this particular time, a half pint of Hennessey would most definitely serve me well.

The bottle of liquor was bought, drained dry and then discarded by the time I delivered the two bundles of base to Ms. Kay in the Fairview section of Camden. Now, twenty minutes later, I found myself parked by a street curb on Spruce Street, sucking on a piece of peppermint candy. With the liquor now coursing warmly throughout every vein in my body, I sighed while staring across the street at the house in which I had spent the greater part of my life.

My mother's house was a tall three-bedroom row home with an open porch which, very much to her disapproval, I paid to have repainted and renovated. The

213

color was changed from a dull grayish tint to a bright lavender shade, the window sills and front door painted white. The rickety wooden planks of the front porch's floor were straightened, refined, and then carpeted with a purple turf-styled rug that matched brilliantly with the screen door and porch steps. It was an earnest attempt to beautify a home that had housed more than two decades of some of the ugliest and most painful childhood memories I had come to know.

The house was almost in the middle of the block, and during the day, its bright and flavorful colors helped distinguish it from the other row homes. But the evening was now upon us, and with the porch light off, the blackness of night which blanketed my neighborhood seemed only to be more intensified when staring at this particular house. The bright lavender color if its walls were dulled, and the white-colored door and window sills now cast an eerie glow about the place.

I stared at the house with a combination of dismay and trepidation. In truth, it was the person living at 1121 Spruce Street, and not the house itself, that filled me with such apprehension. The little old lady more commonly known by the neighborhood as "Momma Ingles" was awaiting my arrival, and deep down inside, I was actually dreading this very moment.

To those who hadn't had the opportunity to experience her sharp tongue and venomous wit, Momma

Ingles was indeed an esteemed woman, worthy of the respect given by both her peers and neighbors alike; she radiated a measure of strength that was easily felt by any and everyone around her.

Those within her more intimate circle, however, had come to know Momma Ingles and her strength as a stark, oppressive force that she was most definitely able to wield with exactness. With my mother, there was never any compromise, or as many would say, a point to which we may "agree-to-disagree." It was either her way or no way at all, and anyone with a good mind to oppose her point of view will quickly find themselves balked at and swiftly rejected.

Unfortunately, I didn't have the luxury of being shunned. I was more than her only son; I was also the father of her only grandchild, which meant she could never truly entertain the notion of completely disowning me. Parting ways will never be an option for neither one of us, and that meant me constantly having to endure the brunt of her verbal assaults.

It took very little effort, on my part, to provoke my mother into berating me. The slightest dislike to something I'd say could easily and most effortlessly trigger her wrath; sometimes all I needed to do was look the wrong way. Through it all, there was never, ever, a time in which she had once apologized for her mental and verbal abuse, let alone a time when she had admitted to maybe going about things a bit too harshly. In my mother's eyes, she was never wrong, and I hated it.

The line between reluctance and fear was growing increasingly thin with each second I spent sitting in the car. With that notion suddenly coming to mind, I now openly frowned at the thought of me being afraid to face my own mother. Like my experience with any other dubious situation, I decided to waste no more time with my hesitating to engage. I exited the car, made my way across the street and up the steps to my mother's home and then rang the doorbell.

The porch light had immediately come to life, illuminating the entire front porch along with myself, forcing my eyes into a momentary squint. The curtain behind a small, diamond-shaped window in the front door had vanished and was instantly replaced by the top portion of my mother's face.

Being only four feet, nine and a half inches tall, she was obviously standing on the tips of her toes; the top half of her eyeglasses and forehead were all that was visible through the glass. The solid, metallic click of a bolt lock had immediately followed her disappearance from the window, and a slight nudge of the doorknob, which allowed the front door to open just a smidgen, was my cue to enter inside.

As usual, the house was immaculate. The wall-to-wall carpeting was a soft-colored lavender and matched perfectly with the living room furniture; the walls were white and speckled lightly with a soft touch of purple. The lights were dimmed and the television was turned off, which lent to an air of relaxation throughout the house.

My mother was seated in a sofa chair which was positioned farthest from the door yet slightly angled towards it. Her tiny frame seemed dwarfed by the very size and plushness of the chair, and while sitting with her legs crossed at the ankles, she looked more like a child in a grown-up's seat. With a brittle body and an overall coarse demeanor, Mrs. Lorraine Martha Ingles appeared more than twenty years older than fifty-four.

Years and years of a grievous and woeful life had seemingly drained her of any element of liveliness. Whatever spark of vitality that may have remained now existed only in the form of scorn and admonishment. It shone brilliantly in her eyes and fueled every malicious word she'd ever strike with. It gave sharp definition to the hard, toughened expression she wore, an expression that would never change, regardless of the emotion she showed. Even when amused, my mother's gaze wouldn't soften; her countenance, even when smiling, resembled the grim carving of a jack-o-lantern.

"How've you been, momma?" I asked while hanging my coat in the closet.

I then kissed her cheek before taking a seat at the end of the sofa.

My mother, as I expected, wasted little time with her cynicism.

"How've I been?" she remarked smartly. "I'm surprised that you got the balls to pretend that you even care about how I've been, Dijuan."

"Come on, momma," I answered back tiredly. "You know that I care."

"Three weeks, Dijuan," she replied rather brusquely. "It's been three weeks since I've last seen you. Did I hurt your feelings that freakin' bad for you not come around for damned near a month? When did you get so damned sensitive?"

Of course, she'd hurt my feelings that much. After enduring more than an hour of her insulting my intelligence and challenging my right to even call myself a man, how could my feelings not be wounded? Moreover, she even topped everything off by swearing to almighty God that I was a "jigaboo" and an "Uncle Tom."

As cool and as unflappable as I may appear to others, I was the total opposite of such a facade when it came to my mother, and she knew it. My mother knew it, and she played on it.

Admitting to my mother that my feelings were hurt by what she had said to me would be like admitting to her that she was right about me not being a man. To Momma Ingles, a woman who had endured one tragedy after another with the resolve of a hardened war veteran, a man was supposed to be a tough-minded individual who not only has the heart to stick with his principles regardless to whom or what, but he is also able to shield any visible signs of mental or physical weakness while doing so.

I did indeed embody all of the qualities my mother would expect in a man, but unfortunately, they were directed in a manner that she adamantly disapproved of. This is what ultimately leads the two of us into an ever-occurring "battle of wills," to which our stalemates often left me feeling like the one whom had truly lost the fight. Yet and still, she was still my mother, and just as it was impossible for her to sever ties with her only son, such was the case with me severing ties with my mother.

"It's not that my feelings was hurt, momma," I lied. "You was talkin' like you ain't wanna see me no more, so I just fell back and gave you a lil' space. That's all. How could I try an' act like I'm cuttin' you off? You're my momma."

My mother only narrowed her eyes while allowing a tight smile. It was a remote, yet genuine smile that matched the faint glimpse of warmth that I recognized in her eyes; it was a sight that I silently welcomed with open arms. Comforted by her genuine show of concern, yet wary of her potential for hostility, I only relaxed my guard instead of dropping it altogether.

"Three weeks, Dijuan," she remarked rather sharply. "That's way too long for you to go without talking to me. Don't ever do that again, son, you hear me?"

Despite being small in stature, she exerted a rather commanding aura; and all in a swift instant, I felt as if I were ten years old again.

"Yes, momma," I meekly replied.

"Very good," she replied. "Now, with all that being said, what have you been doing these past three weeks?"

It was a question that the two of us had already known the answer to. My mother was just as sure that nothing had changed with me just as I knew that nothing had changed with her; both of us knew that my answer would only rekindle her anger.

A knot was now beginning to form in the pit of my stomach.

"What have I been doin'?" I asked.

"Yes," she answered with studying eyes. "What have you been doing while you were on your little vacation away from me?"

Referring to my brief separation from her as a "vacation" was an indirect move towards a fight. The battle was now officially underway.

"Same ol', same ol'," I replied rather guardedly. "Doin' the family thing."

"The family thing?" she remarked with the sarcasm of her question being accented with an arched eyebrow. "What do you mean the family thing? The family thing with who?"

Momma Ingles was an old-fashioned woman and terribly set in her ways. Although she inflexibly disapproved of premarital sex, she despised it even more amongst the youth, females in particular. Moreover, she held a particularly high level of disgust for women with children born out of wedlock and frowned at the men who fathered them; needless to say, I was constantly condemned and looked down upon. For Lakeisha, an unemployed mother of three who hadn't even finished high school, there was absolutely no chance in hell of her appeasing my mother.

Momma Ingles was at least merciful enough to wait until Lakeisha returned home from the hospital with our newborn son to break the news of her disfavor toward our union. I sat in the living room filled with guilt as she explained her disesteem to Lakeisha, who was still struggling to recover from the emergency C-section she received in order for our child to be delivered. The memory of that sorrowful afternoon still stings and haunts me to this day.

"The family thing?" Momma Ingles remarked once more in response to my silence. "I know you ain't talkin' about that fat, lazy-ass girl you've been layin' up with every night."

Despite the admirable front she portrayed, Lakeisha's heart was ripped to shreds while listening to my mother's disapproval. She endured Momma Ingles' rejection with venerable fortitude, and I was reminded of it each time my mother spoke ill of her. I loved Lakeisha with all of my heart; there was no doubt in my mind that I'd kill for her. I was willing to defend her honor against anyone, well, anyone except my mother. She was the only person on Earth whom I allowed to openly disrespect me and get away with it.

"Momma, please," I said rather dejectedly.

"Momma, please, what?" she rasped. "First, you drop out of school to have a child by a whore who is just as simple and as lazy as you are, and then you hang out here in this sorry ass neighborhood, jeopardizing your life out there with the rest of them niggers on the street, thinkin' y'all are somebody important."

Unlike most parents, Momma Ingles didn't overindulge with a flurry of inquiries. Each question and statement was measured and delivered with an acute accuracy for guilt. It was an interrogation of the worst kind; moreover, it was one that I had gotten all-too used to. Although I appeared astute and paying strict attention to every question and statement she fired off, on the inside, however, I was slowly drifting off somewhere else in my mind where none of it really mattered. It was the sound of my cell phone now ringing from inside the coat I left hanging in the closet that deterred me from zoning off into our question and answer session.

"Let me get that," I said while raising up off the sofa and starting towards the closet.

When speaking, Momma Ingles' required my absolute attention. Me abruptly breaking away from our conversation to answer my cell phone was, without a doubt, considered to be disrespectful. While reaching inside my coat pocket, I could feel her contemptuous glare burning deep into the flesh of my back.

I knew there would be hell to pay for allowing our conversation to be disrupted, but I didn't care; I desperately needed a break from her overbearing demeanor. I retrieved my phone, which had stopped ringing only to begin ringing again, and I was somewhat surprised to learn the call was coming from Lakeisha. We both understood that she was only to call this phone in the midst of an extreme emergency.

"Hello?" I announced into the receiver of the cell phone.

"Dijuan?"

The undercurrent of fear in which Lakeisha had spoken my name was severe; it pierced my heart and froze over the blood in my veins. My chest tightened and my breath began to quicken when recognizing her apprehension.

"What's up, babe?" I asked, mindful that my mother was paying astute attention to my conversation.

"Dijuan, come home," she demanded. "Niggas is out her disrespectin' me and our kids. I need you to come home, now."

To say that Lakeisha was distressed would have been a gross understatement. Her voice trembled with each word she spoke, indicating to me just how close she was to becoming hysterical.

"I'm on my way," I replied with an overwhelming sense of urgency. "Gimme ten minutes."

"I love you, Dijuan," said Lakeisha.

"I love you, too, babe," I answered back earnestly. "I'm on my way."

"Hurry up, Dijuan," she said.

"Ten minutes," I assured her.

"Ten minutes," she repeated as if to confirm my statement with the sincere intention of holding me to that specific time limit.

With that, the two of us hung up. I didn't have to look over at my mother to know that she was watching me as I began slipping into my army coat.

"Trouble at home?" she asked.

This time, there wasn't a single hint of sarcasm in Momma Ingles' voice. I could tell that she was thoroughly concerned.

"I really don't know what's goin' on yet," I answered while kissing her on the cheek. "But I'll call you tomorrow and fill you in on what happened."

I stopped at the door and turned to give my mother one last look before leaving. The look in her eyes, this time, was a mixture of both concern and uncertainty. Like myself, Momma Ingles' soft spot was embedded somewhere deep inside of her battle-hardened soul, and it was very hard to get to; however, the idea of her only child entering into what may very well be a perilous and unpredictable situation was troublesome enough to pierce straight to the core.

"You'd better call me tomorrow," she said sharply.

It was the best she could do to relay her feelings of concern; and it was moments like this which inspired me to endure my mother's darker, more volatile ways. My heart was overflowing with emotion, yet I was still careful not to appear infirm. I kept in mind the need for me to display my feelings as prudently as possible.

"Will do, momma," I said before starting out the door. "I'll call you tomorrow."

After a brief and seemingly strained exchange of smiles, I shut the door behind me and started towards whatever may lie ahead of me on the other side of town.

8:30 p.m.

With the thought of my family in danger, it truly felt as if I couldn't get home fast enough. While traveling in what felt to be the greatest sense of urgency ever, I seemed to catch every red light in the city while rushing back home to my and Lakeisha's house. The streets of East Camden were dark and ominous, and as I turned onto Twenty-Fifth Street from Federal Street, I could see the congregation of hustlers huddled together on the corner of Twenty-Fifth and High Street from a short distance away. It was a foreboding sign of the things to come.

Our home was but a few short yards away from the corner, and I as neared our house, the view ahead of me grew larger and more daunting by the second. The heads of those huddled at the corner were staring in my direction as I pulled up and parked in front of my house. They, too, were expecting some sort of confrontation.

Dressed in a pair of sweatpants, a puffy goose-down jacket and a wool-knit skull cap, Lakeisha had suddenly appeared in the doorway. Despite her being enshrouded in the darkness of night, she was still absolutely beautiful. And while staring at Lakeisha through my car window, I couldn't help but to be fond of the way her thick, springy hair flowed freely from beneath the cap on her head, whipping wildly about her face as the wind blew.

Lakeisha was undoubtedly the love of my life, which ultimately made her out as my Achilles' heel to our impending enemies down the street; conscious of just how vulnerable we were appearing to the onlookers at the corner, I quickly snapped out of my adoration of Lakeisha and moved swiftly to usher her inside the house.

"I got the bags, babe," I said to Lakeisha as she started toward the trunk of the car to help me with what I had bought from the mall. "Go back in the house."

Lakeisha glanced up the street and caught a quick glimpse of what I had been taking in since my arrival. There was a deep sense of worry that I had read in her eyes. With a bag clutched tightly in each one of her hands, Lakeisha turned and started back up the steps without bothering to utter a single word. I grabbed the remainder of our bags, shut the trunk of my car, and then took one more peek at the group on the corner; I was quite sure they were eagerly awaiting my next move. Thinking of what lay ahead of me later on tonight, the looming showdown between me and the hustlers on the corner of Twenty-Fifth and High Street was no doubt an untimely glitch in my plans.

This is really some bullshit, I thought dejectedly to myself while making my way inside. *Of all the times to start some dumb shit, these niggas gots to choose tonight.*

I stepped inside of my home to find Lakeisha seated on the couch with her arms folded across her chest; it was the body posture she'd often exhibit when distressed. I placed my shopping bags on the floor where Lakeisha had dropped hers, took off my coat, and then found a seat on the couch beside her. It was extremely important for me to appear as cool, calm, and as level-headed as possible; the both of us couldn't possibly afford to be running high off of our emotions, and Lakeisha visibly appeared to be struggling with her last wits.

"Did you cook?" I asked.

"Did I cook?!" Lakeisha mocked with a building sense of anger. "What do you mean, did I cook? I told you that niggas out here is disrespectin' me and our kids, and you come in here askin' me about some fuckin' food? What . . ."

"My job is to take care of this house and hold the family down," I interrupted. "*Your* job is to take care of me and hold me down. I got my end of the deal covered all day. What about you, though? Can you play your part and bring a nigga his plate, please?"

Lakeisha's face went tight while staring deep into my eyes with a look that could have easily stricken fear into the hustlers who were now outside awaiting my arrival. Despite my urge to spew a joke based on what I was thinking of her facial expression, I decided otherwise.

Moreover, the fact that she had chosen to stare me down instead of moving to prepare my dinner had left me somewhat annoyed. Consequently, I pressed on to further my point.

"Stop actin' like you don't fuckin' hear me, Keisha," I remarked brusquely with my eyes fixed firmly upon hers. "I'm fuckin' hungry as hell. Bring me my dinner and you can tell me what happened while I eat."

To my surprise, Lakeisha's face had grown even tighter, and for a minute, it seemed as if tonight's fight would take place at home instead of on the corner of Twenty-Fifth and High. However, such wasn't the case. Without bothering to utter a response, she rose from out of her seat on the couch and started off into the kitchen. I, in turn, pulled the pistol from out the waistband of my jeans and slid it beneath the sofa.

Lakeisha returned a short moment later with an open bottle of Beck's beer and handed it to me.

"Your food'll be ready in about five minutes," she said rather tersely; then she turned and marched back toward the kitchen.

Unfettered by Lakeisha's palpable attitude, I took a sip of beer and then a drag of my cigarette while reclining back onto the couch. With my plans to retaliate against Jay-Dollar set to materialize just a few hours from now, my mind was overwhelmed with vivid ideas of violence;

all types of thoughts were now swirling about my mind as I struggled to think clearly about the situations at hand.

Lakeisha then returned with my dinner: baked chicken, rice with gravy and green beans. I took another sip of beer, mashed out my cigarette, and then accepted the plate of food. Lakeisha took her seat beside me and waited in silence. I could feel the weight of her impatience pressing for me to converse while eating, but she would have to hold fast. Each second Lakeisha spent waiting only added to the demands I felt to hurry up and indulge her; and I fully understood why. However, I was absolutely famished. After wolfing down a good portion of my dinner, I decided that it was now time for her to speak her piece.

"So, what happened?" I asked in between bites.

All of the children, including Serenity who now had my son draped on her tiny hip, began making their way down the steps.

"I sent Serenity and Milky to the store to go get something to drink for dinner and Serenity came home crying," Lakeisha began. "She said that niggas was outside sellin' drugs in front of our house, and when she said somethin' about it, they cussed her out and told her to go in the house."

I looked over at Serenity who had just placed my son, Dijuan Jr., down on the floor. He immediately began making his way in my direction, smiling as he came. Serenity, however, wasn't as gleeful as her youngest brother, neither was Milky.

"What happened, baby?" I asked Serenity.

"Me and Milky was comin' from the store when we saw them guys sellin' drugs in front of our house," Serenity said shakily. She was obviously still very much perturbed by what had happened. "I told 'em that they wasn't supposed to be in front of our house, and they was like, 'get the eff' out of here' and stuff like that."

Serenity was now visibly trembling. It was clear to see that she had obviously been more affected by what had happened than I previously thought, and I was enraged. I looked over at Milky who was sitting on the bottom step, observing our conversation. As usual, he remained quiet while surveying the scene with sharp, studious eyes. I could imagine him walking with his sister and assessing the situation, even predicting what would happen before it even transpiring only to find his analysis correct all along. Now, I guessed Milky to be watching me from his place at the bottom of the stairway, trying to predict what I would do next; or maybe he already knew.

"Serenity told me what happened, and I went outside an' told them niggas that they ain't got no business bein' in front of my house," Lakeisha continued. 'And they was like 'ain't nobody sellin' nothin' in front of your house . . .' and I was like 'so what . . . y'all niggas ain't even got no business standin' in front of my house.' And then I told 'em that they know damn well they wouldn't even be standing in front of our house if you were here."

Great, I thought silently to myself. *Lakeisha's last statement was undoubtedly an open declaration of war. The crowd outside on the corner weren't waiting to see what I would do, they were most likely waiting for me to go outside and do it.*

The thugs in this particular neighborhood probably would have vacated the premises without any problems had she spoken to them in a rather civil fashion, but Lakeisha was rarely civil. It was bad enough that she had come out of her home to blast them for standing in front of her house, but to say that they definitely wouldn't have been standing there if I were home was a direct strike against their egos. No self-respecting drug dealer, especially one who is young and reckless, would suffer such an insult.

Had their conflict been expressed in a more non-aggressive way, things may have fared differently; but then again, maybe it wouldn't have. In any event, local drug dealers in this area had disrespected Lakeisha and our family, and it was my duty to make things right. The problem was, however, that Twenty-Fifth Street was a premier 'hood in East Camden and not to be taken lightly. This particular section of the city has long ago upheld a well-known reputation for violence, and with that being said, the phrase "anything can happen" is an absolute reality. I tuned back into the here and now to find Lakeisha still going on about what happened today.

"They was like 'Bitch, get the fuck out of here. Fuck you and fuck your mothafuckin' man' and all types of shit like that."

I nearly choked on my food when hearing what Lakeisha had just now said.

"What?" I asked after washing down my dinner with a full swallow of beer. "They called you a bitch? And they said fuck you?"

"Yup," she concurred. "They was talkin' mad shit like you some kind of bitch or somethin' . . . like you ain't gonna do shit to nobody."

I handed my empty plate and silverware to Serenity who immediately scurried off to place them into the kitchen sink. I then grabbed Dijuan Jr. and placed him on my knee. He giggled and smiled as I mounted him onto my hip, and I, too, couldn't help but to smile.

"Ya'll go on upstairs," I said out loud to the children while handing little D.J. back over to Serenity upon her return from the kitchen.

All three children had immediately obeyed, and in a matter of minutes, Lakeisha and I were alone. I rose up from my place on the couch and slipped back into my army coat.

"I told you that I ain't wanna live around here, Dijaun," said Lakeisha who was now on the verge of crying. "Every day, I tell you how much I hate it around here, and every day, you act like you don't fuckin' hear me. Now, do you hear me, Dijuan? Do you fuckin' hear me, now?"

With my mind already set on how I intended to handle the situation, I didn't feel the need to respond.

"What are you gonna do, Dijuan?" asked Lakeisha when spying me pull the pistol from underneath the couch, cock a round into its firing chamber and then place it into the waistband of my jeans.

"I'm gonna go down there an' see what's really good wit' these niggas," I answered coolly. "Just sit tight and wait for me to get back."

"Wit' your gun out?" she asked, this time allowing a bit more of her nervousness to show.

"Yeah," I replied without bothering to glance upon what I was sure to be a most worried expression. "Wit' my gun out."

"Dijuan . . ."

"Listen, Keisha," I fiercely interrupted. "Don't fuckin' 'Dijuan me', all right? Niggas done hung out all in front of my mafuckin' house disrespectin' my family an' shit, and I ain't lettin' it go down like that! Now, I'm just gonna go down the street an' get down to the bottom of this shit, that's all; and I don't need you botherin' me about how I'm gonna go about doin' what I'm supposed to do, Keisha. You hear me?"

Lakeisha fell quiet, her facial expression and body language telling me that she had already admitted defeat. At this particular time, however, I cared little about the look of defeat she was now wearing.

"Just be careful, Dijuan," said Lakeisha. "Please."

"I will, babe," I heard myself reply. "I promise."

While making my way out the door, I silently hoped that I would be able to keep that guarantee.

*   *   *

The night had grown blacker, and its winds had grown even colder since making my way home nearly twenty minutes ago. The crowd on the corner, too, had swelled considerably since then. It was more than obvious that the local riff-raff was very much anticipating my arrival.

While making my way down the street, I silently began to weigh the pros and cons of my situation. Twenty-Fifth and High Street was literally a danger zone, and it was most definitely a bad idea to get violent with them while still living in their neighborhood amongst them. We lived only a few yards away from the heart of their 'hood, and any retaliation on their behalf would be swift and unforgiving. There was no way in the world I could leave home and do what I planned to do tonight if things went badly between me and the dealers on this corner. I had to be as diplomatic as possible. The problem is, however, that there are always at least one or two individuals in every neighborhood who are constantly on a mission to make trouble.

Some would say that approaching such a sticky situation with a pistol hanging so blatantly from the waistband of my jeans would be nothing more than a direct invitation to conflict, and they'd be exactly right. Nevertheless, there was no way in the world that I would approach these hoodlums without openly advertising what is sure to happen if they were to test my courage. I am already on my way into a situation where I'd be outnumbered more than seven-to-one; the gun being held in plain view was nothing more than a sincere warning, a plea even, for anyone not to try me. Again, I had to remind myself that the mission at hand was to remain humble and resolve this situation as smooth as humanly possible.

I stood at the curb and waited for an automobile to continue past as it cruised ever so slowly down the street. The crowd, now standing directly across from me, fell silent as they all cast their eyes in my direction. The atmosphere was electric. My breath began to quicken, and after noticing the slight tremble in my hand, I recognized that I was bit too nervous for my own liking. I frowned before tossing my cigarette into the street and starting towards those whom were all eagerly waiting to see what it is that I planned to do.

All eyes were at first on me, and then on my pistol, as I made my way towards them. It was almost too much of a struggle for me to contain my own emotions, and it somewhat impeded my ability to read the emotions of those now standing before me. Nevertheless, I had more than enough experience with these types of situations to know all of the possible outcomes; the most disturbing fact of it all is that a peaceful end to this conflict was highly unlikely. Something may very well happen tonight, and it may very well be at this moment.

"Hey, yo," I began out loud, not speaking to anyone in particular. "Somebody out here disrespected my wife an' my kids earlier today, an' I ain't tryin' to have them go through that type of shit no more; you know what I'm sayin'? I don't give a fuck who did it or why. I just don't want the shit to happen again, you know what I mean? My family don't fuck wit' nobody around here, an' I don't need nobody around here fuckin' wit' them, feel me? All I give a fuck about is us keepin' the peace wit' each other, you know what I'm sayin'? I just want us to keep on livin' around here without no trouble."

There was a short but ominous moment of silence that I felt resonating from amongst the crowd. The atmosphere, which was at first electric, now seemed filled with an intense mixture of both restlessness and uncertainty. I could see a few of them shift uneasily while standing beneath the jaded street light.

"I'm sayin' though," said a voice from amongst the pack. "Ain't nobody disrespect your family, yo. Matter of fact, she's the one that came outside talkin' mad shit to us . . . poppin' off at the mouth about some bullshit."

"Word up," said someone I recognized in the neighborhood as no more than a local troublemaker. "Ain't nobody disrespect your mafuckin' girl an' shit."

And there it was: a knuckle head using profanity when speaking in reference to my significant other. It was a subtle, yet brash show of disrespect in the midst of a potentially riotous moment. Only those with a thirst for confrontation would recognize and hone in on his disrespect. With Lakeisha and the children less than a few yards away from their corner, I struggled to remain level-headed about the situation. Unfortunately, my attempt to be sensible about the ordeal was well on its way to being in vain.

"I'm sayin' though," said a young Puerto Rican thug I knew only as Oscar. "You talkin' about tryin' to keep the peace an' what not, but you walkin' up on us wit' a gun out an' shit like niggas is supposed to be shook (shook being a slang term for being afraid). The fuck's up wit' that?"

The crowd was now beginning to stir with excitement, and in that instant, I knew that the time for peace-talk had ended. I was now caught in an even more serious dilemma. The gun, which I brandished with the hopes of keeping the predators at bay, seemed only to antagonize them. A few of the bolder hoodlums were now beginning to mouth off, and if I didn't respond accordingly, things will only grow worse by the second.

I was fast approaching a no-win situation. If I were to reach for my pistol and start blasting away, the police would soon be knocking at my door with their guns drawn, that is, if the neighborhood thugs didn't beat them to it. And if I were to keep my pistol tucked inside of my pants, especially after being called out by the enemy, I'd be deemed as both a bluff-artist and a coward, which will ultimately lead the hustlers in this crime-ridden area to consider me a target for harassment. Life in this neighborhood, for me and my family, will take a dreadful spin for the worst, and such a harrowing picture is something that I couldn't bear to stomach. I'd rather die right here in the streets before allowing any one of these individuals to think such a thing would happen to me and mine.

While standing before this now hostile group of thugs, all of these scenarios, and so much more, were racing about my mind in just the blink of an eye. Oscar's question was nothing more than a direct challenge, leaving his words to hang between me and the crowd like icicles. The atmosphere was growing more and more heated by the second, while I, on the other hand, was growing colder.

The blood flowing through my veins felt cold, so much so that I felt myself growing numb to the entire situation. Did Oscar really think that I'd allow him to get away with speaking to me with such a challenging tone of voice? Did any one of these so-called *gangstas* really think that I would give them a free pass to talk to my family any way they chose to? And most important of all, do they *really* think that I don't have the courage to reach for my pistol and start blasting away?

At the very instant, the blood in my veins had instantly gone from ice-cold to red hot. My entire body was now searing with anger when imagining that these persons actually had the nerve to entertain the thought of toying with me and my family, and it was such a concept that prompted me to react the way I had done.

The crowd had immediately grown tense and somewhat afraid as I pulled the pistol from the waistband of my jeans. There was now a stark mixture of fear and uncertainty in the air.

"Listen," I said with my eyes fixed firmly on Oscar's. "I ain't goin' for all this back an' forth shit. We been livin' around here for a nice lil' minute now, and we ain't never had no problems wit' none of y'all niggas. All I'm askin' for is for mafuckas around here to respect us like we respect y'all. And if you or anybody else around this mafucka got a problem wit' that, then we might as well get it over an' done with right now. Now tell me what's good."

"Like we said," remarked a hustler whom I only knew by face. "Wasn't nobody out here disrespectin' your family an' shit. All that comin' down here flashin' your pistol an' shit ain't even necessary."

The crowd shifted once more, this time, with more so a tone of hostility than discomfort. I had now been challenged twice by one of the hustlers out here on Twenty-Fifth Street, this time while holding a pistol in my hand. We've been teetering on the verge of confrontation for the longest time, and I was now beginning to grow tired. Something had to be done in order to show that I meant business, and it had to be done now.

It was the sudden emergence of a black late-model Suburban truck with black-tinted windows that had stolen everyone's attention away from me and the pistol I've been holding in my grasp, its huge fan-like rims still spinning forward as the truck began slowing to a complete stop at the corner where we were all standing. The muffled sound of rap music now blared out loudly as the doors began to open. Four men made their way out of the truck and started their way towards the crowd, all of their facial expressions growing tense when seeing how the conflict was threatening to play itself out. Of the four, there was only one man that I recognized.

Kashflow, who was once a middle school classmate of my brother, was now a high-ranking gang member and an undisputed big-shot in this particular part of town. Since my migration to Twenty-Fifth Street, he and I had crossed paths every now and then, the two of us acknowledging each other with no more than a nod or a simple greeting. He and my brother, Tommy, weren't ever friends, neither were me and Kashflow. Kashflow and I were simply two hustlers from two different parts of Camden who shared a very common respect for one another. There was really no telling how he'd affect the situation at hand.

Dressed in a black goose-down jacket, black denim jeans, and a pair of red-on-black Michael Jordan sneakers, Kashflow and his cronies were now upon us. Standing well over six feet tall, he was indeed a harrowing figure. With eyes as red as the shoe laces in his sneaker and a bandanna which peeked out from beneath a black skullcap, Kashflow remained quiet while surveying the situation as everyone on the corner scrambled to greet him.

"What's goin' on out here?" he asked with his eyes moving back and forth from the gun in my hand to the crowd I'd been facing. "What's poppin'?"

"Niggas was out here disrespectin' my family," I answered, beating them all to the punch of voicing their side of the story. "So I came down here to try an' make peace an' shit, but niggas act like they ain't tryin' to hear it."

The crowd erupted in protest, making the point that it was I, and not them, that was standing smack dab in the middle of their 'hood with a pistol in my hand. They were angry, they were loud, and most of all, they were utterly disrespectful. I forced myself to remain silent as they referred to me as a "bitch-ass nigga" and my wife as a "bitch" while arguing that they were innocent of my charge of them disrespecting my family.

"All right, all right," said Kashflow, who had seemingly grown tired with all of the hoopla. "Enough wit' all the 'he said-she said' shit. Don Juan, come an' take a walk wit' me."

Certain that Kashflow wasn't out to betray me, and also that no one on the corner would try me as long as I was in his presence, I reluctantly tucked the pistol back into the front of my jeans before starting up the street with him. I could see Lakeisha standing in the doorway as we approached my home; and again, I was irked by her making herself visible to our enemies.

"I really don't know you like that, yo, but you seem like a cool dude," said Kashflow. "You can't be comin' out here on the block wit' your gun out an' shit, though, homeboy, you know what I'm sayin'? That shit is bad business for everybody."

Kashflow's only concern was about me making trouble in his neighborhood. His cronies disrespecting my family, which was the reason I had gone down there in the first place, meant absolutely nothing to him; he hadn't even cared to mention a thing about it. Again, I felt myself becoming enraged, but still, I kept my emotions in check. Reasoning had immediately began to check in as I felt my blood began to boil once more.

Even if Kashflow did sincerely care about the well-being of my family, it was his obligation to place the well-being of his 'hood before anything. It was a concept that I completely understood, for I had found myself in that same exact position many times before.

Lakeisha was standing in the doorway of our home with the door closed behind her as Kashflow and I made our way to the front of the house. The thought of her standing outside, still advertising herself as my Achilles' heel, was beginning to aggravate me.

"Go in the house, Keisha," I said out loud while trying as best I could to mask just how irritated I was with her being nosey. "I'll be there in a minute."

Lakeisha dutifully obeyed my request, and I, as she closed the door behind her, turned back to Kashflow.

"I'm a tell you like I told them niggas down the street," I heard myself say to him. "I ain't never had no kind of problems wit' nobody from around here, and I don't want none now. All I want is for mafuckas to respect me an' mines, you know what I'm sayin'? I can't have niggas around here thinkin' that they can just say or do whatever they want to me or my family, yo. I wouldn't be who I am if I was to let shit go down like that . . . like I said, I don't want no problems wit' niggas around here, but I ain't gon' let nobody get away wit' disrespectin' me, either. All I want is for niggas to respect us like we respect them."

"You ain't got to worry about them niggas down there," said Kashflow with a tone of indifference. He stared directly into my eyes as he spoke, and for the first time, I could actually sense the abundant weight of the influence that he held in this particular part of town. "I'm a talk to 'em, doggy. . . you ain't gon' have no more problems out of them niggas . . . trust me. I just need you to fall back wit' all the drama, you know what I'm sayin'?"

Kashflow may have held sway and power over the local hustlers here in this neighborhood, but I wasn't one of the local hustlers from this neighborhood. I wasn't too partial with the "God-like" persona he was conveying; moreover, Kashflow had the audacity to refer to my situation as "drama," and he did so without even bothering to look in my direction. As enraged as I was with his haughtiness, I managed to contain myself with a great enough show of discipline in order to give a respectful response.

"I'm cool," I replied smoothly. "I just don't want niggas out here disrespectin' my family an' shit. That's all."

"You got that," said Kashflow. "That's my word."

And with that, he began making his way back down the street. I, in turn, started up the steps and back into my home. Before going inside, I stopped for a second to peer down the street at Kashflow, who was now conversing with his cronies on the corner just as he had promised; still, it was of little comfort for me to see him talking to them.

I had been terribly offended and couldn't get over just how disrespected I'd felt, not only by the hustlers out here in this neighborhood, but by Kashflow as well. His means of keeping the peace was nothing more than a barefaced show of authority, which did nothing but open the door to me being indebted to him for rescuing me from a bad situation. Contrary to what Kashflow may have thought, I am not, by any means, a low-level drug dealer who depends on the bigger fish for survival. I take a great deal of pride in being able to stand on my own two feet, regardless of the situation; and the last thing I cared for is a big shot, who bleeds just as I bleed, to undermine such an attribute.

While making my way inside the house, I decided to make all of them pay for their disrespect, and I will be sure to do so in a manner than none of them will ever forget.

9:15 p.m.

I entered back inside the house to find Lakeisha sitting on the couch, eagerly awaiting my arrival. The hungry look about her eyes was a telltale sign of her wanting to know every last detail of what had just taken place outside, and it peeved me terribly. I was still mulling over everything that had transpired today while at the same time trying to steel myself for what was to take place later on tonight. Needless to say, I was far from being in the mood to discuss every last element of my confrontation with the hoodlums on the corner; still, Lakeisha deserved to know about everything that had just now happened, and rest assured, she would not allow herself to be denied.

I sighed while setting my pistol back onto safety before flopping down on the couch beside her. I lay back with my hand over my face, not needing to look over at Lakeisha to know that she was now staring at me with a blatant show of impatience. Just as I had suspected, our stark moment of silence was short-lived.

"Well?" she asked out loud with the slight hint of her having an attitude. "What happened?"

"Go get me a beer real quick," I replied tiredly. "And then I'll tell you what happened."

Lakeisha's face drew tight, but she rose to reluctantly obey my wish without argument. With my sweetheart now off to retrieve my drink, I drew a cigarette from its pack while scrambling to figure out how to give her a more abbreviated version of what had recently taken place. But it was all for naught, for Lakeisha was back with my beer in only a matter of seconds.

"So?" Lakeisha asked as I took a sip of my beer. "What happened?"

"Nothin' much," I replied after exhaling a stream of cigarette smoke. "Niggas down the street was startin' to talk slick, an' shit was about to get ugly. But then the dude, Kashflow, rolls up and squashes everything."

I had just given Lakeisha the shortest, most abbreviated version of what had taken place down the street, and just as I'd figured, she wasn't the least bit satisfied. Lakeisha, in this particular case, is a stickler for details, but unfortunately, I wasn't the least bit moved to oblige her.

"Dijuan," she began, not satisfied with the fact that I had withheld all of the juicy, word-for-word details. "Can you go a little bit more in depth with it, or what?"

"There's nothin' to go in depth about," I remarked tiredly. "I just told you what happened."

"What do you mean, you just told me what happened?" she remarked with a combination of both anger and bemusement. "You . . ."

"It means that there's nothin' else to talk about, Keisha!" I replied snappily. Then, I softened my tone of voice before continuing on. "And . . . that we're moving, too."

It was an idea that I was silently entertaining, yet I didn't mean to blurt it out without first thinking through all of the details. Lakeishawas every bit as shocked as I was when hearing myself say such a thing. Her face, with elated eyes, was beaming with joy. She leaped over and wrapped her arms tightly around me, all the while kissing my face and thanking me for making such an executive decision.

"Where're we movin' to?" Lakeisha asked with a controlled show of excitement.

"That's up to you," I replied nonchalantly. "Go out an' look around, and whenever you find a place that you like, we'll be out of here the next day."

"Oh, Dijuan," she sighed while burrowing deep into my embrace. "I love you so much."

"I love you, too, babe," I replied, not being able to resist the feeling of basking in the light of bringing her so much joy.

Oh, yeah, I thought to myself while holding Lakeisha tight in my arms. *I AM the King.*

Being frugal was an inherent trait of mine; therefore, it was practically a natural reflex for me to automatically begin assessing just how much it would cost me to make good on my promise to Lakeisha. Needless to say, the glory of wallowing in my own majesty was soon overshadowed by the figures I was coming up with on my mental calculator.

A nice house in a relatively decent neighborhood will call for well over a thousand dollars a month, not to mention the one month security deposit. That meant me spending more than two thousand dollars fresh off the bat. The idea of moving outside of Camden meant me having to get my car legalized, which translated into me having to pay another few hundred dollars for registration and insurance.

After spending a little more than a thousand dollars tonight at the mall, I was now looking to spend nearly three thousand more the very next day. The forty-six hundred dollar profit that I had bagged up from the cooked-up cocaine earlier today had instantly shriveled up to a figure somewhere in the area of a thousand dollars, and that didn't include gas for my car, food for the family and household bills, not to mention me having to pay Puerto Rican Mannie for his services. I was standing to make absolutely nothing off of this flip, and if

I wasn't careful, I'd find myself digging into the money I already had saved and stashed away.

The sound of Lakeisha calling my name had instantly brought me back to reality. I snapped back to the here and now only to find her staring intently into my eyes with a look of concern.

"You okay?" she asked.

"Yeah," I replied, trying as best I could to straighten out my line of thinking. "I'm good."

"Well, you're gonna be even better once we put the kids to bed," she remarked sexily. "I got a special lil' somethin'- somethin'waitin' in the wings for you, baby, and I'm dyin' to give it to you."

I was already bogged down with thoughts of what lay ahead of me tonight, and now, I was dealing with the guilt of leaving Lakeisha alone on top of everything. It was breaking my heart to abandon her for the sake of my neighborhood's reputation, especially when I know how much she needs my presence right now after what had happened earlier today.

"I gotta go handle some business in a lil' bit," I said while intently stroking Lakeisha's hair. "But I'll be back in a couple hours."

Lakeisha rose up and broke away from me, her facial expression being a mixture of shock, anger and panic.

"What do you mean you gotta go out for a couple hours?!?" she asked rather incredulously. "Dijuan, how . . ."

"Keisha!" I interrupted with almost an exaggerated show of vehemence. "We gon' need a lot of money to get up out of here, yo . . . and we gon' need it now! We gon' need money for this month's rent and we gon' need money for a security deposit . . . we gon' need money to rent a truck to move all of this shit, and on top of all that, we ain't even paid the bills for this month yet!

"Shit, I just spent over a thousand fuckin' dollars on Christmas gifts! We really can't afford to be movin' right now, and I ain't bitchin' about it 'cause we gotta do what we gotta do. But don't act like I ain't gots to go out and get every dollar I can, Keisha. We need that money now more than ever."

Lakeisha remained silent as I ranted on about our need to make money, all the while, her face showing an overwhelming measure of sadness with regards to the fact that I was right. After a few minutes, I found myself spent of all my anger and was now regretting how I had blown up at her for wanting me home tonight. Noticing just how sorrowful Lakeisha was feeling, I moved quickly to remedy some of her melancholy.

"Come here, baby," I said softly to Lakeisha while tightening my embrace around her shoulder. "I'm sorry for snappin' on you like that, babe."

Lakeisha didn't respond; instead, she remained quiet while snuggling deep within the embrace of my one free arm while my other hand moved to resume the task of stroking her hair.

It was then that I had suddenly come up with an idea.

"Babe, do you remember that time when we was in back of Camden High?" I asked.

"Yeah," she replied while sitting up straight to look directly into my eyes. "Why?"

"I ain't talkin' about when I was back there bustin' ya ass, yo," I remarked smartly.

"I know what you talkin' about, nigga!" Lakeisha snapped back with an attitude. "You're talkin' about when you was back there teachin' me how to shoot that big ass gun."

I fought not to smile at Lakeisha's automatic instinct to get sassy with me. It was one of the things that attracted me so strongly to her. My urge to grab Lakeisha and squeeze her ever so tightly was shown only with a purse of my lips.

"You remember what I taught you about shootin' it?" I asked.

Lakeisha took a moment to think, and then, with look of pure concentration, she began to recall out loud.

"You said to grip the handle tight and use my other hand as a brace to keep the gun steady when it kicks back . . . and for me to depend on the strength of my wrist and my forearm to keep the gun steady. You said that too many people underestimate the weight of a pistol or the power of its recoil when you squeeze the trigger. That's why so many shooters miss their marks an' shit. You have to prepare yourself for the kick of the gun when it lets off until you get comfortable with it."

I was absolutely impressed with how accurately Lakeisha had recalled my lesson on shooting a pistol, and again, I found myself fighting not to smile. Instead, I pulled my gun from beneath the sofa, emptied the bullet from out of its firing chamber, and then wiped it clean of my fingerprints before reloading it back into the clip of my pistol. Lakeisha watched all of this with transfixed eyes, at times, slightly flinching from the metallic sounds of the pistol magazine sliding out and then back into its handle.

"The gun we was shootin' in the back of Camden High was a .357 Magnum," I said while showing her the pistol. "This is a Glock-nine; it's made of plastic, and it's way lighter than a .357. It don't kick back as bad as the .357, either. You can handle this one way better. Here . . . hold it."

Lakeisha accepted the pistol, and while slowly weighing it in her grasp, she agreed.

"Damn," she concurred with a slight touch of awe. "You're right, baby. This gun is light as hell."

"You remember how to load and reload?" I asked.

Without speaking a word, Lakeisha checked the side of the pistol and then pointed at the small, mechanical lever. "This is the safety. It won't shoot until I point this switch to the red dot; that means it's on fire."

She gripped the top part of the pistol and slid it back, consequently cocking a round into the chamber of the weapon; her attention to what she was doing only intensified with the loud metallic sound of it now being loaded.

"Now it's ready to be fired," she said."

"All right now," I began with the seriousness of a high school teacher. "I need you to listen to me."

Lakeisha placed the gun beside her on the arm of the sofa and then gave me her complete attention.

"I talked to the dude, Kashflow, and I'm a hundred percent sure that nobody is gonna try no bullshit tonight, but then again, you never know," I said frankly. "I really don't want to leave you here by yourself, baby, but I ain't really got too much of a choice . . . I gots to go out and get this money."

"I know, baby," Lakeisha replied with a sincere show of regret. "I understand that you gotta do what you gotta do."

"I'll be back as soon as I get done," I continued. "But until then, I need you to hold the house down. I need you to "soldier up" for me and our family. I know you can do it, boo. It's one of the reasons why I love you the way I do."

I paused for a moment, all for the sake of dramatizing the message I was so desperately trying to get across to her. I then looked Lakeisha square in the eyes.

"You think you can handle this, baby?"

Lakeisha gripped the pistol tightly, and with a look of sheer determination, nodded her head yes. And in that instant, I fell in love with her all over again. I ran my fingers all so gingerly through Lakeisha's hair before kissing her softly on the lips. Damn, I wanted to make love to her; and, as if reading my mind, Lakeisha smiled.

"Stop wit' all the sentimental shit, and go do what you gotta do, nigga," she said while staring into my eyes with a gaze that was every bit as serious as the tone of voice she was now speaking with. "I got a lot of house shopping to do tomorrow, and you sittin' here all dreamy eyed an' shit ain't helpin' me none."

I kissed Lakeisha once more, this time with a bit more passion than before, and then rose to my feet. Besides my mother and Tamara, she was truly one of the most robust women I had ever known, and I wholeheartedly loved her for it. Before exiting out of the house, I turned and took one more second to gaze at the love of my life. No matter what the situation, no matter what the atmosphere, she always proved herself to be the most beautiful woman I've ever seen; and she did so without the slightest effort.

Now, while standing at the threshold of the doorway, I began to feel a twinge of guilt for never truly expressing to Lakeisha just how much she really meant to me.

I had to say something.

"I love you, baby," I said with a bubbling heart. "I really do."

"Yeah, yeah, yeah," Lakeisha replied toughly. "Hurry up and do what you gotta do so you can bring your black ass home."

I smiled at Lakeisha's hard-nosed response while making my way towards the door. The sound of her calling my name had immediately stopped me from shutting it behind me on my way out. I peeked my head back inside to see what it is that she may have wanted.

"I love you, too, baby," she said earnestly. "And please . . . be careful."

Again, I smiled at Lakeisha's response.

"I will baby," I said while closing the door behind me. "I sure fucking will."

10:00 p.m.

The congregation on the corner of Twenty-Fifth and High Street had dissipated a bit, but a good deal of them were still milling about as I left the house and started towards my car. They all stared as I came to a stop at the corner before making a right onto High Street. The heat which blazed from their unfriendly glares grew cooler and cooler as I increased the distance between us. While turning onto Twenty-Seventh Street, one of East Camden's main roads, I made a mental note for myself not to forget the disrespect that the hustlers from Twenty-Fifth Street had shown me and my family. I very much planned to pay them back for their hostility, and I would do so in spades.

As Twenty-Seventh Street transformed into Baird Boulevard and Baird Boulevard lead me over the Camden High Bridge, I silently began to reflect on the spat that had transpired between Tamara and I earlier this morning; after all, it was indeed her home that I was on my way to so that I could prepare myself for what was soon to take place in just an hour. While cruising down Park Boulevard, I thought about the brief conversation I had with her while driving. She was all too composed when learning that I was on my way to her house, which was far from the confrontational type of person I've known her to be.

I wasn't the least bit fooled by the tranquility of Tamara's voice when speaking to her over the phone. For Tamara, there would definitely be no peace of mind until the two of us came to some type of resolution with regards to our argument; it just wasn't in her nature to simply live and let die. She and my mother were too much alike, which meant that Tamara, too, shared my having a problem with leaving loose ends as they were. With her pretty much having the same personality as I, there would be no doubt about us having a showdown upon my arrival; it was something that scholars would describe as an "inevitability."

It wasn't the thought of facing Tamara that fueled my reluctance, but the timing of it all which troubled me most. My plans were to shower, get dressed, inspect my soon-to-be murder weapons and then use what little time I had left to relax before meeting up with Justice and Peace-Peace. Tamara was supposed to be at work, but for whatever reason, she was at home and awaiting my arrival.

I parked my car on the nine hundred block of Haddon Avenue, which was a short distance away from my 'hood, and then took the back route to Tamara's house. From the outside looking in, one would think that she may have been asleep; once inside, however, I saw that such wasn't the case.

Every light in the house, except for the living room lamp, was turned off. I frowned when recognizing the music she was listening to. "My Life" by Mary J. Blige was one of Tamara's all-time favorite albums; she'd only listen to it when in a sullen mood. I locked the back door behind me and then started towards the living room, the scent of marijuana growing stronger as I approached.

Tamara was curled up into a corner of the couch with her legs folded beneath her, dressed in a way that I'd never seen before. Her shorts were cut exceedingly high, revealing a great portion of her buttocks. The swell of her bosom pressed tightly against the fabric of a shrunken half-shirt, which left little to my imagination as to whether or not she was wearing a bra.

With an elbow propped against the arm of the sofa, Tamara was sitting with the side of her head resting in the palm of her hand, the other one holding a huge joint. Mary J. Blige's sorrowful rendition of the Rose Royce classic, "I'm Goin' Down," filled the room, which only intensified the gloominess of the atmosphere. With the bang of her hair hanging just above her eyebrows, and sprinkled about her forehead, she somewhat resembled the legendary Hip-Hop and R&B diva.

Tamara took a long drag from her joint and then peered through a cloud of marijuana smoke with squinting eyes.

"I thought you changed your mind about coming," she said while shifting her position on the couch. "Sit down."

I've never, ever seen Tamara dressed in such a provocative fashion, and I couldn't help but to glance between her legs as I took a seat beside her. She took another drag of the joint before offering me some, to which I promptly declined.

Tamara shot me a scrupulous look.

"What?" she asked. "You still mad at me or somethin'?"

It was the same question that Tamara had asked me earlier, but this time, it was done so with a great measure of constraint. Just like that, all within a blink of an eye, Tamara had poised herself for contention.

"Mad at you for what?" I asked with forced show of nonchalance. "Nah, Tammy. I'm good, yo. For real."

Tamara's relief was expressed with a simple purse of the lips. Her eyes, however, remained sharp and diligent.

"What, you stressin' or somethin'?" I asked.

"Stressin'?" she remarked rather mockingly through a cloud of newly-exhaled weed smoke. "Stressin' about what? Shit, ain't nobody stressin'."

"Bullshit," I remarked with a slight laugh. "You sittin' up here all by yourself, listenin' to Mary J. Blige an' shit. Yeah, nigga . . . you stressin'. You stressin'like a mafucka."

Tamara frowned while rising to her feet and starting across the living room.

"Whatever, Dijuan," she remarked while on her towards the floor-model stereo system. "I ain't think you was gon' come, so I was like 'fuck it.' I was just layin' around, chillin' an' shit."

I seized the opportunity to ogle her physique as she squatted down to fiddle with the CD player. Every inch of her lower body, from her calves to the lower end of her buttocks, was now ballooning out from beneath her shorts while squatting; her lower body was taut and exceedingly muscular. My wish for her to be more than just my "big sister" increased with each second I spent staring at her.

Reoccurring ideas of lust were now beginning to overshadow my concentration on the events due to take place in less than an hour from now, and I, now began to feel myself needing to go upstairs.

The sound of Mary J. Blige's voice disappeared and was replaced with a momentary silence. R. Kelly's voice now began crooning from the stereo speakers.

"Is that better?" asked Tamara, who was now standing directly in front of me with her hands placed haughtily on her hips.

With the lights dimmed, soft music playing, and a beautiful woman standing directly in my sights, it was impossible for me to do anything but entertain the thought of romance. While observing the scenery Tamara had just now created, I instinctively began pondering whether or not she was entertaining the same idea. The only notion more unthinkable than her coming on to me was the discomfort I felt with the chance of it actually being true.

Tamara was everything a big sister was supposed to be; not only that, but my cheek still burned with shame whenever thinking of how she reacted when I had last made a pass at her. We were both children back then, yet despite her burying the hatchet long ago, there was no erasing the shame of what had happened.

I watched as Tamara made her way in my direction, the muscles of her abdomen twisting and flexing as she approached. She then flopped down beside me, carrying the scent of strawberries along with her. I suddenly found myself struck with the oddity of becoming aroused, and it was driving me crazy.

Was this it? I thought silently to myself. *Is she gon' try to make a move on me or somethin'?*

I was feeling like a high school kid, nervously plotting on how I should make the next move on my first ever girlfriend.

"Everything all right at home?" she asked while mashing the remnants of her joint into an ashtray.

It was a rather unexpected question, and it caught me well off guard.

"Yeah," I answered while casting a suspicious eye. "Why you ask me that?"

"Your mom told me how fast you hauled ass out of there when your little wifey called you on the phone an' shit," she replied curtly. "That's why I asked."

From the bristled manner in which Tamara was now speaking, I could sense that she was just as displeased with my response as I was with her interrogation.

"Oh," I replied, smoothly trying to dismiss Tamara's nosey line of questioning. "There was a little situation at home, but everything is good."

Tamara flashed a smirk as if to say "whatever" and then rose once more, placing her voluptuous rear end directly in front of my face.

"I'm going to take a shower," she said while heading towards the steps. "I'll see you when I get out."

Trying as best I could to appear nonchalant, I pursed my lips and nodded while fishing a cigarette from the pack in my pants pocket. With the cigarette now lit and hanging loosely from my lips, I remained still on the couch, totally perplexed by Tamara's strange and provocative behavior. My mind was now being swamped with a whirlwind of questions.

What were Tamara's intentions? Is she really inviting me to make a pass at her? Or is she simply teasing me? If she's not teasing me, then why? If she IS teasing me, then why?

Maybe it was neither one. Maybe it was just as Tamara had said, that she figured I wouldn't show up and was just lounging around in whatever she felt comfortable with.

Hell no.

Tamara was practically one of the guys. She always preferred a wardrobe of over-sized clothing and was adamantly opposed to the form-fitting, skin-tight outfits other females chose to wear. Plus-sized sweat suits are the norm for Tamara throughout the winter, and on the hottest days of the year, her shorts were never raised more than a few inches above the knee.

Considering Tamara's ultra-conservative personality, it became quite clear to me that she was dressed like this for a specific reason; unfortunately, I wouldn't have the immediate opportunity to indulge in whatever it is that she may have had in mind. I was due to meet Peace-Peace and Justice at ten-thirty tonight, which was exactly one half hour before we were scheduled to retaliate against Jay-Dollar and his crew. It was already a little after ten, which was a clear indication of time being a luxury that I did not have.

Without wasting another second, I rose from off of the couch and began making my way up the stairs. The bathroom door was slightly ajar, making it easy for me to overhear Tamara making herself busy beneath the shower water. The temptation of going inside of the bathroom was all too much for me to bear. Instead of trying my luck, I entered inside of my own bedroom and proceeded to get ready for tonight. I clicked on the bedroom light and then the stereo before doing anything else; I needed a little mood music to soothe the anxiety I felt creeping about my conscience.

I've shot quite a few people during my time on the streets, but never before had it been with the deliberate intention of killing them. Tonight, however, I was planning to commit murder. To walk into a crowded place of business and intentionally shoot someone to death wasn't an easy task for me to do; the fact that I was to also kill a female made it even more difficult for me to digest.

I tried my best to phase out any feelings of unease by singing along with one of my favorite rap songs while retrieving two fully loaded nine millimeter handguns from the top dresser drawer and placing them on top of the bureau. "Scarface" was a popular song made by a member of the Texas-based rap group called the "Geto Boys," and it was considered a national anthem for those like myself who lived the street life. I passionately sang along with the rap artist's tale of murder and street bravado, all the while hoping to ward off any reservations about what I was planning to do.

The idea of blasting away at one's enemies with twin .45 caliber handguns is a concept often romanticized by not only drug dealers and gangster rappers everywhere, but Peace-Peace and Justice as well. I, for one, wasn't too enthused with the notion, and this is what lead me into a most heated debated with the two of them. Desert Eagles were fairly large handguns that produced a powerful recoil similar to that of a .357 Magnum; such large caliber weapons will surely guarantee a successful murder, but its strength and kickback was not to be taken lightly. A strong wrist and an almost vice-like grip on its handle is all but absolutely necessary in order ensure accuracy. In the midst of rapid fire, it would be all too easy for one to lose control and miss the mark, especially with both pistols blasting away at the same time. Not only could I run the risk of shooting an innocent bystander, but I could also allow enough time for a quick-thinker to react and play hero.

To be honest, I preferred thirty-eight caliber revolvers, or even a pair of forty-four caliber revolvers for the job;

they both weighed a lot less and possessed a much weaker recoil. Moreover, revolvers were more attractive to murderers for the simple fact of the pistols not spending and emptying its shells onto the ground; in short, the physical evidence of these shootings will remain inside the pistols' chambers and leave police without much to work with; also, revolvers were less prone to jams and misfires than semi-automatic weapons. I plead my case to Peace-Peace and Justice about this issue, citing my misgivings about using the two Desert Eagles all the while expressing my desire to use one of the smaller-sized revolvers, but neither of them would be dissuaded.

We agreed to both compromise with me using two nine millimeter handguns instead of the Desert Eagles; the revolvers, however, would never have been agreed upon. There was absolutely no way that they'd agree for me to use anything other than semi-automatic handguns, and I completely understood. In the event of meeting some sort of confrontation, it would be much better to have two loaded magazines rather than twelve loaded chambers. Who knows how many bullets I would have to use while inside the bar; I couldn't afford to run the risk of being short of ammunition if, by chance, I'd end up having to shoot my way out of a situation.

Choosing to no longer to dwell on our past debate of semi-automatic handguns versus revolvers, I gathered up my "assassin gear" and then spread them all about my bed: black sweatpants, a black hooded sweatshirt, a black wool-knit ski mask, a black jacket and a pair of latex gloves. After changing into something other than what was already laid out across my bed, I looked over at the clock on my bureau and sighed.

It was almost time.

With only a few minutes to spare, I stretched out across my bed and began thinking about the events that had led me up to this point in time. I completely understood Jay-Dollar's extreme measure of retaliation against my neighborhood. Thinking about what I had just went through with the drug dealers on the corner of Twenty-fifth and High Street, I could only imagine what may have been going on inside of Jay-Dollar's head when returning home to find that his house had been violated. I sympathized with him greatly, yet and still, there was no way in the world he could be allowed to get away with shooting my neighborhood to pieces.

My attention was suddenly diverted from thoughts of violence and towards my bedroom door which had just now opened. I always strove to make a habit of locking the door behind me, and I was now beginning to curse myself for slacking on this routine; such negligence could easily cost me my life one day. The sight of Tamara dressed in nothing but a bath towel was more than enough cause for me to minimize my self-reproof.

"Damn, Tammy," I said while scooting off the bed. "What's up?"

Her gaze ricocheted from me, to my clothing on the bed, to the guns on top of the dresser and then back to me, all in a matter of milliseconds. Her facial expression, like the air between she and I, had instantly grown cold.

"What're you getting ready to do, Dijuan?" she asked crossly.

Here we go, I thought dejectedly to myself. Our cycle of arguments was beginning to grow smaller and much more immediate.

"Listen, Tammy," I said wearily. I got somethin' to do right now, an' I ain't tryin' to argue about it. We'll talk about it sometime tomorrow."

"Hold up," said Tamara before disappearing back into the hallway.

Figuring that she had left out to get dressed, I began hurrying to do the same. By the time I had managed to slip my sweatpants and hooded sweatshirt over what I was already wearing, Tamara had reappeared in the doorway. Dressed in a baggy pair of sweatpants and an oversized tee-shirt, she was back to her normal attire. The bulge against Tamara's tee-shirt gave hint of her still not wearing a bra, and I silently wondered if she was wearing any underwear as well.

We stared at one another in silence; my gaze being one of lust, hers being one of disgust.

"You're gonna go out there and do somethin' stupid."

"Tammy, this ain't nothin' for us to get into right now," I replied while reaching for my jacket.

I clicked off the stereo, collected my weapons, and then started towards the door where Tamara stood, blocking my path. While standing face to face with her, I couldn't help but to feel somewhat aroused. Sensing an urge to forsake everything for a moment of intimacy with her, I immediately went on the offensive.

"Come on now, Tammy," I barked while tucking both pistols into the waistband of my pants. "Stop wit' the bullshit, all right? I gotta go."

"Why're you doin' this, Dijuan?" Tamara asked, still not bothering to move an inch from in front of me. "You gonna get yourself involved in some bullshit over this whack-ass neighborhood?!? That's the same stupid-ass shit that got Rasheed stuck in jail for all of these years . . . you too stupid to see that, or what?"

"I'm gonna ask you one more time to get out of my way, Tammy," I heard myself say in a menacing manner. "Don't make me . . ."

Tamara exploded.

"What?!?" she snapped. "Don't make you what, Dijuan?!? What the fuck are you gonna do?!?"

Tamara pushed hard into my chest with just one of her hands, her strength knocking me a half-step backward. In a vain attempt to shove me once more, she pushed hard into chest, this time, with both her hands. By instinct, I moved deftly to one side and allowed her to slip past me. I then grabbed her from behind; henceforth, the tussle between us had immediately begun. Although short in size, Tamara was terribly scrappy and proved a formidable adversary when wrestling. Fortunately, both my handguns were set on safety and not loaded with a round in their firing chambers. She bumped hard into my guns while turning, gripping, grabbing, and trying her best to counter any moved I used to subdue her as we grappled.

In the end, it was my strength that prevailed. Using my weight as leverage, I was now holding Tamara pinned against the wall. With her tiny wrists held firmly in my grasp and my body pressed firmly against hers, Tamara was rendered helpless; only her eyes maintained the fervent drive of aggression. We stood face to face, our mouths and noses so close together that we could both feel the quickness of our breaths against each other. I found myself incredibly turned on, and something told me that she felt the same.

I don't wanna fight wit' you, Tammy," I said with her wrists still in my grasp. "Chill the fuck out, yo... please."

"Stay here then, Dijuan . . ." she replied quickly. "Just stay here . . . please . . . don't go."

The flair in Tamara's eyes was still very much apparent, but waning. There was a slight tone of desperation that I saw in her gaze, and it was disturbing.

My attempt to respond to her demand for me to stay was thwarted by the full kiss that she had suddenly, and without warning, planted on my lips. It took only a second for me to recover from the shock, and after a moment or two of indulgence, I broke clean away from her.

"Tammy, I gotta go."

Lord knows I didn't want to leave.

"If you leave this house, Dijaun, I swear to God, you'd better not ever come back!" she screamed out loud as I continued to walk past without looking back in her direction.

There was nothing left for me to say.

My love for the 'hood came before any and everything else I've come to know and love, even my life. As far as I was concerned, both my life and my 'hood were one and the same; and there was absolutely no way that I could ever see myself separating the two.

The sounds of Tamara threatening for me to not to leave the house were echoing about my head as I started out the door, and deep down inside, I could only hope that our bond as brother and sister was stronger than her swears to God.

11:00 p.m.

Fourth Street, a road near the westernmost side of Camden, was four or so miles away from my neighborhood and ran parallel with Broadway from one part of the city to the other. The streets that intersected and crossed Fourth Street were just as long, and together, with the rarity of streetlights, they all combined to help paint a rather grim setting for what was soon about to take place.

I was sitting inside of a stolen Honda Accord, which was parked a few feet away from the corner of Fourth and Walnut Street, facing a small Dominican lounge. Jay-Dollar was currently inside this place of business with absolutely no clue as to what was sure to be his demise just a few minutes from now.

The plan was immaculate; the length to which Peace-Peace and Justice had gone in order to ensure its success, however, was even more impressive. Not only had they managed to pinpoint Jay-Dollar's schedule, but they had also managed to convince his lover to position him in a manner to which I'd be able to kill him and escape before anyone would have the chance to gather their wits and piece together what had so suddenly happened. As I handled my business inside the bar, Peace-Peace and Justice will be driving through Jay-Dollar's beloved territory, riddling it with bullets. The murder of Jay-Dollar and the decimation of his neighborhood were to take place simultaneously; its effect would be totally devastating, and it was exactly what the three of us had in mind.

If all things went according to planned, there will be no tangible proof that could link us to the crime, which means even if the police were to figure out how, what, when, and where, they will never be able to prove who and why. The streets talk, and the beef J-Dollar had initiated with my neighborhood will definitely be a topic, but the police will never be able to prove a thing. They may figure out that me and my cohorts had something to do with it, but they definitely won't be able to prove it. The police may have their eyes set on us forever, but so will my city; Camden will finally recognize our neighborhood in a most respectful light. It was a grim, yet grand ambition that I was all too hungry to realize.

Anxious to get things going, yet deathly afraid to make a mistake, I remained inside the car and continued to stare at the entrance of the tiny Latin club, at times, peering across Fourth Street and farther up Walnut Street. Justice and Peace-Peace, too, were sitting inside of a stolen car which was parked a few feet away from the corner of Fourth and Walnut Street, facing me in the opposite direction. Being the only one of the murderous duo with two healthy eyes, Justice was better suited to be the driver; yet and still, he refused to allow his role of being the getaway driver prevent him from lending a hand in the shooting. Instead of staging a conventional drive-by shooting, Justice planned to pull up and hop out of the car along with Peace-Peace, to which he'd brandish a Mac-10 of his own and empty all forty-two rounds into Jay-Dollar's neighborhood before taking flight.

Up the street, I spied a car pulling away from its parking spot, flashing its headlights no more than twice while approaching the corner; it was Justice and Peace-Peace signaling for me to get things underway. My heart rate had begun to increase a thousand times over. It was "do or die" and definitely no time for turning back. I pulled the hoodie over my head and then reached for the two nine millimeters lying on the passenger seat beside me. I tucked one pistol into the waistband of my jeans and the other near the small of my back while exiting the car.

Justice flicked the car's headlights once more before turning the corner, and I felt even more pressed to get things over and done with. Anxious to make it happen, I walked swiftly up the street with my ears fixed firmly on the Latin music booming from inside the club as I neared the curb. I took one last breath and then started across the street, spying the taillights of Justice's car as it disappeared around the corner and off of Fourth Street. I removed my plastic-gloved hands from inside the pocket of my hooded sweatshirt and pulled the ski mask down over my face before retrieving and getting a firm grip on both my pistols. I counted to three and then entered inside the bar.

*   *   *

It was as if I were watching myself on television with the volume muted; from the very moment I had entered inside, it seemed that I could only see and not hear what was going on.

Dressed in all black and with a ski mask pulled over my face, I walked directly into the bar while holding both pistols down by my sides. No one, not even the bartender, noticed my dubious entrance. Everything seemed to be in slow motion. Patrons at the rear of the bar were dancing slowly to a rhythm I did not hear, and it was absolutely bizarre to see people dancing and enjoying themselves in such silence.

I glanced over to my right and recognized Tamika Barlow seated at a booth with Jay-Dollar, the two of them sitting with their backs toward the door as planned. Christian Nutter, one of Jay-Dollar's most trusted henchmen more commonly known as C.N.N., was sitting opposite to the couple in the same booth. The trio was engrossed in a conversation and totally oblivious to my approach. From behind, I could see Jay-Dollar sitting with his arm around Tamika, the two of them listening intently to whatever C.N.N. was so colorfully saying. He was quite an animated fellow. His face beamed with elation as he spoke, laughing heartily with his eyes closed and his mouth wide open. Neither of the three ever saw me approach them.

C.N.N. reopened his eyes just in time to see me as I approached with each gun drawn, one against the back of Jay-Dollar's head and the other aimed directly towards his own self. It was a threatening enough sight to replace the once-jovial expression he wore with a genuine look of dread; it was now panic that gleamed brightly from within the whites of his eyes. To say that I could sense C.N.N.'s fear would have been a gross understatement; in this precise moment, I could very well feel and soak up the dread I felt resonating from the very core his being.

Tamika was the first to read C.N.N.'s facial expression, and from the corner of my eye, I could see her turn halfway in my direction. Her jaw went slack; and her brow was arched high over a pair of eyes that showed a mixture of both surprise and horror. By instinct, Jay-Dollar turned around to see what had stricken his company with such terror, and it was C.N.N. whom unfroze and looked as if he were going to motion for his waist.

It was attempt made in vain.

I squeezed both triggers almost simultaneously. C.N.N.'s head snapped backward with a jet stream of blood exploding from out the back of his head as the force of the nine millimeter slug nearly raised him up and out of the booth. Jay-Dollar's body was propelled headfirst onto Tamika's fear-frozen body, the majority of her face now being plastered with his blood and brain matter; portions of Jay-Dollar's brain and bodily fluids now slickened her once pricey, salon-styled hairdo. With stunned, horror-filled eyes, she stared back and forth at C.N.N. and Jay-Dollar's now-lifeless bodies with her mouth agape. It seemed to me that she was screaming, but again, I was deaf to any sound in the bar.

I angled one of my pistols directly at Tamika's face and then squeezed the trigger. Thick, sponge-like pieces of flesh, bone, and blood splattered the wall behind her. I shot Tamika twice more before turning my pistols back onto C.N.N. and Jay-Dollar's bodies and shooting them a few times more. Not knowing what may lie ahead of me from here to the rendezvous spot, I was careful not to spend all my ammunition; there was no telling if I'd have to shoot it out with anyone while trying to get away. With that in mind, I decided it was time for me to make my exit.

Once outside, all five of my senses had returned at full blast. Justice and Peace-Peace were still on Chestnut Street; the screams of those I'd left inside the bar were loud but didn't register above the gunshots I heard ringing out from around the corner. For the two of them to still be on Jay-Dollar's set after I had already handled my business meant that it didn't take long for me to do what I had set out to do; it must have taken no more than a few minutes.

Still having the murder weapons firmly in my grasp, I tucked them both into the front pocket of my sweatshirt and began walking swiftly down the street with my head tilted a bit downward, so as to hide my ski mask while heading towards the car. Once back inside the Honda, I peeled off my ski mask and tossed the handguns onto the passenger seat of the car before starting it up with a flathead screwdriver.

Despite my overwhelming urge to get away as quick and as fast as humanly possible, I instead, eased from out of my parking space and drove up to the intersection which, by now, had grown crowded with bystanders. No one seemed to notice as I made a right turn onto Fourth Street and cruised ever so smoothly away from the crime scene. It was a show of nonchalance worthy of an Oscar award.

Like Mid Town, the city of Camden itself was rather small in size and consisted of countless alleys, side streets and back roads. I took full advantage of the inner-city labyrinth and cruised smoothly through one back street after another until reaching 36th and Fairmount Street which was clear across town and near desolate at this particular hour.

Fairmount Street was a road with a string of row homes on one side and the rear of Woodrow Wilson High School on the other. With the light post at the end of Woodrow Wilson's rear parking lot being the street's only source of illumination, I found myself feeling a bit safe while driving down this dark and quiet road. A strained sigh of exhaustion had finally escaped my lips as I slowed down and parked a short distance behind my vehicle, which was a short ways up the street and away from the light of the school's parking lot street lamp.

I couldn't remember taking one single breath of air during the entire ordeal, and as I neared my final getaway car, I was still very much trapped in a controlled sense of panic. Despite being able to commit murder three times over and flee the scene without incident, the deed was still incomplete; the need for me to destroy all physical evidence was gnawing at my brain entirely too much for me to experience relief.

I exited the Honda and immediately pitched both pistols into a nearby storm drain; then, I retrieved a canister filled with gasoline from the backseat of my car. After dousing both the interior and exterior of the stolen vehicle with gas, I peeled off my sweats and then tossed them inside the car as well. I was now dressed in a beige pair of khaki pants and a multi-colored sweater, a wardrobe being the exact opposite of what the killer would be described as wearing. In my left pocket was the three thousand dollars I intended to take home tonight, and in the other were a pack of cigarettes, a book of matches, a cigarette lighter and a set of keys. I peeled off my latex gloves and tossed them into the car, retrieved my matches, lit the entire book, and then tossed them inside the Honda as well.

Once inside my own car, I started the engine and drove away from the fiery scene with the same controlled sense of haste I exhibited when leaving the bar on Fourth and Walnut Street. Despite the still looming sense of urgency, I couldn't help but to finally feel a touch of relief as I distanced myself from the now-flaming pile of physical evidence.

I smiled with satisfaction after checking my cell phone and pager to find them empty of any messages. I clipped the pager back onto the waistband of my khaki pants, tossed the cell phone into the car's middle console, and then headed to Justice's apartment in Maple Shade.

11:45 p.m.

By greeting me with a wide toothy smile and a hearty well-felt hug, I could tell that Justice was in good spirits. I felt safe to assume that all had gone well on their end of the job. Our mutual embrace was sincere but brief, and after a few seconds, Justice turned and I followed him inside.

Justice's apartment was kept in the same exact fashion as his car, pristine and meticulously clean. A slight aromatic scent filled his home which mixed well with the classic R&B music playing softly from an expensive stereo system.

Just and his god damned oldies, I thought to myself while removing my boots and placing them onto a shoe rack which was situated by the door.

He returned to his place on the sofa where an attractive pair of women were sitting at opposite ends, the two of them eagerly awaiting his return. One of them appeared to be of Latin descent, the other was obviously Asian; both of them were extremely beautiful. Justice relaxed back against the cushions of the sofa and crossed his legs at the ankles while draping an arm over each woman. Their affectionate reactions to Justice's embrace more than answered my question as to the nature of their relationship to him.

Peace-Peace, always the non-social type, was seated by his self at the table in the dining room. Deciding to leave Justice alone with his female company, I walked past him and began making my way over to Peace-Peace who seemed content all by his lonesome, breaking up mountainous buds of marijuana.

"It's about time you showed up, sun," he said while pulling an already-wrapped blunt from behind his ear. "As long as it took for you to get here, I thought you might've been out makin' the news or some shit . . . you all right?"

I could only smile at Peace-Peace's remark. Concern is concern, no matter how it is displayed, and I appreciated his worry with regards to my well-being, no matter how gruff it came across.

"Everything is good," I replied while taking a seat at the table. "What about y'all?"

"Everything is in its proper order," Peace-Peace replied with his usual sneer.

"Ladies," I heard Justice say from his place in the living room. "I gotta go build wit' my brothers for a minute, so y'all go 'head in the bedroom and keep busy 'til I get there."

I watched as Justice trailed behind the two women as the three of them passed us and headed into the bedroom. He returned almost immediately with a huge bottle of cognac and three wine glasses, to which he then filled them all to the top before passing one to both Peace-Peace and myself. He then lit a blunt of his own before raising his glass as if to propose a toast.

"To empires and the niggas that build them," he said thoughtfully.

Both Peace-Peace and I both raised our glass, and together, we repeated Justice's cheer.

This was not only a defining moment for our neighborhood, but a solidification of my bond with both Peace-Peace and Justice as well. The two of them were already bound together by their culture as Five Percenters, a way of life I wasn't apart of; and at times, I couldn't help but to feel somewhat a bit outside of their circle. But now, my participation with them on this fateful and eventful night had undoubtedly placed me on equal standing; we now held secrets that could easily determine one another's fate.

While taking a sip of liquor and placing my glass back onto the table, I was suddenly struck with an overwhelming feeling. The weight of what I had just done, along with the impact of it all, was now beginning to hit home for me, and it was burdensome. I reached for my glass once more and took a big swallow of liquor.

"Look," said Peace-Peace to Justice. "Don Juan ain't never served "thirty-two below" (Five Percenter term for justice) to a mafucka, yo . . .do the knowledge (a Five Percenter term for "pay attention") to how he's actin' an' shit."

I only looked into Peace-Peace's face as he stared into mine with a stern look of assessment. The distant, yet up close and frighteningly personal gaze Peace-Peace held in his one good eye was more disturbing than the gray lifeless marble in his left socket. From the strained, ill-placed smile that had now surfaced upon his face, I gathered that he was more so expressing a sense of humor. His ever-menacing demeanor always made it difficult for me to determine just how light of a mood he was in.

"Stop tryin' to clown him, God," Justice remarked, rushing to my defense. "I know for a fact that he done gave it to a couple mafuckas in the past, so I'm sure it ain't nothin' for him to bust his gun. On the flip side, though, we all know that servin' justice at point-blank range is a bit harder on the brain than a bullshit drive-by. Wit' all that bein' said, demonstrate a lil' bit of understandin', Lord. That shit is a tough pill to swallow, G . . . let him live."

Justice matched Peace-Peace's menacing glare with a cool, nonchalant look of his own while passing the blunt, and while doing so, a silent understanding was transmitted back and forth between them. There were absolutely no secrets between either of them, which meant that if Justice knew of my criminal caliber, then Peace-Peace definitely knew of it as well. For Justice to utter such a comment without it being challenged by his more disagreeable counterpart was a further indication of Peace-Peace already having knowledge of my criminal history; in short, he was merely having fun with me.

What disturbed me most about the entire situation was how quickly and how effective they were when it came to detecting my anxiety. Peace-Peace had honed in on it and made fun of me for it, and Justice had moved in just as quickly to vindicate me for it. I was now feeling the urge to reaffirm my courage, and with that being said, I began speaking from a more commanding position.

"Listen," I said after taking another huge swallow of cognac. "Fuck how I feel about one thing or the other. What's done is done, and if worse come to worst, I'll do it again. Only dumb niggas and rat niggas talk about the dirt they do, so let's just move on."

"True indeed," Justice agreed. "Let's move on, but first, we got some issues to review."

Peace-Peace passed me the blunt and immediately began rolling another.

"Over the past couple of months, we've been talkin' about how we gon take Mid Town to a whole 'nother level, right?" Justice continued on. "Tonight was the first step, but it ain't really mean much 'cause we already knew that we can do what we did tonight, know what I'm sayin'?"

Justice paused to take another swig of liquor, almost wincing as he did so; it took but a half second for him to recover from the harshness of his drink before continuing on.

"It's more to servin' thirty-two below than murder," Justice went on to say. "It's about bein' able to live with it, and more importantly, it's about bein' able to capitalize off of it, too; and that type of shit calls for mad discipline and intelligence."

Justice took another moment to pause, this time making sure to look me in the eyes with a slight notion of acknowledgement.

"And you're right, my nigga," he said after turning his attention back to the drink in his hand. "Tonight is gonna be the last night that any of us talk about what happened.

"We're all conscious and smart enough to know that there are ways to discuss things without actually sayin' it. Feel me? That's the golden rule, gentlemen, and we all know the penalty for the law not bein' upheld."

"True indeed, God," Peace-Peace remarked. "Actual fuckin' fact."

I remained silent and poured myself another glass of liquor; then, I took a toke of the blunt before passing it to Justice as he continued speaking.

"Check it out," he said while sliding a piece of paper across the table in my direction.

It was a receipt from the Lagoon Motel, complete with my name written in cursive down where the customer's signature is required. According to the information on the receipt, I had checked in at eleven o'clock tonight, which was precisely at the same time I was busy committing an act of triple murder.

Triple murder, I thought to remind myself.

It was a deed that I would've never imagined having to perform. At some point in time, every ambitious drug dealer will be confronted with the possibility of having to kill an enemy or rival; it comes with the territory of drug dealing. But triple murder? Hell no! Not even in my wildest dreams would I have thought that I would ever do what I had done tonight; it was something one would only see in the movies.

In the second it took for me to blink, I could recall the violence that I had perpetrated in the bar not even two hours ago: the screams . . . the thunderous roars of my pistols as I took aim and opened fire . . . the gasps of panic and surprise . . . the blood that spewed from out of their bodies and extremities as I shot them . . . the heavy smell of gunpowder being so thick I could almost taste its grit . . . and so much more. I could still see the blood as it poured from their wounds in what was left of their bullet riddled bodies . . . their mouths and eyes open, staring deeply and blankly into nothingness.

I saw all of this, each time, with every blink of my eye, and it unnerved me. I finished my glass of alcohol with two huge swallows and then turned my attention back to the receipt.

"What the fuck is this?" I asked.

"It's a receipt, my man!" Justice laughed while passing the blunt to Peace-Peace.

Peace-Peace accepted the blunt from my fingertips and then took a sip of cognac from his glass before speaking. "According to that little piece of paper, you are currently at the Lagoon and having the time of your life with a cute little honey . . . and far as hell away from the crime scene when shit hits the fan."

"How . . ."

"Shit was easy," Justice said, interrupting my question as to how he had managed such a task. "I got one of the Gods to throw on a hat and a hoodie and get a room in your name while we took care of business. Fake I.D.'s ain't hard to get, and in this case, white folks thinkin' that we all look alike ain't exactly a bad thing, feel me? If the police were to ever question your whereabouts, you can tell 'em that you was out and about, bonin' some chick and what not. Shit, you got the proof right there in your hands! All you need is some chick to co-sign the fact that she was wit' you, and everything will be all good."

"It'll probably be safer for you to have your wife play that part, though," said Peace-Peace while putting out the remnants of his blunt. "This'll be one lie that your woman won't hesitate to tell."

"Both of y'all got one of these, too?" I asked, not bothering to indulge in the off-color remark Peace-Peace had just made about my woman.

"I don't need one," Peace-Peace replied. "My Earth and young moon are gonna vouch for me like they always do."

"I got one," said Justice. "I'm at the Feather's Nest, though. I got way too much class to be takin' a chick to the Lagoon."

Justice laughed heartily at his own joke. Peace-Peace broke into an uneasy smile. I, caring more so about the details of Justice's plan rather than his wit, remained stoned-faced. I raised the glass up to my lips, but thought better of it and elected to place it back onto the table. Justice's humor, however, lasted only for a few seconds and then faded quickly as he instantly resumed an air of seriousness.

"All jokes aside though," he said rather earnestly. "It would be a good idea for you to use this as an alibi, black man. It's the next best thing to having an eyewitness."

I examined the receipt one last time before folding it and placing it into my pocket. It made one hell of an alibi but still, I had my reservations about involving Lakeisha with any of it. There will indeed be some hard decisions for me to make with regards to who I'd choose to use as a witness to me being at The Lagoon. Nevertheless, I was close to being completely sold on the alibi Peace-Peace and Justice had provided.

"Oh, yeah," I said, this time deciding to take a sip from the glass I had once again raised to my lips. "I'm having a great time at the Lagoon."

Justice smiled while raising his glass as if to be giving a toast to my decision.

Peace-Peace only nodded while pursing his lips.

"And now, for the next order of business," said Justice. "Remember all our talks about the need to network?"

Based on our past conversations, "networking" meant the strengthening of one's own position by aligning themselves with those of the same standing, all for one common cause. Peace-Peace, Justice and I had all agreed that the best way to realize Mid Town's legitimacy was for each of us to monopolize a particular drug racket and then force the rest of the neighborhood into subordination.

If things went according to plan, cornering Mid Town's illegal drug market would be an easy task. Those who'd dare oppose, no matter who they were, will simply disappear. My part will be to control the flow of base cocaine, Justice will handle the marijuana racket and Peace-Peace will try his hand with heroin. The three of us planned to establish ourselves and flourish in our own separate endeavors while simultaneously pooling our resources together to work as one cohesive unit. Once our individual goals have been achieved and our core solidified, we'd look to expand.

Our plans to spread out beyond the borders of Camden City were grandiose; and in our case, Mid Town's expansion meant moving southward. The value of narcotics increased as they traveled farther down south; and in southbound counties like Gloucester and Salem, there were hard-nosed hustlers and drug dealers who'd greatly appreciate the benefits of dealing with "stand-up guys" such as our selves. In states south of New Jersey, this concept was even more so. The main issue, however, is that we must first solidify our positions at home before we could even think of expanding abroad. With that being said, a coalition of fellow hustlers throughout the city was imperative and very, very necessary; before moving out of state, we had to make sure that our core was solid and strong.

One of the things I admired most about the Nation of Gods and Earths was its huge number of members and the wide range and variety of lifestyles it encompassed. Not all Five Percenters were criminals, drug dealers and rap artists. Some were teachers, small businessmen, community activists and family-oriented citizens; there were even some who practiced law and medicine. Another important aspect of their nation, which would also play a vital role in our plans to network, was the loyalty and sense of kinship that is shared by mostly all its members, no matter what the lifestyle.

Peace-Peace, Justice and my ultimate goal is to establish ties with those firmly rooted in the legitimate world, making our organization something resemble that of an organized crime family. I must admit that it is a rather far-fetched vision; however, common people with steadfast and uncommon talents have been known to realize some of the grandest enterprises. The three of us wholeheartedly believe that we possessed the means to realize such an ambition, and we were more than determined to go about doing so.

With all of that in mind, I was prepared to answer Justice's question.

"Yeah, I remember our talks about networking."

Justice acknowledged my answer with a slight nod and a cluck of his tongue before continuing. "Well, after we sit for a minute to see how the streets turn out, I'm gonna introduce you to the God, Ta'kwan from Southwest Philly. Him and his peoples are doin' their thing over there out "Power-He" (a Five Percenter's terminology for Philadelphia); they're sellin' fish-scale for eight hundred an ounce, seven if you want it in powder."

Powder cocaine is manufactured and distributed very much in the same manner as base. Upon reaching the hands of its manufactures, kilograms of raw and pure cocaine are diluted with additives, which decrease its quality but increase its quantity while still in its powdered form. This process, called "adding cut," is the same as stretching the amount of grams while cooking base-cocaine. This newly-cut cocaine will then be packaged and sold to street peddlers in an array of measurements. Given the high demand and availability of base cocaine, powder cocaine is normally more expensive and usually reserved for those higher up on the criminal food chain.

Fish-scale is a premier quality of cocaine with a potency that rings superb regardless to whatever form in which it is delivered. Its potency is such that a dealer could cut the size of his bags in half, yet still have a tremendously successful flip. And for that reason alone, it was sold at a relatively higher price than the "average" grade of cocaine. Eight hundred dollars an ounce for fish-scale was a damn-good deal; more so, seven hundred dollars an ounce was a dream come true. My main concern, however, was the contact. I've never before heard Justice or Peace-Peace speak of this "God" from Southwest Philly until now.

"How well do you know this guy?" I asked after taking a toke of weed and then passing it to Peace-Peace. I then poured myself another full glass of cognac.

"I can vouch for the God," said Peace-Peace while accepting the blunt. "I did time wit' him and his "physical" (Five Percenter term for one's biological relative) down Rahway; them niggas is on the same shit we on. Me an' Just already made "knowledge born" (Five Percenter term for either openly acknowledging something or making sure that someone else does) to them about our rules and regulations, and he knows full well the measure of the rewards and penalties with regards to this cipher."

"Everything is peace," said Justice. "We all good."

"Well, in this case, 'we' means y'all and not me," I interjected. "Because I don't know shit about this mafucka."

A look of impatience was now beginning to show on both Peace-Peace and Justice's faces. Justice accepted the blunt from Peace-Peace and then took a long drag of it before speaking.

"The God knows just as much about you as you do about him," he said behind a cloud of marijuana smoke. "However, I'm vouching for him now just I had vouched for you when I spoke to him. All four of us are gonna sit down and "build" (a Five Percenter term for expressing and sharing ideas), and by the time the conversation is over and done with, you'll know everything you need to know about him: where he lives, where his people lives, everything. Ultimately, the decision is yours, though. If you don't wanna fuck wit' him after you've talked to him, then peace be unto you, sun; that's your choice."

Justice paused to take another drag of the blunt before passing it in my direction. I accepted it and took a drag of my own as he continued on.

"I know you ain't apart of the nation, Don Juan, but damn, have a little faith in God."

Justice took a moment to smile at his own humor.

Peace-Peace remained stone-faced, seemingly more concerned with rolling another blunt than the back-and-forth conversation between me and Justice.

I had already made the decision to accept the alibi Justice offered me, and was also leaning toward his attempt to hook me up with Ta'kwan. Who could resist the chance to buy fish-scale at seven hundred dollars an ounce? More than the offer to meet and sit down with Ta'kwan, I found myself still dwelling on the events that had taken place down on Fourth Street. I zoned back into the here and now to find both Justice and Peace-Peace staring at me.

"Oh, it's all good," I answered. "I can hook up wit' your boy, Ta'kwan, and see what he's about."

Again, Justice recognized my answer with a simple nod and a cluck of the tongue.

"That's peace," he finally said before rising up and backing away from the table. "Now if y'all will excuse a brotha, I got two fine females in the bedroom waitin' for a little sport and play. Peace."

Peace-Peace returned Justice's farewell, while I, on the other hand, remained quiet while smoking the blunt Peace-Peace had handed over to me. It now required a great deal of concentration on my part just to accept the weed being passed, which signified the beginning of my submission to the effects of the alcohol and marijuana.

"You all right?" Peace-Peace asked while looking at me with a mixture of both concern and curiosity.

I finished my drink with two strong swallows and then followed its burning sensation with a puff on the blunt. After a short moment of forced concentration, I was able to reply.

"Hell yeah, I'm all right," I lied. "I'm always all right. I just gotta go lay back for a minute."

I handed the blunt back to Peace-Peace and then snatched the bottle of Remy Martin from off the table before heading into the living room where I made myself comfortable on the sofa. Now on the verge of relaxation, I closed my eyes and gave in to the legion of doubts, misgivings and possible qualms that were lurking about in my brain. These thoughts were springing from a multitude of scenarios, all of them being based upon what I've experienced throughout the course of the day.

I thought of the argument I'd had with Tamara and then of my confrontation with the thugs on 25th Street. I thought of my meeting Michelle and then of my episode with Shakira, wondering what they were both doing at this time of night. I thought of Lakeisha and how she may very well be awake at this hour, still with gun in hand, honing in on every noise that registered within earshot. Overshadowing everything, however, were my recollections of what had happened at the bar on Fourth and Walnut Street. All-too vivid scenes of horror and death had seeped deep into my conscience and were beginning to contaminate my every waking thought. Every sound that had taken place while I was shooting inside the bar, which were absent to my ears at the time, had now returned to haunt me terribly.

Sensing the presence of another, I slowly opened my eyes to find Peace-Peace now taking a seat beside me. His one functioning eye stared sleepily into my face, searching to interpret what I guessed to be a rather tormented facial expression.

"You're fucked up," he noted.

"Where's the weed?" I asked, not bothering to respond to his newfound observation.

"Never mind the weed," Peace-Peace replied while taking the bottle from my hands to pour his self another drink. "Let me tell you the story behind me losing my eye."

I was always curious as to how Peace-Peace had lost his eye, but figuring a person's handicap is usually a sensitive point of conversation, I never bothered to ask. I retrieved the bottle of cognac from Peace-Peace's grasp and then fished a cigarette from inside my pants pocket as he began his tale.

"You already know how I was doin' mines before I got knocked an' shit," he began. "Robbin' mafuckas left and right."

"Shootin' and lootin'," I interrupted with a laugh before taking the bottle directly to my lips for another drink.

Peace-Peace ignored my comment and continued on.

"Well, I ran into one of the mafuckas that I robbed back when I was in the county, and I thought we was gon' be beefin' at first, but he ain't want no problems. The nigga was quiet as hell and kept to his self all the time. I took him to be on some sucka shit, so you know how niggas do . . . I started pushin' up on him for his canteen an' shit. When he ain't come up with it, I knocked his ass out and straight took it from him.

"The very next morning, as soon as the doors bust for breakfast, that same nigga came straight in and stabbed me in the mafuckin' face; and I ain't talkin' 'bout no little ass slice, either. Dude stuck that shit deep as hell into my face and dragged it straight down."

Great, I thought to myself while watching as Peace-Peace re-enacted what had been done to him with a make-pretend shank. *Now, I have the image of Peace-Peace being stabbed and slashed in the face to add into my collection of gruesome images.*

"I spent like a month and a half in the hospital before they shipped me to Rahway, and guess who I see as soon as I get to the yard."

"Ol' boy?" I asked.

"Ol' boy," Peace-Peace confirmed. "I got myself a "banger" (slang term for a shank, a prison-made knife) and hit his ass up the very next time I saw him, left his ass leakin' wit' like nine holes an' shit."

Peace-Peace paused, the anguish of that period in his life still very much evident.

"I remember sittin' in my little one-man cell, stressin' like a mafucka. Shit, it was the first time that I had ever killed a mafucka so out in the open like that. You can't imagine how fucked up in the head I was, stayin' up all night, thinking about what I did . . . rememberin' how it went down over and over again. Man, I was scared as hell to get knocked off for a fuckin' body."

Even now, after more than six and a half years after the incident, Peace-Peace still appeared somewhat bothered by what he had done. I sensed his anxiety; it leaked from out the pores of his skin, forcing him to take another drink. Through it all, however, I couldn't help but to revel in the midst of Peace-Peace's unease; at least I wasn't the only one of the trio who was plagued with the guilt of taking someone's life.

"It wasn't until later on that I realized just what exactly had been stressin' me out," Peace-Peace continued after another brief moment of silence. "It wasn't so much the fact that I had killed a mafucka, but it was more so the reason behind it."

"Shit, the nigga stabbed you in the fuckin' eye," I remarked. "That's a good enough reason for me."

"Yeah, but it wouldn't have happened if I ain't push the nigga to do it," Peace-Peace countered. "The nigga ain't want no problems, but me, bein' unaware of Allah's Mathematics at the time, kept victimizin' this man over and over again like there would be no penalty for my actions."

Peace-Peace stopped for a moment to glance at his wristwatch.

"It ain't twelve o'clock yet," he said. "What's today's mathematics?"

I was caught completely off guard and totally unprepared for Peace-Peace's question. As proud as I was to be well-versed in the "Gods' Language," and as eager as I usually was to prove it, the combination of marijuana, cognac and graphic memories of the crimes I had recently committed were impeding me from doing so. It took an intense moment of concentration for me to remember today's date, let alone translate it into the Five Percenters' style of talk.

It's the twenty-third of December, I thought groggily to myself. I then took a small sip of liquor before answering. "Wisdom-understanding-all borns power."

Peace-Peace produced another cigar and began rolling another blunt.

"And how do you see that?" he asked while unraveling the Dutch.

By taking one last drag of my cigarette and mashing its remnants into the ashtray, I was actually stalling for time. Now wasn't exactly the greatest time to undergo a pop quiz. Once again, I found myself speaking with the hopes of not making a fool of myself.

"Wisdom is the word of God" I began. "And understanding is that crystal clear picture that one draws up in the mind . . . power is the truth."

Peace-Peace had finished rolling his blunt with record timing, all the while seeming unfazed by my answer. He remained quiet, focusing more so with setting fire to the marijuanahe had just fashioned. Satisfied to see the blunt was evenly lit, Peace-Peace then turned his attention towards me.

"You know what wisdom is?" he asked. "Wisdom is more than just wise words bein' spoken; wisdom is the manifestation of one's knowledge. Wisdom is one's ways and actions. Wisdom is the bridge between what you know and what you understand; it is indeed the way. Understanding is the ability to see things for what they are and not for what they appear to be, but you need the wisdom first. You have to be able to demonstrate your intelligence first if you want to see it clearly, you know what I'm sayin'?

"When I say that I wisdom my understandin,' I'm telling you that I'm walkin' and talkin' according to that crystal clear picture which has been drawn up in my mind; that's how I born my power. Power is that force that will either attract or repel. That's what truth is. Truth and power are one and the same. Once you apply your ways and actions to the supreme understanding of what it's all about, the truth is born, and the strength of it bein' born is gon' either bring you towards he who holds it or push you away."

I stared into Peace-Peace's hardened, war-scarred face with my own drunken eyes, fighting to make sense of the things he was saying. While sitting forward with my elbows resting upon my knees, it was a hard enough struggle for me to keep myself from falling over, let alone decipher the words of wisdom Peace-Peace was now uttering.

To put it plainly, I just wasn't in the mood for it.

I fell back against Justice's sofa with my eyes closed, sighing as my body welcomed the relaxation brought about by the comfortable feel of his plush sofa cushions. It was the sound of Peace-Peace's voice that helped me open my eyes.

"You all right, sun?" he asked rather genuinely. "You been drinkin' and smokin' hard as hell ever since you got here. That bullshit stressed you out that bad?"

I leaned forward once more, locking my gaze onto Peace-Peace's critical stare.

"Listen, my nigga," I said rather harshly. "I'll admit that I'm a lil' fucked up over what just went down, but don't get it confused . . . I ain't trippin' not one bit. It is what it is. I'm just hopin' that I ain't never got to turn my guns in my own circle, feel me?"

Peace-Peace accepted my brusque response with a simple purse of the lips. The shiny brown tint of his scar then turned bright red as it began to coil beneath his marble eye and touch the corner of his mouth. He was flashing the most gruesome smile I had ever seen. It was the grin of a bona fide psychopath.

"Understandin'- understood," he remarked while passing me the blunt.

I accepted the blunt and inhaled deeply. The effects of my hard drinking and continuous weed smoking were finally beginning to take its toll. Again, my mind was beginning to become cluttered with vivid recollections of the murders I had just committed not too long ago; so much so, that my mind's eye could perceive nothing more than a hazy fog of violence. Despite me thinking better of it, I took one more puff of the weed before giving it back to Peace-Peace.

"You're fucked up, my nigga," Peace-Peace said as I collapsed back against the couch. "It's time for you to go home an' shit."

"Man, I'm good," I heard myself reply.

"Not good enough to hit the highway, though," he remarked. "I'm gonna go get Just so we can take you the fuck home, sun."

"True," I said while lifting the bottle to my lips once more. "Just let me have one more drink, yo . . . just one more drink."

12:45 a.m.

Instead of another drink, I instead found myself indulging in a few minutes of sleep before being awakened and ushered outside and down the stairs of Justice's apartment. Peace-Peace offered to chauffeur me home by way of my own car; Justice followed behind in his own vehicle and would provide Peace-Peace with a ride home after seeing me off safely.

When first leaving Justice's apartment, the cold December winds were sharp and unforgiving; they seeped into every crevice and opening of my clothing, freezing my entire body while at the same time assaulting my inebriation. I was very much relieved to be inside of my vehicle and away from the harsh arctic temperature. Once inside though, the shelter and warmth of the car began to revitalize the alcohol now stirring about my system, and I soon began to crave some of the cold midnight air that I had just so recently been in a hurry to escape from. After reclining back in my seat, I let down the window just a smidgen to enjoy a touch of the cold air as we pulled off.

Peace-Peace didn't fiddle with the car radio, nor did he bother with conversation; instead, he drove in complete silence. Subsequently, I was left alone to deal with my own thoughts which were now beginning to clear a bit more as I sat enjoying the frigid breeze. I closed my eyes once more, and again, I began to relive the horrific deeds I had committed just an hour or so ago. While doing so, I fought to convince myself that it was more so the liquor, and not what I was seeing in my mind's eye, that had began to turn my stomach.

After what seemed like me closing my eyes for only a minute, I found myself being awakened by the sound of my car door being opened. Peace-Peace was hard enough to look at with sober eyes, but for me to awaken at the sight of him staring directly at me was downright heart-stopping; the view of his ghastly face was frightening enough to trigger an automatic reaction for me to reach down for a pistol that was no longer by my waist, but my drunkenness prevented me from doing so. Instead, I slowly raised my hand over the top of my forehead and then lazily dragged it down over my face.

"Let's go, sun," Peace-Peace said. "It's time for you to go beddie-bye."

I lolled my head leftward, and through strained and blurry vision, I could see Lakeisha posted in the doorway of our home. The very sight of her standing and awaiting my return was more than enough encouragement for me to gather my senses and try as best I could to exit the car. With a mighty heave, I scooted from out of the car and soon found myself on unsteady footing. It took less than a second for me to learn that my legs couldn't support the weight of my own body. Had it not been for Peace-Peace and his cat-like reflexes, I surely would have crashed hard onto the pavement. He swooped down with lightening speed and hooked both his massive arms beneath each one of my armpits as I toppled forward. Both Justice and Lakeisha rushed to my side, the two of them eager to assist me.

"I got him," Lakeisha said while bustling past Justice and hastening to my aid.

With one arm around Peace-Peace's neck and the other around Lakeisha's, I was practically dragged around the car and to the front of my home. Justice crept up from behind and slipped my keys into my coat pocket as I hobbled weakly up the stairs and through the door. Satisfied that I'd made it home safely, both Justice and Peace-Peace bid their farewells while heading back into Justice's car which was still parked in the middle of the street with the engine idling.

Once inside the house, Lakeisha moved swiftly to lock the door behind us, and for those brief matter of minutes alone, I remained woozily on my feet; the sight of the couch beside me was looking more and more inviting by the second. No less than a moment later, it was all too much for me to resist. I collapsed down onto it almost at the drop of a dime.

"Uh-uh, motherfucker," she said when returning to find me sprawled out on the couch. "Ain't no way in hell you gon' go to sleep down here."

Lakeisha then grabbed me by the wrist, and with a surprising show of strength, she jerked me off of the couch and halfway onto her shoulder. Now, while riskily standing on her two small feet, Lakeisha adjusted her own self beneath the weight of my body and began what was literally an uphill battle.

With one arm wrapped around my waist and the other braced against the banister for support, Lakeisha somehow managed to lumber up the stairs with a two hundred pound burden of man on her back. With our bodies intertwined and clambering up the stairs with each other, I was quite sure the two of us could have easily passed for a two-headed, four-legged creature straight out of a science-fiction movie. It was I, however, that felt more so like the scientific experiment.

By the time we'd made it inside of our bedroom, I was a miserable wreck. My insides were terribly knotted and felt as if they were on fire. My head was pounding and also beginning to spin wildly around in circles. Worst of all, a highlight of each and every one of today's events were popping in and out of my conscience like the fastest, most evil merry-go-round ride ever.

I collapsed down onto our queen-size bed and welcomed how the plush feel of its mattress seemed as if to caress my tired body. To say that I was more than anxious to go to sleep would have been an understatement; I wasted little time making myself comfortable. With closed eyes and open ears, I could hear Lakeisha complaining about me not bothering to get undressed before lying down. All-too intoxicated to respond, I instead exerted what little energy I had left to twist and turn whatever direction necessary to help her remove my clothing.

Lakeisha carefully unlaced my boots before slipping them off my feet and then eased one arm after the other from inside of my sweater before pulling it over my head and off of my body.

"Where's your chain at, Dijuan?" Lakeisha asked. "Don't tell me you lost it."

In my drunk, high and guilt-stricken mind, I found the mental strength to recall leaving the necklace in my bedroom at Tamara's house before leaving out to kill Jay-Dollar. It was then that I remembered my fight with Tamara and grew a bit disheartened at the idea of having to see her again so soon. I really wanted to give things a good deal of time to blow over before having to deal with Tamara right away, but my chain wouldn't allow me to wait.

I was then struck with another thought. Lakeisha was sure to notice my change of clothing just as she had saw that my necklace was missing, and if she were to discover the motel receipt in my pants pocket, there would be a great chance that I, myself, would soon become a murder victim.

"I left it at Just's house," I drunkenly lied.

"Just's house, huh?" she remarked while unbuttoning my pants.

The tone of Lakeisha's voice was a bit on the testy side, a forewarning of storms to come first thing in the morning.

"Hold up," I said as she began pulling down my pants. I then reached into my pocket and pulled out the three bundles of money that I had brought from my stash in Tamara's house. "You know what this is, right?"

Of course, Lakeisha knew what I was holding in my hand-in my grasp lie the immediate solution to a great deal of her troubles; and just like that, her keen mode of observation was dulled by the tangible proof of her truly being able to leave this God-forsaken neighborhood.

"It's the money we need to move, right?" she asked with what I guessed to be wild, excited eyes. I could sense the childlike wonderment in Lakeisha's words as she spoke; and for a moment, it seemed as if there were five children in the house instead of four. "That looks like a lot of money, babe. How much is it?"

"It's enough for us to pay on the bills we owe, get a U-Haul truck and move somewhere outside of Camden as soon as you find us a place," I answered with a touch of drunken exasperation. "Put the money on the dresser for me."

While Lakeisha did as I asked, I moved just as fast to stash the receipt. I retrieved the motel slip from inside of my pocket, and while feigning the need to stretch my limbs, I reached over my head and dropped it behind the bed. Lakeisha returned to her place on the mattress beside me and resumed the job of getting me out of my clothing.

After stripping me out of everything except my boxer shorts, she folded my clothing, put them away and then got onto the bed beside me, pulling the blanket over both our bodies while snuggling close by my side. She now lie curled up against my body with her legs intertwined with mine. With one arm across my chest, she allowed her fingers to trace the side of my face while kissing me along my neck and jaw line. I reciprocated Lakeisha's show of affection by running my fingers through her hair and occasionally kissing the top of her head, all the while silently trying to sort out and make sense of everything that had happened today.

Reflecting on my conflict with the dealers here on Twenty-Fifth Street, the responsibility I had left on Lakeisha's shoulders to guard our home in my absence proved to be the most significant.

"Everything all right?" I asked.

"Now that you're here," she said while tightening her embrace and kissing me on the side of my mouth. "I couldn't wait to feel your body next to mine."

"I'm talkin' about them niggas outside."

"Everything's fine," she said while kissing me on the mouth once more.

"Where's the strap?" I asked, referring to the gun that I had left in her care.

"It's in the closet, on the top shelf," she replied in between kisses. "I took the clip out and cleaned my fingerprints off it and everything."

"Good girl," I said while kissing the top of Lakeisha's head once more. "That's my baby."

Despite the slight sense of satisfaction I felt about my conflict with the hustlers on Twenty-Fifth and High being somewhat resolved without incident, there was little to no room for celebration. The truce between me and them was a fragile one, held together only on the strength of one person. Moreover, I was sure that it was only a matter of time before someone violates this agreement; I've been in these situations one too many times in my own neighborhood to expect otherwise.

And that was just one of many other things that had taken place today. There were other issues that still lacked closure, and to be honest, they all seemed daunting. The relationship between me and Tamara was definitely up in the air. She had never before approached me in such a sexual and overly aggressive manner as she had; the ramifications of me leaving her high and dry were scary and unpredictable. Sheed's predictions were true, and they were every bit as haunting as the ultimatum I had pretended to ignore while leaving her in what I guessed to be a mixture of both anger and embarrassment.

The idea of Sheed coming home, too, was a discomforting thought. He knew very little of my alliance with Justice and Peace-Peace, and through past conversations, I knew that Sheed didn't care too much for either one of them. Knowing Sheed's temperament, I was quite sure that he wouldn't take too kindly to the way Peace-Peace, Justice and I would have things set up and arranged by the time he'd be released.

Sheed was, is and always will be, Mid Town's greatest living legend; and it seemed impossible for me to imagine him coming home to share the reins of power with individuals whom he had little to no respect for. With Sheed and his followers pitted against the three of us for control of MidTown, the 'hood will undoubtedly be torn in half. Bloodshed will be inevitable, and everything we've struggled and worked so hard for will soon face the threat of going up in smoke.

The only logical means of avoiding such a predicament would be to eliminate Sheed as quickly and as quietly as possible. It was the most rational solution, but still, it was terribly heart-wrenching. The thought of me being pitted against my childhood hero was awfully disturbing; moreover, it pained me even more to find myself pondering the idea of betraying and quite possibly killing him.

First his woman, and then, his life, I thought dejectedly to myself. *So much for loyalty.*

I turned halfway into Lakeisha and tightened my embrace around her soft, tender, frame while fighting not to admit that I may have gotten in far too deep over my head. Tonight, I've taken the lives of three people, and I was now entertaining the thought of killing the only person I've ever looked up to in my entire life, all for the sake of drug money. I've now crossed over into a world in which I'd have to look over my shoulder for the rest of my life. The thirst for revenge may indeed last a lifetime, yet the only thing promised to last longer than the threat of retaliation is the statute of limitations for capital murder; be it next week, next month, or thirty years from now, I could be snatched away by the authorities and sent off to prison for the rest of my natural life.

The feel of Lakeisha's body fidgeting around to get comfortable in my arms made it clear to me the heartbreak our household will suffer if such a thing was to happen. The impact that my incarceration would have on all of my loved ones was all too tragic to imagine, yet horribly clear. I sighed sleepily while adjusting my embrace on Lakeisha's still-squirming body.

As if reading my thoughts, she stirred for a moment more before craning her neck upward to kiss me on the lips.

"Stop stressin', baby," Lakeisha said sleepily. "I'm gonna get up first thing in the morning and go find us a place to stay. We gon' get the fuck out of Camden, baby, and we gon' start all over again. Everything's gonna be all right, baby. Trust me. It's late, Dijuan . . . relax your mind, close your eyes, and go to sleep."

With that, Lakeisha buried her head deep into my chest and again, left me alone with my own whirlwind of thoughts. While lying comfortably beside my woman, I thought of both Shakira and Michelle, and decided to end my dealings with the two of them; not only will I do away with Shakira and Michelle, but Lisa and Charmaine as well.

My decision to become monogamous wasn't an epiphany that had just now come from out of the blue, nor was it based strictly on the premise that Lakeisha is a good woman that deserves better. Frankly, it was more so about it being safer for me in this line of work to be a one-woman man than anything.

Many hustlers get all too comfortable with the women they either cheat on or cheat with; subsequently, they unwittingly let their guard down by foolishly entertaining the thought of being the only man she's pleasing. With that comes a chink in one's mental guard, opening him up to be betrayed by either his main woman or his side chick. Females, from my experience, have shown themselves to be a combination of fickle, emotional, and devious; all of that, combined with a poor understanding with respect to the art of repercussions of street justice make for a most fatal elixir. Only a fool would create such a dangerous scenario to live in, and too many hustlers like me often find themselves flirting all too close to this potential disaster.

Such reckless abandon, as Jay-Dollar had proven tonight, is often a most fatal mistake. The stakes have been raised, and there is no way in the world I could see myself losing it all on the account of having a mistress, especially when the woman I'm currently with has proven time and time again that she is worthy of my trust. Yes, I can honestly say that tonight will be my last night as an adulterer.

Tomorrow is a new day, and with that new day comes a fresh start. Lakeisha will be out first thing in the morning, thanking the Lord for blessing her with such a "good man" while shopping around for a safer environment in which we can live and raise our children; moreover, on the 25th of December, we will be in the living room of our new home, exchanging and opening

Christmas gifts. We'll be a safe distance away from the miseries of poverty, all due to my hard work and dedication.

The safety and happiness of my family are just some of the very few things that help my conscience endure the guilt of me doing whatever it is that I have to do to put food on the table. There is absolutely no way I could support Lakeisha and all four of our children with a low-level job. Ten dollars an hour isn't going to keep our lights on, it won't keep our home warm, and it damned sure won't feed the six of us; and that doesn't even include clothing, haircuts and other miscellaneous things.

Yeah, I'd do whatever I have to do to ensure the comfort of me and my family. Like now, the warmth of Lakeisha's body next to mine, along with the satisfaction of knowing that our children are safe and in the comfort of sleep, seemed very much worth the punishment I may face for any crimes I commit. Until the time of my demise, I will continue to support my family as a drug dealer; no, not just a drug dealer, but as a drug dealer and a murderer as well.

The fruits of my labor are bountiful enough for me to sustain the well-being of me, Lakeisha and all four of our children, and no matter how filthy and blood-soaked the soil in which they are tilled, we all lived fairly well from the seeds I have sown. It was of no use for me to express shame or remorse for the things that I have done and continue to do because I don't feel any.

Although I absolutely don't want to break any laws to support my family, I damned sure didn't want to work seventy to eighty hours a week to earn only half of what I have now. If it calls for me to sell drugs and take the lives of others just to provide for those whom I love, then so be it. What's done is done, and there's no turning back. For me, the only option other than prison or death is to be careful and live my life one day at a time until that time comes.

Yeah, I thought groggily to myself while drifting off to sleep. *That's just how I'm gonna live my life . . . one day at time.*

The End

Made in the USA
Middletown, DE
24 May 2019